John Marrs, auth... ...ppeared

'Engrossing, compelling and twisty from the first page to the
shocking ending. This book grabbed me and didn't let go'
Michele Campbell, author of *It's Always the Husband*

'Unique and utterly compelling. This twisty
psychological thriller will chill you to the bones'
Gemma Metcalfe, author of *Trust Me*

'A stellar and original concept, brilliantly executed.
The final chapters had my heart in my throat!
O'Sullivan is certainly one to watch'
Phoebe Morgan, author of *The Doll House*

'I was gripped by this taut and emotional thriller.'
Louise Jensen, author of *The Sister*.

'I thought it was absolutely brilliant – really fast-paced,
and packed full of action.'
Lisa Hall, author of *Between You and Me*

DARREN O'SULLIVAN is the No.1 best-selling author of psychological thrillers *Our Little Secret*, *Close Your Eyes* and *Closer Than You Think*. Formerly an actor, theatre director, and teacher, Darren was accepted onto the Faber & Faber novel writing programme in 2015. After completing their extensive six-month training, his debut was born. Darren lives in Peterborough where he's currently writing his fourth dark and unsettling novel which is due for publication in 2020. Darren loves to chat to readers and spends too much time on twitter, you can find him on @darrensully.

Also by Darren O'Sullivan

Our Little Secret
Close Your Eyes

Closer Than You Think

DARREN O'SULLIVAN

ONE PLACE. MANY STORIES

HQ
An imprint of HarperCollins*Publishers* Ltd
1 London Bridge Street
London SE1 9GF

This paperback edition 2019

First published in Great Britain by
HQ, an imprint of HarperCollins*Publishers* Ltd 2019

Copyright © Darren O'Sullivan 2019

Darren O'Sullivan asserts the moral right to be
identified as the author of this work.
A catalogue record for this book is
available from the British Library.

ISBN: 9780008330859

MIX
Paper from
responsible sources
FSC www.fsc.org   **FSC™ C007454**

This book is produced from independently certified FSC™ paper
to ensure responsible forest management.

For more information visit: www.harpercollins.co.uk/green

Typeset by Palimpsest Book Production Ltd, Falkirk, Stirlingshire
Printed and bound in Great Britain by
CPI Group (UK) Ltd, Melksham, SN12 6TR

For my family

Prologue

The eighth

He once read somewhere that people become who they are based on their environment and experiences. Their childhood memories, the interactions with friends and profound moments, good and bad, experiences create the building blocks of existence, and once those blocks are set, they are solid, like a castle wall. Some people are kind, some passionate, some victors, some victims. Some are violent. He knew that more than most. And although people couldn't fundamentally change, he knew, from personal experience, they could evolve. Transform. A switch could be thrown, showing a different way to be, without really being any different at all. It happened in nature: the caterpillar doesn't change its DNA when it becomes a butterfly, but unlocks a part of itself that has lain dormant, patiently waiting for the right moment to create a cocoon. He had experienced several evolutions which had altered the direction of his thoughts and actions. But these didn't change who he was. He would always be someone who killed.

And it wouldn't be long before he would kill again. A matter of an hour or so. He wanted to fulfil his purpose now, but knew he had to wait, be patient, and watch. Standing in the shadow of a wide tree, he looked into the eighth's bedroom window, waiting to see her enter, and he thought about when he would be in that room with her just before he ended her life. He knew she would panic and cry and scream before he sedated and killed her, because they always did.

He had planned to be outside her house after dark. But, with it being such a long time since he had done the one thing that made him feel alive, the thing that made him feel like he was flying, he arrived early and took time to enjoy that forgotten sense of anticipation. This also gave him a moment to reflect on the last person he'd failed to kill in this manner. A woman named Claire Moore. She played on his mind more than she should. The one that got away, so to speak.

Before coming to Bethesda, he'd felt compelled to write a letter to Claire. He wanted to explain the reasons for his absence from the world. He revealed to her that after their eventful night a decade before, he needed to regroup, re-evaluate. After her, he never intended to kill in the same manner as he would tonight. But then he discovered she was moving on, leaving that night, their night, in May of 2008 behind. He wrote that he had learnt she was becoming the same person he felt the need to visit before. Which told him she was forgetting him, and he didn't want his last survivor to forget him, because if she did, everyone else would.

He knew, one day, she would read his letter. Perhaps, before then, he would write more. If so, he would let her read them all, right before he ended her life. He could have killed Claire Moore several times in the past few months but decided not to. He wanted to wait, savour the moment. He wanted her to know him as well as he knew her, and to understand his reasons.

He wanted to be able to taste the connection they once shared on the tip of his tongue, as the light in her eyes faded. Claire

2

Moore would die, as she nearly did by his hand all those years ago, but not yet, not until he was in buried in the centre of her soul once more. He wanted every voice to sound like his, every shadow to be one cast by his frame blocking the light. It was the reason he was in Bethesda, and why the woman whose window he looked into would die.

The knowledge of what would happen within the next hour, and what would follow over the coming weeks – the speculation, the fear – coursed through his veins so hard his skin itched. He knew he needed to focus, to contain his excitement, until night staked its claim over the day. He centred on his breathing, regulated his heart rate. He pushed thoughts of what he would do to the woman in the house opposite him out of his head.

Then she, the eighth, walked into her bedroom. He watched her step out of her work clothes, her light skirt falling effortlessly around her ankles. He enjoyed the sight of her slim frame in just her underwear, and the tingle that carried from behind his eyes to his crotch. It was a feeling he hadn't felt in a very long time. There had been plenty of kills since 2008, but not one reignited the fire he remembered from a decade before. For the past ten years, when the itch had been unbearable, he had scratched it discreetly, and taken those no one cared for. The old and alone, the homeless, the migrant. But this one was to be a spectacle, like in those wonderful days in Ireland, putting him back where he belonged, in people's minds, in Claire's mind – a destructive force touching everyone like cancer.

He missed being someone who was feared. In the days when a simple power outage caused widespread terror, he would often kill the electricity to a street, just to watch people panic, thinking they would be next. He especially enjoyed one occasion, three months after that night with Claire Moore, when a storm swept off the Atlantic and cut the power in Shannon. It caused the whole town to descend into terror, thinking he had visited. Police took to the streets, people locked their doors. News helicopters circled, expecting to see a house fire in the aftermath – his other calling card. But there was no fire, no death as he was in Greece on that day, on the island of Rhodes, enjoying the sunshine without a care in the world. He intended that trip to be one in which he learnt to be the man he would become, the man he had evolved into. But, seeing the news, the terror coming out of Ireland, drove the desire to kill once more. It was there, on the sun-bleached Aegean coast, that his metamorphosis began, as he felt a more primal calling. He needed to kill, not because it was his purpose, but for the thrill of it. After a brief search he found his victim, an unaccompanied male who had survived the Mediterranean Sea to start a new life in Europe, and he ended his life, luxuriating in the power he felt while doing so.

But the power didn't last long, because no one cared about this man's death. And upon returning home to Ireland, he could sense he was being forgotten. Over time, only the areas he had visited remembered the horror of those months between April 2006 and May 2008. To try and cling on to his power, he would still toy with their memories, killing the electricity from time to time, just to see the panic unfold. He would walk through the town and watch as whole families squashed together in one candlelit room. But time heals all wounds, and their outright terror diminished to a quiet readiness. Eventually, a power cut became just an annoyance once more.

The eighth hadn't closed her bathroom door and he could see as she unclipped her bra and dropped it on the floor. He glimpsed her breasts, and the tingle intensified. But he didn't want to fuck her; the very idea was repugnant to him. His pleasure came from somewhere else.

He visualised his approach as he waited for the sun to set. Once darkness held, he would go to the single distribution substation. It was less than two hundred metres away, and he knew it supplied the power to her house, along with a few hundred others. The enclosed five-metre wall containing the substation was built in the Nineties, along with the houses it supplied, and was secured with a padlock on its front gates. The bolt cutters that sat heavy in his rucksack would make light work of that. Then it was a case of isolating the switch gear and using a rewired portable generator that would intentionally overheat and blow. This simple and well-practised task would black out the entire street and beyond.

He pictured the walk from the substation to her back door, and then breaking in. He knew he would find her stumbling around upstairs with her phone as a torch. He suspected she would be in her nightwear. He thought about what he would do to her. The fun he would have. The joy he would feel feeding off her fear.

Then, once satisfied, he would place her body in the bathtub, douse her with petrol and ignite her. He would leave before the heat cracked the windows and smoke billowed into the sky. He would go home and cook himself a meal, a pasta dish to replenish the burnt carbohydrates from his evening's work, as he knew from experience work drove his appetite. Then, full and content, he would watch the news, waiting to see what he did featured on it, and the assumptions they would make. And he knew he would get away with it, because he'd gotten away with it before.

His kills in Ireland landed in the lap of a brute of a man named Tommy Kay. Kay was a drug dealer with a reputation for being heavy-handed if a favour or loan hadn't been repaid. He was sent to prison for running down a man in his Range Rover, nearly killing him over a hundred-pound debt. Kay's arrest and that night with Claire Moore were a few months apart, and although Kay was never charged with the murders in Ireland, he was widely believed to be the serial killer that haunted the country, never saying otherwise. Perhaps he enjoyed the notoriety it gave him?

But Kay's motivations for tacitly claiming his kills weren't his concern, because one day they would know how wrong they had been. Until then, he would play on what the media would no doubt suggest: because Kay was now dead, tonight was a copycat.

After ten minutes the eighth came out of her bathroom, a towel around her body, another wrapped around her hair. She turned on her TV, then stepped towards the window, her arm outstretched to close her bedroom curtains. She couldn't see him. He knew it. The fading sun directly behind him was low. The trees tall. She wouldn't be able to see anything beyond the dusty orange skyline. But still he pressed himself further into the tree's shadow. She paused before drawing the curtains, her eyes looking out above his head. The last line of sun painted colours in the evening sky. A perfect disguise for him. Hide the ugly thing that he had become in something equally beautiful.

It was almost time. Another thirty minutes and it would be dark enough to work. He smiled, knowing how tomorrow's newspapers would read.

Chapter 1

6th May 2018
St Ives, Cambridgeshire

As I lay on my right side, left arm under the pillow that my head rested on, I fiddled with my necklace, counting the keys that hung from the thick silver chain. Four keys. Front door, back door and two smaller window keys, one up, one down. I watched the alarm clock flick from one minute to the next. I had done so for the last hour, waiting for it to say 05:05, then the alarm would sound, and I could get up. I'd wanted to get up at three minutes to four, a dream of fire waking me, but forced myself not to. By doing so, I hoped I could present myself as a woman who wasn't struggling to sleep. Although, I don't know who I was trying to kid. I *was* struggling to sleep, I always do at this time of year.

I watched the minutes turn into hours and waited for my alarm before rising, because it felt like a victory over myself. It was me telling myself I could be normal if I worked hard at it. And that was important, to be as normal as I could be. This daily victory was one of the few things I liked about the month of May. It seemed small, maybe even pointless, but the small things

7

mattered more than I could have possibly foreseen. I had no choice but to enjoy the little things. Like the morning sunshine and the sound of the breeze in the trees; the buzz of bees in my garden collecting nectar from one of the many flowers I grew. If I focused on these details, I would get through the month I dreaded. Then June would come, and I would survive another year.

Rolling over to face the window, I looked through the small gap in my curtains to see pale blue sky outside. Not a cloud in sight. It made me smile. A cloudless morning was another victory. Stretching, I uncurled my arms and straightened my legs groaning as my muscles pulled, and blood flowed in my limbs. A feeling I liked. Reaching over, I turned off my bedside light and picked up my phone, checking the date. I didn't know why I did that. I knew exactly what day it was. I had been checking and counting down for weeks now. The date that was the source of my sleepless nights, the date that ruined the month for me was only thirteen days away. Thirteen long days until I could reclaim the night for its intended purpose. I couldn't help but feel a rising trepidation that started just below my belly button and slowly oozed up through my stomach and chest. I sat upright and tricked myself into thinking gravity would stem the flow. With a few deep breaths, it worked.

This year marked ten years since it happened. My mother had somehow convinced me it would be healthy to go back to Ireland, back home. I didn't like flying; I didn't like the idea of going back there again. But Mum stressed it would be good for me. It would cleanse me, and, she said, would help me remove the guilt I was feeling for enjoying the time I was spending with my new friend, Paul. She was right, of course, but it didn't make me feel any better about it.

The red digital display flicked to 05:05, and the buzz made me jump. Gently, I hit the off button with my left hand. I looked at my emails on my phone. There wasn't much going on aside from some spam emails from Groupon, trying to sell me unmissable deals on spa weekends. This was exactly what I needed, and yet another thing I couldn't do.

There was also one unread Facebook message. Sighing, I opened the app and I saw who had sent it. Killian. He had messaged at 03:19. I shouldn't have read it. But I did anyway.

Hi, Claire, how are you? Is everything OK? We keep missing each other. I've been thinking about you, being May and all... I hope you are all right. I am here to talk if you need a friend.

I went to reply but stopped myself. Instead I clicked on his profile, seeing his photo hadn't been changed in all the years I had known him. The same lopsided smile, same thumbs-up gesture. The same mountain range behind him. I scrolled down to see the group page he was an administrator for: the Claire Moore Support Page. Tapping the bold letters, the next image I saw was a picture of me. I couldn't bring myself to read things from the past written there, as kind as the words were. I just wanted to see if there was anything new. The last post was from January.

Claire, on behalf of everyone here at CMSP, we want to wish you a Happy New Year. 2018 will be a good one.

I hadn't responded to the message, but remembered that shortly after a cheque came through the post from the support group, with a note attached saying I should go away somewhere nice.

I didn't spend it, I never did.

I threw the phone on my bed and rolled onto my back. I regretted reading the message. The group have always been supportive, but recently, Killian unnerved me in a way I couldn't put my finger on. To stop myself overthinking and ruining the day before it had begun, I looked towards the window. Lazy dawn light filtered through the thin curtains, casting beams of honey across the ceiling. I focused on the colours, letting myself enjoy the softness for a moment. Owen would have loved me observing this; he would tell me to enjoy the moment for as long as possible, as all things are short-lived. If only he knew how right he had been. I could almost hear him saying it, his voice light and melodic. I stopped myself. Perhaps one day it wouldn't hurt so much.

Lifting myself out of bed I slowly placed my feet on the cool wooden floor and walked quietly into my bathroom, careful not to disrupt Mum and Geoff who were asleep in the room next to me. I hadn't intended to stay the night at Mum's. I'd only wanted to come for a quick cuppa and book the online tickets for our flight to Ireland, tickets she insisted she paid for. But a quick cuppa ended in me staying for dinner and then it was late. Going home by myself was too daunting. Mum knew this, and once it had crept past eight and the daylight had faded, she offered the spare room so I didn't have to ask.

Closing the bathroom door behind me I switched on the light and waited as my eyes adjusted. Then, stretching again, feeling the blood move around my body, I considered how much I hurt. I did most mornings. Sometimes it was excruciating, sometimes tolerable. This morning I was OK. The only part of me that felt discomfort was my right foot – it always seemed to ache more in May than at any other time in the year, suggesting my pain was more psychological than physical. I popped a codeine tablet, just to be safe. Considering the mirror, I noticed that my eyes looked dark and heavy. Age was doing its dance on my face. Not that age really mattered anyway, it was all just borrowed time I would have to give back. I realised that getting older and watching a face wrinkle was a gift some didn't receive.

I heard footsteps in the hallway, followed by my mum's sleepy voice.

'I'm outside.'

'Thanks, Mum.'

She knew I was in the bathroom and had gotten out of bed, so I knew she had an eye on me. It meant I could have a shower.

10

Something I cannot do unless I know I am safe, even after all this time. Removing my necklace, I hung it on the back of the door before stepping into the shower and turning the water on. After the initial shock of cold water hitting me, it quickly warmed until it was so hot my skin turned pink as I washed the night away. Another night survived. Another night in the countdown completed.

As the hot water poured over my head, I focused on the heat on my scalp. I couldn't help wondering, as with most mornings recently, what I had been doing exactly ten years ago when my life had been so very different. Owen and I were probably still in bed, his heavy arm draped over me, our bedroom windows wide open, letting the cool breeze waft our net curtains, making them float like ghosts. We would get up, shower, maybe together, and then have breakfast before going our separate ways to work. He would kiss me goodbye at the door before jumping into his car and driving down the lane towards Cork. He might have been back that day, or he might have been going off-site for a few days in another part of the country. With his car out of view, I would climb into mine and drive to the pre-school where I worked. The children would arrive, and I would spend the next six hours playing, reading, cooking and helping with toilet breaks, giving gold stars to the little ones who went all by themselves. I would then come home, cook for us both, and go to bed with the windows wide open once more – oblivious to pain, heartbreak. Evil.

I knew it wasn't healthy to reminisce; that wasn't my life anymore and nothing would bring it back. I turned my attention to the torrent of hot water that ran over my forehead and into my eyes, sticking my lashes together. It stung a little, but that was good. It stopped my dark memories pushing forwards. I stayed there, head against the tiles, until thoughts of what my life had been like a decade ago washed down the plughole.

Wrapping myself in my dressing gown that I'd brought round

to Mum's a few months ago and left here, I put my necklace back on, comforted by the weight of the four keys, and walked down the narrow corridor of Mum's bungalow into the kitchen. As I passed her room I could hear Geoff snoring. No sooner had I flicked on the kettle, the cat, Baloo, greeted me. He was named after the bear in *The Jungle Book* because of his colour and the huge paws he'd had as a kitten. He meowed and stared at me, unblinking.

'Are you hungry, little man?'

He rubbed himself up against my shin to tell me yes, and acting on cue I rolled up my dressing gown sleeves and took out a pouch of his food from the cupboard beside the bin. As soon as I'd emptied the pouch into his bowl, he dismissed me. The bloody cat didn't like anyone.

I made a cup of green tea, adding a slice of lemon, and walked to the back door, needing to take some measured breaths before opening it. With my heart beating faster than before, the door creaked open, letting the rousing spring morning flood in. The air was clean and fresh, making goose bumps rise on my exposed forearms.

Dawn was my favourite time of the day. The world was still asleep, and felt somehow different. The air smelt cleaner, richer, as if the lack of cars and noise and bustle of people wrapped up in their own sense of importance allowed the trees to sigh. Dawn brought a sense of peace and magic that didn't exist at any other time in the day and, for a short while every morning, I felt like I had it all to myself. I drank it in, the peace. Again, it was in the small things, things I had only let myself see in recent years.

I stepped barefoot onto the lawn. The morning had not warmed the dew enough to evaporate it. As I walked towards the bench in the middle of the lawn, I felt the cold creep through my feet, soothing them. Broken blades of grass from yesterday's cut stuck to my soles. I couldn't look; the grass cuttings served as a powerful reminder of something I longed to forget.

I looked back towards the bungalow to see if Mum had come into the kitchen to make sure I was all right. The kitchen was empty. But I could see my footprints in the dew, perfect shapes that caught a glimmer from the rising sun. My eye was drawn to the impressions of my right foot. I had to look away. Then, sitting on the bench under a maple tree, I allowed myself to momentarily forget where I was, letting my thoughts and anxieties dissolve like sugar in hot water. This feeling of serenity wouldn't last long, so I let myself be wrapped up in it. Although the sun was weak, I could feel it warm my skin. Undoing my dressing gown, I let it touch my neck and collarbones. I focused on what I had been taught by my doctor a long time ago: enjoy the sunshine on your skin. I took a deep breath and focused on my neck which was gently warming, and drew in the smell of morning dew.

After about five minutes the moment faltered, and without warning my mind drifted back to the thoughts of flying home with Mum in ten days' time. It had been a long time since I'd last travelled any distance, and I wasn't sure how I would cope. I felt the small ice-cold hand I'd housed for a decade pluck my diaphragm like a guitar string, making the next few breaths hard to draw. I didn't want to go, but I knew I needed to. It was the right thing to do. I owed it to him, at the very least. But really, I owed him more than I could ever repay. Sighing, I sipped my now-cool tea and waited for the noise of the day to start. I heard a dog barking a few doors down, then a front door somewhere along the row of houses attached to mine opened and closed.

The world was awake, and it wasn't mine anymore. Going back into the bungalow I tried and failed to not look at my footprints.

Chapter 2

6th May 2018
St Ives, Cambridgeshire

I sat quietly in the kitchen for half an hour, thinking about how I hadn't been to see my doctor for a very long time. Dr Porter had been great. She listened. She knew how I felt about most things. But the last few visits, we went around in circles, discussing nothing new. And so, I stopped going to see her. Dr Porter knew most of my secrets. Most. But not all. Some things I couldn't say, and some things I wouldn't ever say. My thoughts were interrupted when I heard Mum and Geoff moving around their room, and wondered when they'd join me in the kitchen. Eventually, Geoff crossed to the bathroom and called out good morning as he did.

'Morning, I'll make you both a brew,' I called back.

'Thanks, love,' he shouted through the door.

As the kettle began to boil, I felt my phone vibrate in my dressing-gown pocket. I couldn't help but smile to see who the message was from.

So, it turns out I'm not needed on site anymore. I'm coming back later today. Do you fancy a takeaway? No pressure to say yes.

Paul wasn't due back till the weekend, and then he was seeing his daughters who lived in Cambridge. With my trip to Ireland in ten days, I wasn't likely to see him again for another few weeks. I guess that was why our ... whatever we were, worked. We were taking things slow, because we had to. Paul was also older than me, quite a few years older. He was divorced and had no intention of having more children, which made things less complicated. At first, knowing his children were adults felt weird. It was one of the first things I had commented on when Mum told me how old they were. But, if we became anything other than two adults getting to know each other, I would cross that bridge when I came to it. With everything else going on – every other bridge I had to cross on a daily basis – it didn't seem that important.

We'd been spending time together for a few months now. We'd met online, which was something I wasn't sure I wanted to do but Mum, the most forward thinking sixty-four-year-old I had ever known, insisted it would do me good to meet new people, get me out and about. She had been trying for years, so, finally I said yes. She crafted my profile, stating I was Claire O'Healy, her new surname after marrying Geoff. If she put my surname it would have undoubtedly drawn the wrong attention. She wrote things in the 'about me' section I wasn't sure were entirely true, things she insisted were accurate but told me I couldn't see. She cropped a photo of me and her in my garden from last year and then hit complete, making me real in the digital world. I didn't want to see what was being said, assuming people would be unkind. And if I was honest, meeting someone was so terrifying I convinced myself I was happy on my own. It had taken me a long time to get to a place where I could manage my own company, and I wasn't sure I was ready to share that with anyone. But still, under the fear, I was also lonely.

Mum told me she would vet the potential 'friends' I would talk to and be discreet in doing so. She told me most were just looking for sex, but this didn't faze her. There were a few who appeared desperate, and only one she had seen who seemed nice. So, on a wet night a few months ago, both of us sat at my kitchen table between a pot of fresh tea and she told me all about him. A man named Paul.

When she stated he was forty-eight, I blew on my tea and raised an eyebrow. He was fourteen years older than me, and only fourteen younger than her. But after she read his profile to me, I understood why he'd made the shortlist. He seemed genuine, kind. Devoted to his children. Hard-working. He was a divorcee, but he didn't seem to have baggage, and I believed it as divorce was so common these days, lots of people didn't have complications after separation. That was the thing I was most drawn to – Paul appeared to be uncomplicated. Something I wasn't. With my curiosity piqued, I asked her to show me his message.

Hello, I'm Paul. I'm new to this so not sure what the right etiquette is. You look nice, and it's nice to be around nice people.

She showed me his photo on the dating website. He looked great. His hair was grey, but in a sexy George Clooney way, and he looked athletic and tall. Mum joked that if I didn't want to meet him she would, stating that Geoff wouldn't mind. We both chuckled at the idea. Mum and Geoff had their difficulties, as all couples did. But they loved one another dearly.

Looking back to the picture, in which he was grinning, standing by a river or lake somewhere, I could feel my hesitation rising. Meeting new people had become nearly impossible for me. With each introduction came a fresh wave of panic about who they were and what motivated them. An online introduction was unchartered territory I didn't feel I could navigate. I didn't know how you could get to know someone without seeing them face to face and reading their eyes?

'I'm not saying you have to shack up with anyone,' Mum said, interrupting my thoughts.

'Shack up? Does anyone say that anymore?' I replied, smiling.

16

'Claire, stop deflecting. It will be good for you.'

I dropped the smile. She was right; I was trying to sidestep the conversation. 'Mum, it's been a long time.'

'I know, that's why we're doing this. You shouldn't be on your own.'

'I'm not, I've got Penny.'

'A friend who has a family of her own.'

'I've got you and Geoff.'

'And we've got each other, Claire – you know what I mean.'

'I'm not sure I can, you know... be around somebody else.'

'You can.'

'Fine, I'm not sure I want to.'

'That's just your fear talking, Claire. After everything you've been through you deserve to have someone nice in your life.'

'But what about—'

She cut me off by reaching over the table and resting her hand on my forearm, on my scar, and although it had faded and lost its raised texture, it was still there – a permanent reminder of the past. I pulled away awkwardly, and knowing why, she apologised.

'Claire, we both know Owen would be all right with it, it's been long enough.'

'I have no idea how to do this.'

'Do what? All you're doing is saying hello. Getting to know him. The best thing about doing it this way is if it's too much for you, if you decide you don't like him, you close the app and lock your phone. God, I wish they had this when I was in the market after your dad.'

'Mum!'

I'd taken another week to pluck up the courage to say hello. Our chat was slow, both he and I not responding quickly to one another. I half expected him to rush in, overload me with messages. But he seemed as tentative as I was. We kept our conversation light, commenting on the weather and things

17

happening in the local news. Eventually we both opened up a little and spoke of musical interests, our hobbies and our jobs – well, his anyway. I wasn't sure if it was weird or fated that Paul was in a similar line of work to Owen. But while Owen had worked on building sites, installing cables and switches into homes before they were decorated, Paul oversaw the building projects at a more senior level. I wondered, for a moment, if they might have met, but quickly quashed the ridiculous thought. When Paul asked me about what I did, I lied and told him I was taking time away from childcare. Well, part lied. Technically, I *was* taking time out: nearly ten years, in fact.

He spoke of his children often, and I spoke of not having any. We didn't talk about our pasts and I was glad he didn't ask. We exchanged emails, eventually numbers, and when we spoke over the phone, I couldn't hide the nerves. My voice shook as I fumbled for words to say. He commented on my accent, asking where in Ireland I was from and I was surprised he knew the area. Paul had family near Limerick and had visited a few times when he was younger. Then, after a month or so of chatting, we had our first dinner with Mum and Geoff. As weird as it sounds to be going on a double date with my mother, I was glad she suggested it. I couldn't face it alone.

We met at an Italian place in nearby Huntingdon. He made me laugh – made us all laugh, in fact – and appeared to be completely composed despite telling me after, via message, that he was nervous all evening. He was kind, we all could see it. Geoff, who was protective over me, treating me like his own daughter, told me as we drove home that night that he liked Paul a lot. When Mum noticed he didn't drink after he opted for a soda and lime when we had a bottle of red, she was won over. I wasn't so sure; both Mum and Geoff had to convince me I should see him again. Our next date, if you could call it that, was break-fast at a café nearby. I went alone, and for our short but lovely meet, the past didn't matter; the future wasn't real. We were just 'in the moment'. Two people talking and sharing and laughing like nothing else mattered. I almost felt normal again.

What I liked about Paul the most was his patience. We had shared a few kisses, each time becoming more fervent. But no further than that – I wasn't sure how ready I was for anything more. It had taken me years to be comfortable in my own skin.

It was a lovely surprise to know he would be back today. And, although I was still trying to be cautious, I couldn't help feel excited by the idea of us spending time together. He was the first person in a long time I had let myself become close to (other than Penny, of course, but that was different).

Now he knew who I once was, and what I was. He didn't know much, as he hadn't followed the story when it happened, but he knew enough to not need an excuse to head for the hills. But here he was, for now. I wasn't expecting it to be for ever. Not once he knew everything. And over the next few weeks, with the anniversary approaching, it was likely he would know most of the details. Someone, somewhere would dig up the past and force me to relive what happened in some magazine or online blog. Then the messages of support would come back, and my quiet life that I fought so hard to maintain would become noisy once more.

My phone vibrated again, lifting me from my daydream, as another message came through.

Or, if you prefer we could eat out somewhere?

I replied, the smile staying firmly in place.

No, a takeaway would be lovely.

His reply was instant.

Perfect. I'll be leaving the site in a few hours, then another few to get home (if the traffic gods are kind).

Don't rush, I'm not going anywhere.

Watching my screen, I saw the three dots telling me he was messaging back. It seemed to last a lifetime. Eventually he responded.

I hope not.

Regardless of the fact I was older and wiser and more battle-scarred than a teenager, I couldn't help, for a moment, feeling like one. My heart fluttered.

Geoff walked from the bathroom back into his room as Mum came into the kitchen. I turned my back, busying myself with the tea. I hoped she didn't see my cheeks had flushed. When I turned to face her she smiled, still groggy from sleep. She was wrapped in her dressing gown, which was frighteningly similar to mine. Was she young-looking, or was I dressing myself as an older lady? I wasn't sure. She kissed me on the cheek, sat at the kitchen table and asked me what my plans were for the day, expecting the answer to be as it was most days: 'Oh nothing, I'm just going to potter around.' When I sat opposite her and flippantly said Paul was coming over for a takeaway, she couldn't hide the mischievous glint in her eyes.

'Oh.'

'Mum! I know what that smile means, don't be so crude!'

Geoff walked into the kitchen scratching his stomach and yawning, like an old bear waking after a winter's sleep. He noticed I was blushing. It didn't shock me; Geoff was one to notice the small things.

'You two all right?' he asked.

'Oh, more than all right, I'd say,' Mum replied, her tone playful and teasing.

'Oh yeah?'

'Claire is on a promise.'

'I'm not on a promise, Mum! Who even says that anymore? Paul's just coming around for a bite to eat.'

'Yeah, Geoff did the same thing nearly twenty years ago.'

'She's not been able to get rid of me since,' he said, laughing and squeezing Mum's shoulder with his wide calloused hand before sitting at the table beside her.

20

'You two are hopeless,' I said, smiling at them before getting up to grab the mugs.

'So, what time is he coming over?' Geoff continued, blowing on his tea.

'I don't know, later?'

'Want us to pop out and get a bottle of wine or something?'

'No, I'll go,' I said, and both Mum and Geoff looked at me a little too quickly.

'Claire, shall I come with you?' Mum asked delicately.

'I'll be fine.'

'Are you sure?'

'Yeah, I want to go for myself.'

'Good for you!' Geoff replied, a little too eagerly.

It wasn't every day I had something to look forward to. It wasn't every day I even needed to get dressed. Paul coming back and wanting to see me filled me with an unexpected sense of purpose. I needed to do something before seeing him. I decided I wanted to be out in the world, to get us a bottle of wine and something for dessert; I wanted to be the one to do it.

I had to prepare myself first.

Chapter 3

April 2006
Ballybunnion, West Ireland

The first

The wind gusting across the Atlantic hadn't let up all day, and now dusk had settled and night taken hold, it intensified. The gusts roared so ferociously he could hear the trees that lined the Ballybunnion golf course moaning, their aching limbs struggling against the onslaught. The relentless wind, buffeting against his right side, had caused an earache that spread down to his jaw and behind his eye. But it didn't deter him from what he had to do. If anything, the ache made the moment more poignant, his suffering reminding him of the necessity of his task.

Despite the weather, he didn't walk fast, the pain in his ear a steadying friend. As he passed the ninth hole, he stopped and looked back to the bay that nestled against the town centre. His mother would have loved the view. The golf course itself was closed, meaning he could enjoy the last of the weak spring sun cast out to sea without the need to be mindful of other people. Once pitch black – a blackness you didn't get in cities, a blackness that wrapped itself around you, a blackness that became a consuming void – he would carry out his violent act. He would work in a way God didn't and he would punish the one his research told him needed to be punished.

The act he would commit was something his inner voice had whispered about for years, but he hadn't listened. It wasn't until his father died, and he had no one else in the world to listen to, that he allowed himself to hear what it had to say. It told him what to do, and why he was to do it. It was rational in its argument, composed, clear, and it made perfect sense to him. Once he allowed himself to fully commit to the thing that had monopolised his subconscious thoughts since he was young, he gained a purpose to his life.

It had taken another few months to find the right man to be the first. He had to fit the description he knew well; he had to be someone who needed punishing. So, he set about his research, compiling a list of his potential victim's desirable attributes, and then sought him out based on the list. Opting to go to pubs both in the area and further afield, he'd listen as men drank and then bragged about how good their lives were, and if one of them said something of interest, he made a mental note of it. To these men he was Jim or Jimmy, Frank or Donny, and he said just enough for them to think they knew who he was, so then he could listen to what they said. Most he talked to weren't of interest. But the few who stirred something inside, he obsessed over. He made a point of 'bumping' into them and then, after they were comfortable in his presence, he would help them get blind drunk so he could offer to drive them home and learn where they lived. They thanked him, thinking they were entirely safe with their new drinking buddy. Then he would watch their homes, watch how they lived once the front door was closed. His instincts about the ones that interested him were always right. They were the right breed of men. After a few months he had his shortlist, but knew he had to whittle it down to just one.

Blair Patterson.

Stopping to look at the violent waves rolling into shore he thought about the four others he had ruled out, and felt formidable knowing it was entirely his decision to let them live. One resided in a flat in Kanturk; another on a busy main road just outside Limerick. He would visit those when he felt more confident, if no other options became available. The other two had children, and he hoped that after the world knew who he was targeting, they would take heed and change their ways – if not, the children would become fatherless. It wasn't ideal, but, he argued, it was perhaps better to have no father at all than one who was like his own. For a moment, he wondered what kind of man he could have been if someone like him had been around to change his own father's ways. Or to have killed him before he could inflict the harm he had.

Blair, his first, had a house in the remote, furthest south part of Ballybunnion, along with half a dozen other houses. Behind the small, detached home was the closed golf course he walked across, and in front, an estuary to the Atlantic. The nearest neighbour was close, probably only thirty feet away, but he knew the noise emanating from Blair's house would be minimal.

Darkness descended and, knowing it was time, he left the golf course via a small gap in the furthest corner that backed on to a car park for people wanting to walk along the estuary sands. Then, joining the footpath, he walked back past the house where his victim lived. He looked inside the window to see him sat in front of the television: one arm folded across his belly, his legs wide apart, and a bottle of lager in his other hand. In the other window at the front of the house, visible from the footpath, he saw Josephine, his wife. A nice lady he had met on the few occasions when he was invited in after dropping Blair home from yet another pub session. She was busy washing up after her man, her expression tired and numb. When he entered to kill Blair, she

24

would be out of the house, because it was a Wednesday, and she always went to work on a Wednesday night.

Pressing himself against a tree, he sat and watched inside the house. Josephine fluttered around the kitchen, trying to keep busy. Blair sat motionless, staring at the TV. She would leave soon. He didn't mind waiting. Watching them was exciting, because he knew that after tonight one would be dead, and the other would be free.

An hour later, Josephine put on her coat, said goodnight to her husband and left the house to start her night shift at the supermarket. He deduced she worked nights to have one night a week avoiding Blair. Watching her drive down Sandhill Road, he stood up, knowing it was time to begin something that would become talked about not just here, but all over Ireland, and eventually, the world.

Two hundred yards past the house was the sub-generator he needed to access. The three-foot green metal box contained the power supply for this small cluster of houses, and another few hundred at the other end of the golf course, closer to the town. Removing his bolt cutters, he let himself inside the fenced-off area and opened the door. Carefully, he removed the transformer and watched as the power died in the surrounding area. Then he hit the generator with his bolt cutters, to make it look like the break-in was carried out by an amateur. He slowly walked back towards his chosen house, watching as torches and candles lit up the others, the people inside unharassed, unafraid. Just as he hoped.

Turning off the main path he quietly walked behind Blair's house and climbed over the back fence, torchlight shining out from the dining-room window. He could see Blair shuffling back into the lounge. Opening the back door, he stepped inside and quietly closed it behind him. Moving to the doorway between the two rooms he watched his target trip over the coffee table, swearing loudly as he did. Blair steadied himself, turned and headed back towards the kitchen. Without panicking, he stepped into the space behind the open door and held his breath. His victim walked into the kitchen and using his phone, opened a small cupboard where the fuse box lived.

Pointless looking there, he thought with a wry smile.

After Blair flicked on and off the fuse switches half a dozen times, he swore to himself before giving up and saying out loud that he may as well fuck off to bed. As Blair stumbled past him hiding in the shadows between the dining room and kitchen, he could feel the air move.

He listened as the kitchen clock ticked from one minute to the next for ten cycles of the second hand before quietly walking up the stairs behind Blair, who was now snoring in his bed. Pausing in the doorway he watched the mound of flesh rise and fall with each deep, vibrating breath and smiled to himself. Blair was oblivious to the fact his time on this earth had completely run out.

Crouching beside him, he observed his features. He looked entirely relaxed; he slept like a man without a care in the world. A man with no demons. Watching him and knowing what he was about to do, he couldn't help but think of that summer from 1989 when he was just seven. His first ever kill.

It was so hot that summer the ground in his back garden had cracked, exposing inch-deep ravines. He had run away again, running until the tears stopped falling and exhaustion crept into his stomach. He came to his regular hiding space beside the old court, a seventeenth-century castle on the outskirts of Kanturk. Once there, he pressed his back against the cool rock of the ancient ninety-foot wall and struggled to catch his breath. Above him, birds fluttered from one side of the walls to the other. He knew he would be in a lot of trouble for running away again, but he couldn't bear it, not anymore. His father's voice shouting was like a whisper channelled directly into his eardrum, his mother's muffled cries were deafening. He didn't know it then, but what happened next would define who he was.

Under the trees that lined the castle was a black and white cat. It was playing with something, toying with it, slapping it with its paws, claws out. At first, he assumed it was a frog or a rat, and so did nothing, but when the little bird tried to fly away and was caught again, he took more notice. Frogs were rife, and rats carried diseases. But the little bird hadn't done anything but fly and sing. Beautiful things. Anything that sang so sweetly shouldn't be subjected to pain. He threw a stone, narrowly missing the cat, and jumped up shouting at it. The cat panicked and dropped the bird before running away, leaving the bird on the floor at his feet, its body broken, but still breathing. He picked it up, held the little bird in his hands, watching it fight to survive. Its tiny stomach lay open, the contents sticking to his fingers. He knew the bird was suffering, suffering because of another creature and he knew that despite his desperation for the bird to fly away to sing sweetly once more, it would die painfully. Gently he lay it on the ground and raising his boot high into the air he stamped on its little head. After he scraped the remains of the animal from the bottom of his shoe, he thought of his mother.

Something shifted that day. He knew if he wanted to, he could be powerful beyond compare. He could be in charge of it all – watching Blair sleep up close he felt the same wave of power as he had when he was seven.

Standing up, he undressed and calmly folded his clothes, leaving them by the door. What was coming next would be messy.

Afterwards, with raised goose bumps on his naked skin, he walked back to the bay he knew his mother would have loved. Behind him, the fire was starting to grow, soon to be all-consuming. Once in the bay the wind was less fierce, the bay protected by the cliffs on three sides. Even in the total blackness he could still see the beauty of the place. Yes, his mother would have loved it here. She would have brought a picnic and they would have sat and eaten it on a quiet midweek day, the sun beating down on their heads. She would walk in the sea shin-deep and stare out to the vast blue, trying to see beyond the horizon, and he knew he wouldn't have interrupted it. She would look beautiful, and in peace.

Thinking about his mother made him realise he was covered in blood and needed to be cleansed. Carefully placing his clothes against the cliff, he walked into the icy sea. He let the cold water surge over him, relinquishing control. Because nature was the only thing that was incapable of punishing someone, even at its most violent.

Washing himself in the tide, he heard sirens in the distance. He looked back from where he'd just come: the house itself too far away and with a cliff blocking it from view, but in the sky, he could see his mark, the black clouds smudged with an orange glow as the fire raged. They would put it out, and then they would find Blair Patterson. His body, burnt beyond recognition, likely unidentifiable without the use of dental records.

It would remain a mystery, the power cut, the lack of clear motive, and then, just when the murder felt like yesterday's news, he would do it all over again.

Chapter 4

6th May 2018
St Ives, Cambridgeshire

An hour after deciding to go to the shops on my own, Geoff walked me home and checked the house. Once satisfied, he offered to come with me to the shops again, insisting it was no bother. I said I was OK, and he smiled, told me I was more than OK before kissing me on the head and leaving.

I prepared myself for the walk into town. I messaged Penny, telling her I was venturing out. She messaged back an emoji, the one with the bicep curling. I think she was telling me to be strong, but I didn't really get emojis. Her message, although designed to be light was anything but, because it was obvious she was trying not to make a big deal out of something that was a huge deal. I wished I hadn't messaged.

It took another two hours for me to leave the front door. It wasn't often I went out my own. But today I felt bolstered, brave. I blamed the unexpected text from Paul and my even more unexpected reaction to it. I thought I would feel anxious at

29

spending time with him, but far from it – I felt excited, nervous, but the kind that makes you smile.

I was only minutes from my front door, only minutes into my courageous day, and my smile was gone. The half-mile walk into the town centre was stressful, the footpaths busier than I would have liked. Mothers with glazed expressions through sleep deprivation pushed their babies in buggies; their children's eyes shone in contrast as they drank in their new environments. Older people ambled as if they had all the time in the world – somehow defying its passing, as they gently walked for a morning shop. There were those who were on a day off or like me, unemployed. People. Lots, too many of them, all going about their day. Not one paying any attention to the small woman who scuttled through them.

And yet, I couldn't help but feel I was being watched, a feeling I couldn't shake despite the obvious truth. No one cared anymore. I was now just another face in the crowd. But I felt it, regardless. That was just how it was. A long time ago I had tried to combat the insecurity I felt in public, but it was a battle that wasn't mine to win, so I learnt to make peace with feeling both watched and overlooked. The rational side of me knew there were worse problems to have, worse things going on. But still, the battle remained.

To help stop my fear from taking control and rendering me useless, I played with my necklace, fingering the four keys that hung from the chain. Front door, back door, downstairs windows, upstairs windows. As I repeated my mantra, I focused on the used chewing gum someone had trodden into the ground and counted each piece. I hoped once I made it into the supermarket, I would feel safe.

By the time I made it to Tesco Express I had counted forty-seven pieces of old gum and my hand ached from continually moving the keys back and forth. It was disgusting to think about, the amount of gum, all those germs, but counting helped. I thought I would feel better being indoors again, but I felt worse. Grabbing a basket, I walked down the aisles, acutely aware of the exit becoming further and further away. Each step became hard to take but I took them, regardless. I didn't think I would ever remove the hand inside my chest which held me down and kept me afraid.

Heading into the back corner, the smell of fresh bread comforting me, I wrestled my headphones out of my bag. I put them in and pressed play, and as the sound of my music drowned out my own anxious thoughts, I moved on, grabbing the essentials, before heading towards the wine section to get a bottle of red, although I wasn't sure if Paul drank wine. He wasn't a drinker, that much I knew.

But as I turned towards the shelves of alcohol, my thoughts of enjoying an intimate glass of wine with Paul (both warming and nerve-wracking) were hijacked by thoughts of Owen, bringing me to a halt. A memory flashed of our honeymoon in a caravan near Tralee on the west coast of Ireland. It was all we could afford being so young and poor, but it was a magical five days. The wind kept us awake most of the night, the cold creeping in through the vents, and we drank wine, lots of it, to keep ourselves warm. But we wouldn't have had it any other way. We would have lazy mornings in bed and then walk along the coastline, our hands interlinked.

Then my memories took me somewhere else, somewhere darker, and the warm feeling left as quickly as it came. The icy hand was back on my diaphragm, playing its tune. The same one it always played until I forced myself to move again. As I looked for a bottle of red wine I could afford, I felt I was being watched, but this time it felt different. This wasn't me being controlled by my own fear. This was real. The air hung thickly around me, and my body reacted to it before I could think.

Looking to my right I locked eyes with a woman who was staring at me: short dark hair, pale skin. Maybe in her mid-twenties. Her expression was one I had seen countless times before, although not recently. I grabbed the nearest bottle and walked away. Just before turning the corner I looked back, and she was moving towards me, talking with a man who had joined her. He was confident and intimidating, and I felt a surge of terror, but I quickly quelled it. He was too young to be who my fractured mind told me it was. And I knew it couldn't be him, because he, Tommy Kay, died in prison four years ago. Still, it didn't stop me thinking the person following me was involved somehow, despite being told on countless occasions that Tommy Kay, the man who was widely believed to be the Black-Out Killer, was a lone wolf, a solo act. A loner.

I increased my pace, which made the ache in my right foot develop into a sharp pain. I tried to hide my limp. It was hard and painful to do, but I didn't want anyone to notice. As I got to the till, I breathed a sigh of relief that there wasn't a queue. I loaded my things onto the checkout belt quickly and looked over my shoulder as the couple attempted to discreetly watched me, pretending they were examining the contents of the tinned soup aisle, not fooling anyone.

'Thirty-two pounds eighteen, please,' said the cashier after scanning my items. I looked at her, realising I hadn't until that moment. She was young, probably seventeen or eighteen with a ring in her nose and filled-in eyebrows. Her body language told me she didn't want to be there any more than I did. I took out my headphones.

'Sorry, how much?'

'Thirty-two pounds eighteen,' she replied like I was hard of hearing or stupid.

'Are you sure, that seems like a lot?'

'That's what the till says.'

'I see.' I looked at the items sat crushed together, in the recess where they slide after being scanned, waiting to be bagged. 'I'm sorry, can you tell me how much the wine is please?'

'Pardon?'

'Sorry, the wine, could you tell me how much it is, please?'

The young girl rolled her eyes and looked at the display. Quickly looking over my shoulder, I noticed the couple were inching closer. I needed to get out. I needed to go home.

'Twenty-one pounds fifty.'

'Oh.'

I didn't have enough to pay for a bottle that much, but looked in my purse anyway, counting my money. Small coins included, I had around seventeen, maybe eighteen pounds at a stretch. I could feel my cheeks warm as panic began to set in. I could feel the young girl watching me, as were three people with baskets now queued behind me. Behind them, I couldn't see the couple anymore. Perhaps the commotion had startled them away; they couldn't follow me if I wasn't moving. I took my bank card from my purse and mumbled an apology, hoping by some miracle it would go through. As expected, it declined.

'Have you got another card?' asked the girl, irritated by my delay. Another person had joined the queue. Impatience filled the air. I could almost hear their thoughts. 'Come on dole dosser, move it along. Unlike you, we have places to go.'

'Sorry. I'm sorry,' I mumbled. 'Let me count my cash.'

I don't know why I said it; I knew I didn't have enough. My hands shook, my breathing no longer something that was mine to control. I dropped my purse and coins clattered on the metal surface of the till scanner. A quick glance, another person in the queue. All eyes on me. Pity, annoyance, frustration. I could see it all on their faces. I tried to scramble back my money, counting as I did.

Is that three pounds or four? *Concentrate, Claire. Concentrate.*

'I'm so sorry. I... um...'

'If you haven't got enough, I can take something off your bill?'

'No, it'll be OK,' I said, again, not knowing why. The easiest thing would be to take the wine off, but my mind was swimming. With all the fallen coins back in my numbing hands I counted pointlessly, knowing I was well short. I couldn't think. I wanted to leave. I wanted to abandon the shopping and get out of there as quickly as I could. My body moved, about to bolt for the door, and as I looked up the eyes of the pale woman and confident man were before me. Blocking my path.

The woman bagged my things, a small smile on her face. The man stepped past me to speak with the cashier, placing me between them both. Trapped.

Chapter 5

6th May 2018
St Ives, Cambridgeshire

'How much does she owe?'

'Thirty-two pounds eighteen.'

'Here you are.'

'Are you serious?' asked the checkout girl incredulously.

'Yes.' The man pushed his card into the card reader and I heard four quick beeps as he entered his pin. Then the fifth, confirming the payment. The woman backed away, giving me space to run if I needed to, my shopping in her bag. She held out her hand, her eyes firmly on mine, and for reasons that baffled me I took it. She guided me from the tight space between cashiers to the entrance and outside. We stopped at a bench that sat next to a Postman Pat ride for children, the red paint cracked and faded.

The sun that had warmed my skin this morning was gone, dark clouds hiding it. Rain fell like a drifting mist, but that wouldn't be for long. Somewhere in the distance the rumble of thunder sounded. An angry god. The smell of the cold rain water hitting the hot tarmac reminded me of being a little girl again, playing happily on the street outside my house.

I sat on the bench, the pale woman standing close.

'Are you OK?' she asked. I didn't respond. I didn't want them to pay for my shopping, I didn't want a bottle of wine that cost twenty-one pounds fifty. I didn't want charity. I didn't want to be out. I wanted to go back to the morning when the sun kissed my collarbones and the feeling that the day might be mine.

'Here,' the pale lady said, placing the shopping bag at my feet. Her eyes staying fixed on mine as she sat on the other end of the bench.

'Yes, sorry. I'm fine. You shouldn't have paid for my shopping.'

'We wanted to. Can we take you anywhere?' said the man, his voice deep and calming.

'No, I'm fine, thank you.'

'Can we walk you to your car?'

'I'm walking home, thank you.'

'Do you have an umbrella?'

I didn't respond; the answer was obvious. The man dashed out into the rain into the car park, as a flash of lightning streaked across the sky. I counted, like I had as a child in the meadow behind my house, waiting for the thunder to clap. One, two, three, four, five, six, seven, eight, eight, eight... I couldn't get past that number, I doubted I ever would.

The clouds slapped together, making me jump, and I saw the man had returned with a small black umbrella. He gave it to the pale woman, keeping his distance, as if he understood. She placed it on the bench beside me.

'Are you sure we can't give you a lift? Those storm clouds look pretty ominous. It's only going to get worse out here.'

I looked up at her. Her eyes filled with compassion.

'You shouldn't have bought my shopping.'

'Again, we wanted to.'

'I saw you and panicked and picked up the wrong wine.'

'Then we needed to pay for it. I'm sorry we startled you.'

'I can pay you back, if you give me your details.'

'I don't want you to pay me back.'

'I'm so embarrassed.'

'The only embarrassing thing is that we live in a world where someone like you needs help.'

I felt pathetic, a grown woman in her mid-thirties, ten years older than the girl before her, unable to pay for her own shopping. I wanted to cry. But not here, not now. Above our heads the rain started to fall with more force. The drumming of thousands of drops hitting the metal roof sounding like an ocean rolling in. We both looked up.

'Please, can we give you a lift?'

'No, thank you. I need to walk. I can't explain why.'

'I think I understand.'

'Do you?'

'Yes.'

'Then could you tell me, because I don't,' I said, smiling, hoping it didn't look as sad as I felt.

'I think you walking home in a storm is a *fuck you*...'

I laughed quietly, her words unexpected and true.

'Yeah, that's exactly it. It's a *fuck you*.'

The woman rose to her feet and touched my shoulder before walking towards her partner who, out of respect, kept some distance. Just before they left she turned once more.

'Claire Moore. You are the most courageous person I have ever met. That's why it stopped. Never forget that.'

She smiled at me and though I desperately wanted to smile back, I couldn't. I stared at her as she and the kind man walked away, climbed into their car and left.

Gathering the broken bits of my dignity I rose, replacing the headphones in my ears. Before stepping out into what would soon become a deluge, I scrolled through my playlist and chose some music. Opening the umbrella, I stepped into the rain.

Another flash of lightning shot across the sky.

One, two, three, four, five...

Another clap louder than the music in my ears. The storm was drawing in.

With my head down, I set off. The music drowned out the noise of the rain hitting the roofs of parked cars. My return home was far less stressful than the walk in, the footpaths deserted, the air fresh and clean. I took my time despite the rain hitting the ground so hard it bounced and soaked the hem of my trousers. I felt safe when everyone else hid.

The music finished, the end of the short playlist, and silence ensued. The sounds of the world returned. Cars driving through the puddles, splashing water over the footpaths that drained into the puddles once more. Another clap of thunder, which made me jump. Not a surprised jump, but one laced with fear. I hadn't seen the lightning before. The rain hit the top of the umbrella, tiny crackles like a thousand exploding fireworks, their rhythm transfixing, seducing. It stopped me in my tracks, took the world away, the roads, the houses. The tarmac, the daytime. And I was back in the dark, lying on my side, covered in grass cuttings, raindrops forcing me to keep my eyes closed. My head hurting, my stomach screaming. My foot twisted in agony. Sodden soil covered me because of the distance I had crawled. Under my nails, in my hair. In the gum line of my teeth. I tried to keep my eyes open, see what was coming. Face it head on. A coat, lowered over me, making a canopy, blocking the rain. The sound similar to the one I heard right now, the sound of a thousand fireworks.

A car driving past splashed my feet, snatching me away from my thoughts. I hesitated to understand where I was. Then, hoping I hadn't been seen zoning out, I made my way up the road and to my front door.

It took me a moment to get my keys out and in the lock. Closing it behind me, I pressed my back into the wall. Told myself to breathe. Sliding down the wall I sat, the shopping bag to my right, and removed my sodden shoes and socks. My feet felt hot, the veins bulging across the tops. My eyes were drawn to the edge of my right foot. The skin was still bright pink even after all these years and as hard as I tried, I couldn't remember what my foot used to look like before two of my toes had been cut off. But I could still remember that moment as clear as if it was yesterday. I could hear the sound that came from my mouth, the sound of the bolt cutters slamming shut. These memories were always there, just behind my eyes in a box I kept locked, but its lid wasn't airtight, the dark light spilled through the cracks and keyhole when my vigilance slipped.

I wanted to text Mum but stopped myself. I knew what had happened. I knew how I was feeling and what my response to my feelings would be. It had happened before. I knew, despite not feeling like I could at the moment, that I would manage this and then my skin would be just that bit thicker. Hopefully, after enough of these moments, my skin would be so thick they would stop troubling me entirely. Hopefully.

Pushing the awful thoughts back I sighed, defeated, and took my phone out, knowing how the rest of the day would pan out. Opening my messages, I tapped the thread with Paul, my excitement clear to see in the brief words we had exchanged.

What a difference a few hours can make.

Paul, I'm sorry but can we rearrange? Perhaps tomorrow we could go for breakfast somewhere, or a walk in a park. I'm OK, nothing to worry about. Just had a rough trip to the shops. I'm not feeling myself. I'm really sorry.

I hated sending it, I wanted to see him. But not like this, and this would not shift until a new day had begun. Flopping onto my sofa, I turned on the TV and opened my Netflix account. I would find a new show to get into and I would stay there until I fell asleep. Then, I would get up tomorrow and try again.

As I was told, nearly ten years ago when recovering, tomorrow was another day, a chance to start anew.

Hello, Claire,

I came to visit you today. I watched you battle with a carrier bag and umbrella against the rain. Jumping when thunder crashed above our heads. You walked past me, on the other side of the street, twenty feet from me, your right foot clearly causing you discomfort, which I found comforting. Just before you turned onto your road, towards your house, you stopped, lost in your thoughts. I wonder if you were thinking about me? I wanted you to turn and see me across the road – I thought for a moment you did see me out of the corner of your eye. But the storm above us was beautiful, its power undeniable, and you couldn't see anything because of it.

I don't know why I came today, I hadn't planned to. Perhaps it was because it's so close to a milestone date of our brief and climactic moment together. Our past, our night, created an improbable bond, a closeness, an understanding. What we have is something no one else has. And I know I am in your thoughts as much as you are in mine. Our past has drawn me to you once more.

You're probably shocked to read that I came to visit you. Don't be. I would be lying if I said this was my first visit. There is something about you that draws me in, something that I cannot shake. I know it's linked to the intensity of that night, and with the anniversary of that encounter looming, the feeling is heightened. The psychological term is Lima Syndrome. I care for you because I want to kill you, and the absence created by not killing you only fuels the fire within.

And so, I'm compelled to write to you. I know it will be a long time before you read this. But one day, you will know everything. And I want to make sure you understand why – that you know the truth.

The first time I came to you was only weeks after our night. I came to you at a doctor's surgery when you were waiting for your therapy session to begin. I sat behind you, so close I could smell the citrus of your shampoo. But you don't seem to go to these sessions anymore. Is it because you have deluded yourself into thinking you are cured, or have you given up hope?

More recently I've watched you sitting in the park, enjoying the sunshine on your face. I have seen you in a coffee shop with your mother. I've only ever wanted to observe you, to see you as you are now, to see how you're enduring, what you were achieving. What I have seen from you used to make me feel a sense of pride, but recently that sense has gone.

I'm disappointed, Claire. You are not the woman I thought you would become after me, but there is time to change that. I will make you see who you are – who you still *are – and I will make you understand the mistakes you have made. I never intended to return. I have evolved, become something new. But I have watched you, Claire, and I know you have gone full circle, back where you started all those years ago. Only, you are remembering me less. And that is why I will come back for you.*

You'll thank me one day, Claire. Until then, I am never far away. **Closer than you think.**

Chapter 6

9th May 2018
St Ives, Cambridgeshire

Wrapping my dressing gown tightly around me, I opened my back door and let the clean morning air flood in. I still felt weary, uneasy after my last trip outside. It had taken me three days to feel well enough to consider stepping out of the house. Three days of checking and double-checking locked windows and doors, unable to remove the keys from around my neck because I couldn't bear the idea of not having my only means of escape on me. Three days of not being able to have a shower, even when Mum came over and sat on the landing. The sight of the water running made me feel sick and the noise dulled my hearing. Three days of sleeping on the sofa, jumping every time Baloo, who Mum decided should stay with me to keep me company, moved upstairs. The moment in the supermarket, as innocent and kind it was, rocked me to my core. I felt like a temporary prisoner in my own home.

I hadn't felt like this in over a year, and although Mum told me to not be so hard on myself, that relapses happened, I couldn't help but feel like a failure for the backwards step. She suggested I ring Dr Porter and tell her how I was feeling. But I didn't see the point. I knew why I felt this way. Someone had recognised me. I had let myself believe the life in which I found myself labelled a 'hero' had passed me by. I thought I had completely vanished from people's minds. I thought I had become a ghost, but I hadn't. If two strangers could see me, who else could? The supermarket incident told me I wasn't a no one as I had hoped, which meant I had to be someone. The woman who was out, unable to pay for her own shopping, she was a victim. I couldn't bear to be her. For the past three days, I had placed myself under house arrest, crippled by paranoia. I couldn't be her either, and thankfully I could feel her ebbing away, as I started to feel like myself again. Whoever that was.

After messaging Paul to say I couldn't see him, he responded as he had the other times I had blown him out. He was supportive, understanding, telling me there was no rush and he would be around when I was ready, and his kindness made me feel guilty. With each passing week Paul and I were getting closer. We were learning the things about one another that other people might not know. And one day, I felt like I might just be able to tell him what happened ten years ago. More than the basic facts he already knew, more than the obvious truth that I had survived being murdered. I was sure it would shock him, even though a lot of the details were in public domain – a lot, but thankfully not all. Some were too horrific, even for the vultures of the world's media.

I wasn't worried that he'd run away when I told him. The problem was, I knew after I bared all, I would be the one to run away. In my mind it was inevitable. My attachment disorder meant I kept people at arm's length. Everyone understood why, even me. But I didn't like the term 'attachment disorder', it was too generic. I would have preferred if they used the term everyone was thinking but never said – I-think-everyone-is-going-to-try-to-kill-me disorder. A disorder that over the past year was showing signs of being managed – managed well, I thought, right until that moment in the supermarket.

I had realised over these past few days of being locked up at home, my mental health would always be complex. I would always be challenging to be around as I couldn't predict when I would have a good day or a bad day. It wasn't fair to expect or ask anyone to get caught up in my complicated little life. And with the fact I was flying back to Ireland in exactly a week, to visit the grave of my husband for the first time, I knew in coming weeks, maybe even months, my mental state would be even more delicate than usual. The supermarket taught me that although I sometimes thought I could be normal, it was only a delusion.

Paul didn't need the shit I'd bring to a relationship. I would upset him, I would be too difficult, impossible to be around. I knew I had to call it off. I had messaged Penny, telling her I would cool things with Paul and she tried to talk me out of it. She told me I wasn't baggage despite having it, and that to smooth over the 'tricky' few days I had, she should come over with her husband Robbie, so Paul and he could get to know one another. I knew what she was trying to do; she was trying to make my life normal. But really, was that ever going to happen? I politely declined, but promised I'd see her when I got back from Ireland.

Ireland. Just thinking about it made me feel sick.

I had enough to worry about without mistreating the only man I had let myself be close to since Owen died. I would miss Paul, but it was for the greater good. I'd wanted to call him the day after the supermarket and tell him I needed some space, but I wasn't feeling strong enough to do anything but binge on Netflix box sets. Today, I was feeling much better about the world, and that meant I had to do what was right.

I never had identified what snapped me from my funks (my polite phrase for complete and utter meltdowns) but last night I managed to sleep a good six hours, and as soon as I awoke and saw the blue sky, I felt the need to be outside under it. So, I took the steps that only twenty-four hours ago had felt impossible, walked into my garden – away from the house, the place I could lock myself in – and wandered to the patio table where I sat and read most mornings. I aimed to convince myself it was just like any other morning, though I couldn't stop my heart from racing. I tried to settle my hands, but needed to fidget with the keys around my neck. It helped, and stopped me from wanting to run back inside.

Sitting down on a cast iron chair, I leant my elbow on the round table and enjoyed the cold dew seeping through my dressing gown elbow. I pushed down the anxiety by watching small white clouds that smudged the deep blue of the sky. I tried to see animals in them, like I did as a child. Like I had with Owen in the days before we married. We would sit in the garden pointing out the things we saw in the clouds that floated past. Usually with a glass of wine. We did it so often the memories blurred into the same moment. All besides one. It was a mild autumn afternoon, the sun was moving towards the horizon, painting the sky the most beautiful colours. In the clouds I saw a bear, he saw a bird, one I couldn't find, and then, as I was looking to see more animals, Owen dropped to one knee and asked me to be his wife.

I stopped myself thinking anymore. It was too painful.

I tried to see something in the clouds again, but I couldn't. They were just clouds.

Disappointed, I took my phone from my pocket and held it in my hands, the black screen reflecting the sky above me. I needed to talk with Paul, but what I needed to say wasn't something I could say over a text message. I didn't want it to be misread or misinterpreted. He needed to hear my voice.

I dialled and held my breath. It rang and rang and just as it clicked into voicemail I hung up. Selfishly I was disappointed he was busy and didn't answer. Then I realised, I didn't even know the time. Looking at the clock on my phone I saw it was before six. He wasn't busy; he was asleep. Putting my phone beside me I looked back to the sky and could feel the tension of making the call slowly travel from my chest into my stomach before leaving my body through my feet. I focused on the sound of the breeze and birdsong, the combination transporting me to a different time.

I let myself drift to where my mind wanted me to go, if only to keep me from thinking of Paul. The long summers in Ireland before my life changed. I used to wake at a reasonable time in those days, but still early enough to need to tiptoe out of the bedroom so as not to disturb Owen who was a light sleeper. I would get my running gear on and head out. The deserted lane where we lived near Newmarket was a perfect place to run. No traffic, no noise, besides the pigeons calling to one another. It was so quiet I would sometimes see a fox crossing the road or deer in the meadows who watched me run by. I used to run miles every day and if I thought about it, it was the thing I missed the most about my life before. Other than Owen.

Losing myself in the past, I didn't notice my phone vibrating on the bench beside me until I scooped it up to see a missed call from Paul. Calling back, he picked up before the first ring finished.

'Hey,' he said quietly.

'Hey.'

'Are you all right?'

'Hi, Paul, yes I'm fine, sorry, I didn't realise it was so early.'

'No, it's OK, as long as you're OK.'

'I'm feeling much better.'

'Pleased to hear it.'

The line went quiet and I could feel the nervous energy between us building. The silence awoke tiny white butterflies in my stomach. I knew he wasn't speaking because he was waiting for me to lead.

'Listen, Paul—'

'You don't have to say sorry for anything, Claire.'

'But I feel like…'

'I'm not upset or annoyed.'

'But this thing…'

'… is whatever it will be.'

'Will you let me finish?' I said, more forcefully than I intended, the butterflies in my stomach growing bigger by the second.

'Yes. Sorry, I'm talking over you. Carry on.'

I curled my toes on my left foot in the grass and took a breath. 'I don't like that I mess you around. My life is… complicated, and although I manage better, I still have my days. It's not fair to subject you to it.'

I knew what I should have said next, but I couldn't form the words in my mouth, and that was selfish of me, weak of me. But then again, that's what I was, wasn't it? A weak woman.

'Can I speak now?' Paul whispered, snapping me back into breathing, though I was unaware I was holding it to begin with. 'I know you think you should call it quits on us spending time together, thinking it would do me a favour, but it won't. I know you have a complicated past, and because of that I know you have your off days… Christ, if anyone alive is allowed to have problems it's…'

'You think I have problems?'

'No, problem is the wrong word.'

'What, the right word is baggage?'

'No.'

'What is it then?'

'I mean your anxiety issues.'

'So, I have mental health problems?'

'Yes, but that's not a bad thing.'

'It's a good thing?' I said, my voice raising, ready for an argument I didn't want to have, but my attachment disorder would ensure I did have, anyway.

'No, Claire, it's just a thing. We all have something, and it's OK to call it what it is.'

'You have something too?' I asked, wishing I could take it back instantly.

47

'Yes, no, right now I don't. But I used to. And I still carry it with me. Everyone has something. A trauma, a grief. A mistake,' he said, after a beat. I could hear something heavy in his voice.

I wanted to know which one of those three was connected to him. Was he grieving too? Had he suffered something traumatic as well? Had he made a mistake, or done something wrong in his past, like me. It made sense that I felt a connection to him. We both had a shadow.

'Claire?'

'I'm not mental,' I said, trying and failing to stop myself causing a fight and making it easier to walk away.

'Of course you're not. Claire, we both know, the entire world knows who you are. And how brave and strong you have been. You are so strong, even with all of the struggles you have had to face.'

Somehow his words floored me and the fight in me dissolved. No one except Dr Porter had ever said out loud it was OK to have mental health struggles. It was refreshing to hear it called what it was. And unusual. My mum referred to my health as my 'quirks'. It was anything but quirky.

'Paul, this isn't fair.'

'What isn't?'

'Us, you know, getting close.'

'Not fair on who?'

'You.'

'Maybe I should decide what is fair on me and what's not. Yes, if I'm honest, it's hard when you disappear…'

'Then maybe—'

He cut me off, but this time it was OK. 'But it's only hard because I care about you. Claire, I'm old enough to know life is hard, and for you, harder than most, and that sometimes, you need to take a step back. I understand. It's OK. I think you're brilliant as you are.'

I felt tears begin press against the backs of my eyes and I let them out, forming a glaze over my vision, turning the bushes I was looking at in my garden into an underwater reef. As I blinked, a tear dropped onto my right foot, and with clear vision I looked at the matted pink scar tissue that ran from the place my toes used to be up my calf. As if knowing I needed comfort, Baloo had wandered out of the kitchen and rubbed his back against my leg. Reaching down I gently stroked the back of his neck.

'Paul, I will never be uncomplicated.'

'It doesn't matter, you be who you need to be. We are all complicated, that's just how it is.'

Another tear fell, and I had to move the phone away from my face, worried he would hear my jagged breathing as I fought to hold on. Baloo jumped onto my lap and stroking him calmed me. After a moment, I felt like I could speak again.

'Paul, I don't want to hurt you.'

'Then don't. Don't run away. Not yet. I know you don't want to.'

'I don't,' I replied honestly. 'But I might one day.'

'And we'll deal with that then. As hard as it is, let's try being in the moment. Just two adults, enjoying talking to each other.'

I couldn't stop myself from smiling.

'And when I need to back away, like I have done this week—'

'Then we'll text, and I'll get on with on with the rest of my life – work, my girls. I've got lots of other things to do, you know.'

I laughed and wiped my eyes. He was right, of course he was. He had his own life, an adult life. I let myself forget that, instead assuming that things between us might be how Owen and I were. But it wasn't; Owen and I, we were both just kids when we met. No jobs, no children, no mortgages, no worries. No scars. Just each other. This was different. We understood things kids couldn't, we knew things kids didn't. I needed to try and remember that.

'So, what are you doing this morning?' he asked, his tone suggesting he was smiling, like I was.

'If I've not completely balls'd it up, seeing you?'

Chapter 7

9th May 2018
St Ives, Cambridgeshire

Paul and I mutually agreed to meet in St Ives town centre at a popular little café situated on the River Great Ouse. I went with Mum occasionally, and it always felt welcoming, safe. As I got ready, I couldn't believe I'd been so sure about calling it off with Paul and yet I hadn't. I questioned what that meant, and whether we had become honest and trusting friends, or something more? I didn't know. It made me wonder for the first time, could I get back to where I was before? Could I be normal? In all of my battles over the past decade, I fought to find a 'tomorrow'. But could it be, that tomorrow was finally here? Wondering hurt my head so I stopped myself. One thing was for sure, whatever Paul and I were, it was about to take a step forward. I just didn't know which foot it would step on first.

I got ready to leave, dressing and changing a few times until I had an outfit I felt was right for the occasion. A pair of black skinny jeans and a loose-fitting, long-sleeved jade-green top. I felt daunted because I couldn't wait to see him. I was still scared to leave the house, still carrying the icy hand that rested in my chest, waiting to pull my diaphragm into a panic attack. But sometimes, like now, it let me have a break, and I knew I had to seize the opportunity it presented.

I appraised myself in the mirror, making sure all the parts of my skin I wanted hidden were concealed. I wasn't as slim as I was back when I ran, but I didn't feel hideous for a change. I felt good, nervous, but good. Until today I hadn't thought about how I looked – or rather, how I presented myself – in ages, and I'd missed the feeling. I hadn't even considered what to wear on our first 'date', but let my mum guide my outfit decision. One that, in hindsight, made me look similar to her.

Slipping on my cream pumps I walked towards my front door, and the light feeling in my chest was gone. I was so caught up in the idea of being opposite Paul, hearing his voice, learning about his week, apologising for my behaviour, I had forgotten I needed to be in the world first. Before I could see Paul, I had to open my door and take that first step outside. The innocuous white UPC portal acted like a gateway. A passage to a place where I didn't know who was behind me, I didn't know what was around the next corner. Stepping towards it I quietly peered through the peep hole before removing the safety chain. Satisfied there was no one there I lowered myself enough for the long necklace to reach the lock and slid the key hanging from it in the door. I turned it slowly, hearing the lock snap open. Sliding the key out I grabbed the handle and readied myself to push down. The mechanics inside the doorframe would then slide the two latches in the top and bottom of the door and it would open. I had one more check through the peep hole and as I did, there was movement outside. A person walking away.

I panicked and stumbled backwards, grabbing the doorframe to the lounge to stop me falling. I crouched and moved into my living room and looked through the window so I could see the street. There was nobody there. I needed to lock the door again and had to fight against the paralysis in my muscles. I could feel myself shaking as I crept back to the door and lifted the handle, so it couldn't be opened from the outside. I fumbled with unsteady hands at the chain around my neck to grab the right key. Sliding it back in the lock I turned, the snap of the mechanics engaging like music to my ears. Taking a few measured breaths, I placed my eye to the peep hole once more. The street outside my house was empty. I thought maybe, after being recognised in the supermarket, the young couple who helped me might have sold me out to the press, and they were doing a follow-up story about the 'woman who lived'. But that was ridiculous, it was just a person, on their way to the shops or something. And I had blown it out of proportion.

'Shit, Claire. Get a grip.'

Holding my breath, pulse hammering in my neck, I opened my front door and stepped rather hastily into the street. Locking the door behind me I felt my fingertips tingle with each surge of adrenaline that coursed through my veins. Lowering my head, I started to move, hoping I wouldn't pass out. I focused on two things. The mid-morning sun was warm on the back of my neck and the patch of ground where my shadow and feet connected. As always, I counted, this time deciding to find and log cigarette butts. It was harder than counting chewing gum as there seemed to fewer of them these days, but this meant I had to look harder and so it served its purpose. I found one still burning, its end glowing a brilliant red as the hot embers died. I stopped and watched the small fire within fade to black.

I only saw a handful of people, all on the other side of the road and thankfully, heading in the opposite direction. As I turned onto London Road, I could see the beautiful St Ives Bridge that crossed the River Great Ouse, which distracted me, until I heard the sound of a man coughing behind me. I hadn't noticed anyone follow me when leaving the house, which meant that they were already on London Road. I knew I shouldn't panic. It was a busy road and a nice morning; I was bound to have someone behind me. And yet, I felt my blood move through my body that bit quicker. He coughed again, this time a little louder, or perhaps a little closer. I couldn't tell. Up ahead was the bridge, and just on the other side, the café where I was meeting Paul. I knew as soon as I saw him I would feel calmer, so I upped my pace.

I stepped onto the bridge, heard the cough again, and this time I was sure it was closer. Whoever it was, they were gaining on me and my anxiety was turning into a panic attack. I felt that icy hand on my diaphragm once more, plucking like a harpist, playing its tune as it had for years, and it took every ounce of my willpower to stop myself running as fast as I could. But I knew it was a battle I was losing. I heard a sniff, only a matter of feet away and, looking at the floor, I could see the tip of his shadow stretching out over my right shoulder. His head was disproportionately long, like a monster. I wanted to look behind but knew I shouldn't, so instead I took my phone from my pocket and using the glass like a mirror I snuck a peek behind me.

It was hard to make out his features but I could just see that the man behind me was older. His hair was thin, his face pitted with signs of wrinkles. I watched as he coughed again, lowering his head. Then when he looked up, I was sure his eyes locked onto mine though the screen and the icy hand pulled so hard I thought my lungs would tear away from my chest wall. My eyes began to brim, and my flight mechanism tried to power my legs into a hobbled run. But I knew if I ran now, I would run for years, as I had done for the last ten. I was tired of it, and I thought I had beaten it in recent months. I thought by agreeing to go to Ireland, by letting myself meet another man, by slowing down on my doctor appointments until I no longer went, and weaning myself off my medication, I was beating it. Evidently, I wasn't. That part of me that wanted to create distance and then hide was still with me. The part of me that ended up cowering behind a tree or in a shop doorway hadn't gone.

I wasn't supposed to be that person. I wasn't supposed to be what Tommy Kay wanted me to be. He'd wanted me dead, like the others, like Owen, and being like this, someone who was too scared to be outside, I might as well be dead.

But I couldn't let myself hide anymore. I couldn't let myself wish I was invisible. So, despite my head's instruction to run, I didn't. I stopped, turned and looked onto the river, pretending to immerse myself in the swans swimming towards the bridge, a mother followed by two cygnets. I leant on the ancient wall, my hands gripping the stone to pin me to my place.

In my peripheral vision I saw the man come very close. He looked at me, and gave a smile that said, '*I know all about you, Claire,*' and I drew a breath, holding it deep in my lungs. I stood firm. I would not run, I would not freak out. I would hold my ground. This was my patch of earth, my space, and I didn't want to give it away. He passed so close I felt the air between us stir, and as he continued past me I kept my eyes on the swan with her babies. He turned left at the end of the bridge and walk along the river bank. Then, seeing him a safe distance away, I let out my breath. He looked back at me just before disappearing into a butcher shop, and I did something uncharacteristic. I waved. I told him, *yes, I have seen you watching. I know you were there. And I'm not scared of you.*

He didn't wave back but stepped inside and closed the door behind him.

I knew he wasn't anyone I needed to be scared of. I knew he was just some man, and he looked at me because he was nosey or inquisitive. Smiling because he was being polite. I knew I didn't need to be afraid, but I was anyway. And I had waved. Because of the wave, I felt like I had won. I was a victor, not a victim.

And, after watching the swan and her young swim under the bridge I continued to walk towards the café, holding my head a little higher. I didn't count cigarette butts. I didn't try to hide in plain sight. I just walked, like anyone else would. And it felt bloody fantastic.

Walking along the river, past the butcher's that the man had gone into, I saw Paul up ahead, leaning against the wall to the café. As I drew closer, he squinted to see me properly and smiled broadly. I smiled back, and the invisible hand on my diaphragm loosened its grip.

Paul wasn't sure how to greet me, I could tell in his body language, his shuffling feet, his arms not outstretched but not by his side either. So, to help him know, I stepped into his space and wrapped my arms around his waist. I felt his lungs contract as he let out a long sigh, his arms became heavy on my shoulders as I felt tension release. Then he kissed me on the top of my head.

'Hey,' he said quietly, as he stepped back to meet my eye, a smile firmly on his face.

'Hey.'

'Hungry?'

'Yeah, I could eat. Are you?'

'Starved.'

'Starved? Well, we'd better go in, hadn't we?'

Taking his hand, I led us towards the door and opened it. I could see he wanted to take the lead and gesture me inside, but I insisted and awkwardly he followed. The café was busy, mainly filled with pensioners having tea. There were also a few mums scattered around a table, surrounded by buggies. They were all talking as they fed or held or rocked their little ones. One dad, sat near the window on his own was holding his newborn and stared vacantly out the window, wrapped up in his own thoughts. As Paul asked for a table for two, I watched the dad kiss his baby on the head before returning to his contentment. The scene forced a tingling sensation at the top of my nose, but before it could force its way up and become a tear Paul gently touched my arm, making my insides jump, and told me our table was in the far corner. I hoped he didn't notice me staring at the man and baby.

As Paul got up to order, I surveyed the room: noting where

the exits were, how many people were seated, whether anyone seemed suspicious or anxious. As far as I could tell, only I fitted that description. I watched the dad who was lost in thought get up, pack his things away and leave. I watched the mums chatting loudly and an older couple becoming increasingly irritated by it. I listened to people's conversations, my hearing flipping from one to the next, trying to gauge the mood of the room. I tuned into the music playing quietly behind. An old one by Stereophonics that I used to love. I plotted the route I would take if I needed to get out quickly, and what I could use in defense if required. I did all of this in the few minutes Paul was at the counter. It was something I always did when I wasn't at home. My brain was programmed to know how to escape.

Paul sat down and we chatted about nothing, the way normal people did. He spoke of work, how he was managing a difficult contract near Liverpool where the building of two hundred houses was behind schedule – as the contract manager for the estate which was being developed, it was his responsibly to get it back on track.

As he spoke, the stress of the workload clear across the lines in his forehead, I wondered again, might he have ever met Owen? Could they have been in the same place, at the same time? And again, I dismissed it, it was silly to connect them. I wondered if I was doing it to make myself feel better or worse? He must have sensed my thoughts were wandering and, assuming I was bored he stopped and changed the subject to one of his girls and the book by Harlan Coben he'd recently devoured. He was speaking a little quickly, as if my presence made him nervous. He hadn't the last time we'd met up, but last time I hadn't suggested ending our... whatever it was.

As our brunch came the tension lifted and we both focused on our food. I tucked into my poached eggs, enjoying the fact I could eat in front of him comfortably, and watched as he lost himself in his bacon sandwich. I knew I needed to offer something to get conversation flowing and just as I was about to talk about my impending trip to Ireland, and how nervous I was about it, my phone buzzed in my pocket. I took it out, expecting it to be a message from Mum. I couldn't hide my concerned expression as I saw it was another Facebook message from Killian.

As I opened it, Paul stopped eating and watched me.

Claire. I really want to talk, to see how you are. I want to help. I know next week will be hard for you, and I want to be there, as a friend.

Locking the phone, I put it face down on the table.

'Everything all right?' Paul wondered, his brow furrowed intently at me.

'Yes, fine.'

'Are you sure?'

'Honestly, it's fine.'

'Claire, you don't look fine.'

'It's just an old…' I stopped myself. 'Just someone I know who is behaving a little off lately.'

'Off?' Paul asked.

'Yes, it's hard to explain. I used to talk with him often, but over the past year he's become a little… it's hard to explain.'

'Is he giving you grief?'

'No, no he's not, but he's changed, and I don't like it.'

'What are you going to do?' he asked, and I liked the question. He didn't ask what he could do about it but trusted me to deal with it myself.

'I don't know yet. I think he'll understand I don't wish to talk and back away.'

He smiled at me, but I could see he was worried, concerned, curious, trying to piece together what might be going on in my head. I knew he wanted to understand me and the reasons I did things, and I thought it would be easier to not tell him anything and distance myself. But I didn't want to. Taking a deep breath, I prepared myself.

'Paul? How much do you know about what happened? You know, when I was in Ireland?'

'A bit.'

'Would you like to know more? I mean, more than the papers printed.'

'I've never read a newspaper story about you.'

'Never?'

'No, I don't follow the news much.'

'And you've not been curious since we met?'

'Yes, but only so I can understand you more. Out of respect, I've not looked – I figured if you wanted me to know, you'd tell me.'

'Really?'

'I'm not interested in pitying your past. I want to be a part of your future.'

'OK,' I said, knowing it was the right thing to do as soon as he said he didn't want to pity me; I'd had a lifetime of it already. Leaning over the table he took me by my hands, his touch warming them after the adrenaline of the bridge incident had sucked the blood from them. As he spoke, he focused on his thumb which gently stroked mine.

'But you don't have to tell me anything, Claire, you don't.'

Squeezing his hand, I brought my head up, our eyes meeting.

'You're right, Paul, I don't. But I want to, I do, and although I can't right now. I want you to know, one day I will tell you.'

Chapter 8

August 2007
Churchtown, Ireland

The second, third and fourth

Turning off the N20, he drove along the single-track road that stretched towards the setting sun in the distance. Either side of the narrow lane, the endless miles of Irish countryside were punctuated by the spotting of cows. On the CD player 'Paper Cut' by Linkin Park played as it had done on repeat since leaving his house an hour before. Listening to the song didn't send his adrenaline surging; if he was honest, he didn't particularly like it. But he listened anyway, over and over again on his drive to the village where the third lived, because, by accident, he stumbled upon the power of music for stimulating memory recall with his second kill.

The second was a man named Jamie Connell. A man who had divorced and remarried by the age of twenty-five, his first wife having the sense of mind to leave when his drinking and subsequent rage became something more than just a niggling concern. He hadn't learnt to change his ways when marrying his younger bride, Felicity, and it didn't take her long to learn Jamie ruled his home with a heavy hand.

He met the second in the O'Callaghan's pub in the middle of Coachford, a small village twenty miles outside Cork, a few days after his first kill. The media had just learnt that the victim died before the fire started, and his body had been the fuel used to ignite the house. Blair's wife's alibi was airtight, and images of her sobbing for her husband were everywhere. It was while watching a reporter talking about the fire that he struck up a conversation with Jamie, the murder being an easy way to lead into an 'innocent' chat. He noticed how people didn't bond over the positive things in the world. A story about a good deed or heroic act wouldn't be discussed out loud with a stranger. It was the darker things in life that drew humanity in, like a moth to the flame. He didn't speak to Jamie to determine if the man beside him belonged on his list but instead, wanted to speak out loud about the murder he had committed, and to watch how his new 'friend' would react without ever knowing he was talking to the perpetrator. As they spoke, he enjoyed the power that came with the truth only he had knowledge of. Jamie Connell unknowingly called him a monster, the devil incarnate, and as he agreed he fought to suppress his smile at how wrong Jamie was. He wasn't the devil; he was the opposite. He was doing God's work and, although he didn't know it yet, the man sat beside him was one of the real monsters in the world.

That night they drank and got to know one another. As they played pool, Jamie was inebriated enough to speak of more personal matters: his work, his hobbies, his wife. As soon as Jamie mentioned her name, the energy changed, and recognising why, his senses heightened. He watched his drunk acquaintance with more intent, and listened a little closer. He discovered a person of interest. The others on the list would possibly have to wait. He suspected his new friend was right for his list not because of anything he said about his wife, but the way he said it. His tone, and the slight curl of his lip suggested she was below him, a lesser person. Jamie didn't talk of his wife for long, but enough to awaken his instincts, and listen. They told him the man before him, Jamie Connell, was next. Jamie moved onto football, specifically the 2002 World Cup and the magnificent 1-1 draw with Germany, and the dreaded penalty shoot-out against Spain which ended the plucky boys in green's run. He almost felt normal as they spoke, but not quite, because he was focusing more on the man Jamie was. His height, weight, whether he was left- or right-handed. Details that would be important to know later on.

As they chatted and played, he noticed Jamie's pint was empty and went to the bar to get two more, opting for a lager-shandy for himself. He didn't want to be drunk but wanted to appear to be drinking. As he returned, Jamie was talking quietly into his phone, speaking with his wife. He listened as Jamie told her she couldn't go out with her friends as he needed her to be at home when he returned. She must have asked what time that would be because after a pause he said, he would be home 'when he fucking well pleased'. As Jamie hung up, he pretended he hadn't heard the call and passed his new buddy his pint, knowing for sure, now, that Jamie Connell would be the second.

It was on a cold and wet January, eight months after he first met Jamie, that he killed the power to his house and the seven others in the close he lived in. He knew from the months of learning, months of watching, that Jamie would be alone. Felicity, his wife, was visiting her mother who lived in a nursing home. She only visited once a week, on a Tuesday, because this was the only night Jamie would let her go out, despite him being in the pub most nights. His wife did as she was told because she was afraid of his temper. But not now. He had lifted her from her fear and punished the man who created her suffering. On the night he killed the second, a Radiohead song played in the background. He knew Jamie loved this particular song, he'd mentioned he liked to fall asleep to it when he was drunk. As he worked on

Jamie, preparing the body and the house to be incinerated, the song played, barely audible though his victim's headphones, but enough to immortalise the moment in his mind. Now, when he heard that song, he felt the same emotions, adrenaline and excitement he did that night.

As was Radiohead to Jamie, Linkin Park would be for ever linked with the night of the third, because the third mentioned once that 'Paper Cut' was his favourite song when it came on in the pub they were drinking in. From tonight, every time he heard that song, he would be reliving the final moments of thirty-eight-year-old Jack Merrill.

Driving past the sign welcoming him to Churchtown he turned down the car stereo and calmly drove into the village. Parking his car opposite the Boss Murphy pub, the place he met the third, he collected himself before climbing out. Opening the boot, he grabbed his rucksack which housed the tools needed for the job. The bag was lighter than with the first two. He had fine-tuned exactly what was needed for his kill. Slowly, he made his way past the pub in which he met Jack and up the hill towards his house. His hands tingled with the knowledge of how tonight would be different – an evolution, God moving though him to ensure his message would be heard as it should be. Tonight, he would do something new. Something he only recently considered. Tonight, he would punish not just the husband; tonight, he would punish the wife as well.

When the thought first came into his head, he dismissed it. But, in the aftermath of the second and the country making the connection between the crimes, which led the media to suggest he may well be the first serial killer in the Republic of Ireland since the 1900s, he watched the victims' families and friends say what saints they were. He listened as they called him a monster, while the dead were, by contrast, funny, kind, caring men. Men who didn't deserve to die. Men who were now watching down from heaven above. And none spoke louder and with more conviction than the wives, the women who knew as much as he did that they deserved to die. He watched as they lied time after time to the cameras, crocodile tears falling. He watched them both declare they would love their husbands until the day they joined them in heaven. At first, he was stunned – he expected them to be happy that they were at last free, but he realised something. The men were on his list for two reasons. One: they had chosen to inflict hurt and suffering, they chose to be like his father. The second reason surprised him. The wives hadn't left them, because they were weak. If he wanted change, men like his father and women like his mother needed to understand they had to look at themselves, alter their choices, evolve. If they didn't, he would come for them.

Life was about making choices, and these women, just like his own poor mother, were fated to die unhappy.

The sub-generator was located at the end of the row of houses where the third and his wife lived. As before, killing the power was an easy task. This generator ran most of the village and from his elevated position he watched the houses below descend into darkness. Then, within minutes, the torches and candles shone, the dim light bleeding through the curtains. Although he couldn't see anyone, he could almost taste their trepidation, their fear that quietly bubbled. Most would no doubt dismiss it out of hand, rationalising that it was just a power cut, nothing more. Because bad things didn't happen to them.

He entered the house via the back door, and once inside, he took the protective coverall from his bag and dressed over his clothes. Once confident he was suitably covered, with none of his skin or hair exposed and able to leave DNA, he waited quietly in the corner of the kitchen whilst the third and his wife moved around the house, Jack blaming her for the power outage. Quietly he took a roll of tape from his bag and waited. Ideally, the wife would come into the kitchen. Then he would grab her from behind, covering her mouth and tell her if she made a noise, he would kill her. Once she was bound and gagged, he could go to work on the husband. He hoped the shock and fear meant she would comply – if not, he would have to suffocate her.

Eventually, the door between the hallway and kitchen opened, and in walked the slight frame of the wife. As she moved gingerly in the low light, he padded towards her and in one swift movement he placed his hand over her mouth, his other arm wrapping around her throat. He whispered his demands, and her body went limp as she passed out. It made gagging her and binding her wrists and ankles together, like a pig ready for the spit, far easier than he could possibly have hoped. Satisfied she couldn't move or shout for help, he stood and stretched his back. Then, as he heard Jack's voice carried from the living room, he held his breath.

'Charlotte?'

Putting the tape on the kitchen countertop, he removed the bolt cutters from his rucksack and sidestepped to the doorway. He held them above his head, like a baseball bat.

'Charlotte?' Jack called again, more agitated. That was good, it meant he would come into the kitchen soon, charging in like the bull he was.

'Charlotte?' he shouted, angry and full of contempt.

He heard him mumble 'for fuck's sake' before his heavy footsteps bounded towards the kitchen. As the third opened the door he spoke, only managing a few words before the bolt cutters silenced him as he was hit square in the face. In the low light he almost laughed as Jack's legs flew up, cartoon-like, before his head hit the floor. Surprisingly, the blow didn't render him unconscious, not fully. He lay mumbling incoherently. Blood oozed from his mouth and nose, and his jaw was badly broken. Standing over him, he picked up the gaffer tape and wrapped it around his distorted face, trapping in the screams that Jack tried to voice as his broken jaw tugged and squeezed. The pain was evidently too much, and like his wife, Jack passed out.

Leaving him on the floor, blood still seeping from his nose, he dragged Charlotte by the ankle to the foot of the stairs, then lifted her over his shoulder and carried her up, placing her beside the radiator in the bathroom. She lay at a funny angle, and he had to check her pulse to ensure she wasn't already dead. Her jugular vein thumped under his fingertips, for now. Using the tape, he bound her to the radiator, just in case she woke. Then going back downstairs, he stepped over Jack to get to the kitchen sink, filled up a glass of water and threw it on his face, waking him with a start.

For a moment the victim didn't know where he was, or what had happened, and he enjoyed the moment the realisation came, the fear in his eyes. The shock spasmed Jack's body involuntarily, and he squirmed, trying to escape. Dragging him to his feet he punched him again in the jaw, the sound of it breaking further reverberating through the house, and Jack's knees buckled. Calmly, he bound Jack's wrists and ankles together, and throwing his backpack over his shoulder, he dragged him up the stairs, heaving him in the bathtub beside his unconscious wife. Jack tried to climb out but slipped. He hit him again, and the pain robbed Jack of his ability to use his body properly. The third looked like a bee drowning in a glass of water.

With the first two kills he played with his victim before this moment, but he learnt that the anticipation of pain, real pain, was far more terrifying than experiencing it. Jack wouldn't be cut like the other men were, he wouldn't be maimed. He'd learnt with the first two that when experiencing real pain, people retreat into themselves, the shock too much for their conscious minds to take. They didn't face their fate but hid from it, like the cowards they were. No, he wouldn't hurt him, instead he'd suggest he might, ensuring Jack would remain present. After a few minutes of toying with his victim he took his bag off his back and removed a small canister and poured its contents over Jack. The smell of petrol on his skin made him panic, and Jack tried to climb out of the bath but again was struck hard for trying, and again, he fell limp. He wondered if it wasn't for the tape holding Jack's face together, would his jaw still be attached?

Jack was no longer a concern, he wasn't going anywhere now, and so he turned to look at his wife. She had regained consciousness and sat paralysed by her fear. Her eyes were the only part of her moving as they darted from side to side, her mind unable to comprehend, unable to process what she was seeing. A part of him was still sad that he had to do this to her. She had suffered at her husband's hand for long enough. But then he remembered, it was her choice to be here now, not his. And he was doing the work God wouldn't do. If he killed more, others would listen. Men would change, women would leave. What he was doing was for the greater good. Like when the rains came for forty days and forty nights to rid the evil in the world. Now, he was the rain.

He opened the bolt cutters and placed one blade resting on the toes of Charlotte's right foot. Knowing what he was about to do, she passed out again and he couldn't help but feel mildly disappointed. Then, closing the cutters, he removed her toes. A symbol for her not running when she could. He expected it to be harder to do, but it wasn't dissimilar to when he cut his buddleia after letting it grow wildly all summer. A small amount of pressure and the handles met. Collecting her toes, he dropped them in the bath and just before leaving he lit a match and threw it on Jack's leg. The petrol ignited his trousers, spreading quickly to his torso.

Jack's burning body lit the room amply, almost romantically, and using that light he collected his belongings. Once content he hadn't left any trace of himself, he removed the coverall, dropping it on the fire, and left the house. A few minutes later he was back in his car and driving away.

It wasn't until he was on the N20 heading north did he see the first of the fire engines rushing past in the opposite direction. He wondered if they already knew, before arriving to the scene, that he had struck again.

Chapter 9

16th May 2018
A14, en route to Stansted Airport

Sat in the back of the taxi I watched the early morning world rush by. The blur of cars from the other side of the unmoving A14 became a constant stream of metal. I was vaguely aware Mum was saying something beside me, but I couldn't pick out her words. I was unable to think about anything other than the pulsing sensation in my hands, which were clasped together so tightly my fingertips tingled. I considered prising them apart, but thought if I did, my anxiety would spill out of my palms.

'Claire?'

'Sorry, Mum, I was miles away.'

'I can see that. How are you feeling?'

I looked at her and she gave a smile back, one that told me she knew it was a stupid question.

'It will be OK.'

'Will it?'

'Yes, this will do you good. I think it will do us both good.'

I hadn't considered that before. How Mum might need this

67

as much as I did. She too loved Owen and the home that was all but destroyed in the fire had once been hers. And Ireland, that was her home too, before she left and moved to England to be nearer to Geoff. It wasn't just me who hadn't been back to Ireland in ten years, but her also.

'Mum, how are you feeling about going?'

'I'm nervous... scared, even. It's been a long time.'

'It has. I'm scared, too, I guess.'

'There's nothing wrong with that.'

'So why do I feel like there is?'

'Only you can answer that. Claire, how about me and you, we get through it together?'

'That sounds great.'

'And just know, if you want to talk about it – any of it – you can, and I won't pass judgement, I won't react. You can tell me anything, OK?'

'Thanks, Mum.'

I smiled as best I could and turned my attention back to the window. The sun rising in front of us bounced off the damp road, blinding me. I knew what she was hinting at. Despite Mum being by my side for the last ten years, I hadn't really talked about that night with her. Our response to the events that had changed who I was, the events that killed Owen, was only ever reactive. We dealt with the immediate recovery, or responded to the panic attacks, the media, the trauma. But we never looked back. We never talked through what happened. We only ever tried to move forward. I felt that this trip wasn't about saying goodbye to the past but allowing me to talk about it openly.

The taxi slowed, and I heard the indicator ticking as we veered left. In front I saw the terminal building for Stansted Airport. And the icy hand plucked inside me once more.

Chapter 10

Because Mum was just as mischievous now as she was as a teenager, she carried a walking stick to make her seem more elderly. It meant people gave us some distance and allowed her to move freely through the busy airport crowds. We breezed along to the check-in desk. Mum pretended to struggle with her bags, so I helped her load her obscenely over-packed bag onto the conveyor belt. Its weight was a couple of kilograms over the 15kg limit. The man at the desk smiled, his teeth whiter than I thought possible and said sympathetically he'd let her off the extra weight, just this once. Mum thanked him with a fake tired smile.

I couldn't help wondering if she was laying it on thick because she hated queues, something she regularly told me and Geoff, or if she did it for my benefit – to give us space to make sure people were looking at her instead of me. I knew the answer was the latter without needing to ask, and I bloody loved my mum for it. If I mentioned it, asking if she pretended to be immobile for me, she would deny it, saying she was just abusing her position in life, followed up with something like, 'It's not always about you, Claire.' So, I didn't bother, and instead loaded my case on to the conveyor belt and watched nervously as it disappeared behind the check-in desks, hoping I would see it again in a few hours once we landed at Shannon Airport.

We joined the queue for security clearance and I watched as people calmly removed their belts, emptied their pockets, stepped through the metal detector and collected their things seamlessly, barely blinking as they moved on to the duty-free shopping area. I also watched others stop when instructed to and have their bodies scrutinised with the wand to check for metal, sometimes being physically prodded. Most didn't seem fazed by the airport security patting them down; one man even smiled, then apologised saying he was ticklish.

As we got closer to the front of the line, I didn't feel ready to go through, so stepped to the side, the people behind me giving me strange looks as they squeezed past me and through security before heading into the departure lounge. I realised that I must have looked suspicious, and just hoped people assumed I was a nervous flyer, not anything else. I knew I had nothing to worry about. I wasn't carrying anything I shouldn't be. But because I hesitated and kept letting people past, the security staff also gave me quizzical looks and, feeling them assessing me, I tried to turn and walk away. Before I completed my first step back towards the exit, and eventually home, Mum grabbed my arm, her thumb pressing into one of my scars by accident.

'Mum, let go.'

'Claire, we are doing this.'

'I was just…'

'I know what you were going to do, love, I'm your mum. We can do this. *You* can do—'

'Mum, I can't, I can't. I want to, believe me I do, but I can't. I want to go home.'

'I know you do, and you will, after you have done this. You're not alone, I'm with you, and I'll look after you.'

'How on earth would you…' I stopped myself before I finished my thought.

Mum opened her mouth to speak, but before she could, she was cut off by an approaching airport staff member, a big man with a deep voice.

'Excuse me, is everything all right?'

His voice startled me, and I instinctively took a step away, covering my abdomen. Even though it was a subtle movement, it caught the full attention of the man.

'Miss, is everything OK?'

'Yes, sorry, I'm just a nervous flyer.'

'I see. Well, you know you're more likely to die on the way to the airport than you are in a plane crash.'

'Yes, thank you,' I said flashing a glance to Mum who struggled not to laugh.

'Happy to help,' he replied, sounding pleased with himself.

As he walked back to scrutinise the approaching passengers, I glanced at Mum who was looking at the floor, trying to hold herself together. I knew her well enough to know she wouldn't be able to do it for long and as soon as she lifted her head and met my eye she laughed, her shoulders bouncing up and down as she did. Her contagious chuckle swept over me and I laughed too. The security guard's awkward comment wasn't that funny, not really. But it lifted the tension so, oddly, he helped.

Before I realised what was happening, Mum and I were at the front of the queue. She approached the scanners first, her walking stick beeping as she stepped through, and I watched as they took out their wands. Then it was my turn. I walked through without incident, and just as I let out my breath, thinking I was all right, the security guard who was eyeing me from afar walked over, and asked me to step to one side. I did as instructed. My rational side knew he was only asking because I had looked suspicious in the queue. But my rational side wasn't in the driving seat. A

71

female officer came over and asked me to raise my arms. She felt across the tops of my shoulders and forearms, slowing when she felt the skin on my right one was different. Not knowing it was scar tissue, she asked me to lift my sleeves.

'Do I have to? I haven't got anything on me.'

'Please, madam, roll up your sleeves.'

I did as she asked, trying to find Mum who had been ushered to one side to allow other people to collect their belongings. I raised my left sleeve and paused before rolling up my right. As soon as I did, I saw her expression change from suspicion to something else – shock perhaps, or pity.

'Thank you,' she said, unable to hold my eye.

'It's OK,' I replied, my voice quieter than I thought it would be.

She checked my legs and sides, pausing again when she found scar tissue. I saw Mum, who had battled her way back to be in my eye line. She stood, unblinking, looking directly at me. I tried to smile and only managed a weak one. She nodded at me, telling me she was there. She was with me.

'Could you take your shoes off, please?'

'What?'

'Your shoes, please.'

'Do I have to?'

'I'm afraid so, airport procedure.'

'Please,' I begged, and I could see she didn't want to have me remove them.

'I'm sorry. It's procedure.'

Nodding, I slipped my left shoe off and then slowly removed my right. I was wearing pop socks, but even through them you could see the deformed mass that was once a foot.

'Thank you, madam,' she said as she stood, meeting my eye. Her shock or pity turned into recognition. 'I'm sorry I stopped you.'

'It's all right, you're just doing your job.'

'Some things are more important, though, aren't they?'

Turning, she picked up my bag from the conveyor belt and handed it to me.

'Mrs Moore, it's been an honour to meet you.'

I nodded and stepped past her, clutching my bag to my chest. As I joined Mum, she didn't say anything but squeezed my shoulder and I nodded at her, telling her I was all right. Walking away, I looked back to the security checkpoint and saw the woman who had searched me standing next to her male colleague, both looking in my direction. They smiled, and I turned away. Mum linked her arm through mine as we headed into the busy departure lounge.

Chapter 11

16th May 2018
Southern Ireland

I was glad Mum insisted on getting an automatic, so she could drive, because as we headed southbound on the N18 I couldn't stop my right leg from shaking. It had been this way since just after the pilot announced we were making our descent into Shannon Airport. At first, I tried to hide it from Mum, but that was a pointless notion because as soon as it started she placed her hand on my knee, trying to calm me. It worked, too, just for that split second.

Mum drove in silence, as we covered mile after mile, drawing ever closer to Newmarket, to home. I looked out into the windows of passing cars, the drivers in their own metal bubbles like us, with their own worries and adventures and thoughts. None of which I would ever know. As they passed us by – Mum was an impossibly slow driver – I looked beyond to the views of the rolling countryside that lined the motorway. It looked so alien and yet it was something I once had known very well. The chlorophyll from the grass used to course through my veins. The pollen once filled my lungs. I was a stranger to something that was as much a part of me as anything else, and I hadn't realised how sad that made me feel. I was sure Mum could sense my longing and interrupted my thoughts before I could spiral into a gloomy reflection.

'Claire, do you want to do it tonight?' She didn't need to say what the 'it' was. We both knew.

'No, Mum, I don't think I'm ready.'

'I understand, love, but tomorrow we have to, whether you think you're ready or not. We need to get this done,' she said hastily.

I turned in my chair to face her; she didn't look back but focused on the fast-moving motorway ahead. 'Get this done? Mum, this is hard for me, it's not like we're just popping over to visit a place I once knew. Owen...'

I didn't finish, I couldn't. It was so difficult to keep my emotions in check without speaking about the events of a decade ago. Saying them out loud would undo me. And I couldn't be useless here. Not again. Mum turned to look at me, just for a second, before her eyes went back to the road and I watched something change in her, the steely persona dropped. And she looked, for the first time since I could remember, fallible.

'Sorry, love, I'm just as anxious about it as you are. I mean, it is the place I nearly lost you.' She paused, taking a deep breath. 'You know, that night, when the call came in telling me what had happened I thought it was some kind of cruel joke, and I was angry at you for playing it. It wasn't until I turned on the TV and saw that image, that image of you...' She paused, unable to finish her sentence. And I was grateful. That image, the one of me the world saw that night, has haunted me ever since. I've not seen it in years, but I can remember every detail, even now.

'I don't always look at things through someone else's perspective,' I said softly.

'And you shouldn't, it's not your job to empathise with how others might be feeling.'

'But I never recognise how hard it must have been for you.'

I watched as Mum's chin quivered slightly, before she took a deep breath, quelling it. Brushing the indicator, she manoeuvred on to the hard shoulder, pulled up the handbrake and turned on the hazard lights. As she spoke, her voice was as fragile as newly formed ice.

'I would be lying if I didn't say that night nearly killed me too, Claire. But it didn't, and we survived. You survived, not just that night, but every night since. It doesn't matter what *I'm* feeling, your only job is to look after how *you're* feeling.'

'I know but...'

'But nothing,' she said, taking my hands in hers. 'Claire, yes, it's hard for me to be here, but I cannot begin to imagine what is going on in your head. You take as much time as you need. I'm sorry I snapped at you.'

'I promise to be more mindful too, Mum. We'll help each other through this.'

'You and me.'

'Yes, Mum, you and me.'

She nodded in the way she did once her mind was made up about something, and putting the car in gear, we rejoined the motorway heading towards Newmarket.

Chapter 12

16th May 2018
South of Newmarket, Ireland

As the miles passed, the motorway became an A-road that became a winding country lane. After about an hour, I saw a sign for Freemount. Owen and I once had a picnic there, about a year after we married, but I couldn't remember why we'd gone there specifically. There was nothing notable like a castle or lake. But it may have been the nicest picnic we'd ever shared. We found a quiet, open park and lay our blanket in the shadow of a huge old oak, with limbs as thick as the trunk, that bowed under the strain of their weight. We didn't have a lot of money then, so our picnic was modest, consisting of a few sandwiches, some crisps, and a bottle of lemonade we drank from plastic champagne flutes. We spoke about everything and nothing and found shapes in the clouds. At one point a young family came and played in the swing park on the other side of the huge expanse of grass. The children's laughs and delighted squeals hung on the warm breeze and floated over to us. As the sound drifted over our heads, I could see something in the way he was looking at the children imbue his gaze in way words couldn't. There was a sadness about the way he looked at me afterwards, if something was missing. It told me that maybe – just maybe – Owen Moore, the man who didn't want to have kids, had changed his mind.

As we passed the road that led to that park I hoped to glimpse the old oak across the fields. There was a half-built house blocking it. Disappointed, I faced the road again and tried not to look as we passed the turning on the right which, if we went down for about two miles, would lead to where I'd lived. Driving past Newmarket, the place I grew up, fell in love and eventually fled, we continued to our B&B in Cullen, thirteen miles south. We could have stayed closer, in Churchtown, Mallow or Kanturk. But they all had significance. There were victims from Churchtown, and Mallow was where Owen and I had married. Kanturk was a place I would visit tomorrow, for it was the place where they'd laid his body to rest. I knew of Cullen but had never been, and I guess that's why subconsciously I chose it.

Once we pulled up outside, I took a moment to pluck up the courage to get out of the car. We were in the middle of nowhere, and no one expected that I would ever come back to Ireland, yet I couldn't shift the thought I was being watched. Mum struggling with our bags forced me into action, and though she spoke as we walked up to the front of the farmhouse, I couldn't hear the words she was saying – instead, my senses where heightened to focus only on my surroundings, the sounds of nature. I thought I heard something directly behind and spun quickly, my fear taking momentary control over me, before my rational mind wrestled it back.

'Claire?'

'I'm fine, just a little jumpy.'

We checked into our farmhouse-style room with twin beds and as I sat on mine, I suddenly felt exhausted. Mum said she would freshen up and disappeared into the bathroom. Shortly after I could hear the shower running so I changed into something more comfortable, a pair of loose-fitting tracksuit bottoms and a baggy top, and lay on the bed nearest the window. Digging my phone from my bag, I switched it on and noticed I had two messages come through. The first was from Paul. It was short, but sweet.

I hope you and your mum got there OK, I'm thinking of you. X

I responded that we were fine, and I was tired. I wanted to say I was going to miss him but felt like I shouldn't. The second message was from Penny.

Hey, you, just wanted to say, what you are doing is bloody brilliant. Give me a ring whenever, you know me, always on my phone.

I smiled – even in text messages she was bubbly and caring. I didn't respond. I knew that I would probably call her later instead. I checked my emails, same old nonsense, and then checked my Facebook. I had a message. As I clicked on it I could feel that same unease creeping from my diaphragm again, the icy hand ready to play. When I saw who it was from, it played its tune, and as I opened the message it soared to a crescendo, sending vibrations through my body, literally making me shake.

I had another message from Killian.

Hi, Claire, I hear you're back in Ireland. I would love to see you if you get the chance.

The phone slipped from my hands and bounced on the hard wood floor. I left it there and jumped up to lock the door before turning and slumping to the ground.

Only Paul, Penny and Geoff knew that I was in Ireland. How did he know I was back?

Chapter 13

17th May 2018
Cullen, Ireland

I didn't sleep well, every sound that the farmhouse made turned into something bigger. The creaking of the old floorboards became, in my imagination, footsteps approaching. The door closing to the room next to ours morphed into the sound of someone breaking in and, in my half-asleep state, I was convinced what happened ten years ago was about to happen all over again.

When it was quiet enough for me to relax into my surroundings, my mind raced with questions of how Killian knew I was in Ireland. Killian unnerved me, and while his behaviour over the past year hadn't drastically changed, I felt there something different about him. He seemed to linger longer, wanting to speak more – like he was trying to push my buttons. Something that told me to keep my distance. In the early days I leant on him a lot. I guess it was partly because he was kind, he listened, and partly because he reminded me of Owen a little.

I'd told Killian things I hadn't told others. He knew about my dreams and my fear of going outside. He knew of a lot of the trauma I faced on that night in 2008. I wished now I hadn't told him. He meant well, but when he created the Facebook group 'in my honour' as he told me, things got a little too personal, too involved. The gifts and money were bad enough. But the group knowing my movements, congratulating me every time I left the house... it made me feel like I was always being watched. He even took it upon himself a few years ago to set up a group investigation of their own to try and prove categorically that Tommy Kay was or wasn't the Black-Out Killer. It made me feel sick, and when I asked him to stop, he seemed annoyed that I didn't understand he was doing all of this for me. And now somehow, he knew I was back, and all I could do was hope I didn't bump into him.

Eventually, exhaustion took over enough for me to stop thinking of Killian and drift off to sleep, and once I had dozed, I dreamt of the moment I smashed the bathroom window and fell out of it, landing heavily on my side, knocking the wind out of me. I could still feel the pouring rain beating down hard against my almost naked skin. I felt the pain as I dragged myself away from the house, I recalled my body covered in cold wet soil. It made moving difficult as I was heavy and sticky. And then I was lying at the bottom of my garden, curled into a ball, too exhausted to lift myself over the three-foot fence into the farmer's field behind my house that was now a raging inferno. A man ran towards me, his features unidentifiable in front of the intense blaze. Then lights from a helicopter beamed down on me, a beam from the heavens.

In the early days of dreaming this dream I woke screaming in terror, remembering the pain as if it was fresh. Gradually the terror was replaced with waking and sobbing into my pillow. About five years ago the tears stopped, and my heart pounding in my chest was all I felt. Now I was so desensitised to dreaming about it, my heart only skipped enough to open my eyes.

Once awake, the creaks and doors banging and wind howling

outside and thoughts of Killian all returned, and behind them lay the sense of dread knowing this was the day I was going to Kanturk to see Owen. Today was the day before the ten-year anniversary of that night. I didn't want to go to see Owen on the anniversary of the day he died. I didn't think it was right, because I wouldn't remember him for the life he lived, but the way he passed. It had taken me years to push that out of my mind, and I didn't want the image back. Also, Penny suggested the media might be there as it was a big anniversary, and I couldn't bear the thought of being in the papers again.

I wanted to recall what we'd been doing on our final full day together, but I couldn't recall anything. That day had always remained hazy, so it must have been just like any other day. Just another wet night in May. And knowing that I might not ever remember details of our final day together was desperately sad. The clearest thing I had of that night was the image of Owen's arm, hanging out of the bath tub. I forced myself to stop thinking, and instead I propped myself up by folding my pillow and looked out of the window, watching the sky change colour as the sun rose. The rising sun threw a narrow beam of light onto the wall opposite the window. As the minutes passed the beam of light moved until it fell over Mum in her bed, making her stir. She rolled over and stretched, and I couldn't help but feel a pang of envy at how well she slept. She clearly had dealt with the demons of the past, and I didn't know why that shocked me. She, like all of her generation, seemed like trees to me. The older they grew, the stronger they were. My mum's wrinkles were like the rings of a wide trunk, each one connected to the earth.

I hoped it would be the case for me as I got older.

As soon as she stirred enough for her eyes to focus on me, she knew I had had a rough night.

'Are you OK, love?'

'Yeah, fine. Just didn't sleep too well. Fancy a cuppa?'

'I thought you'd never ask.'

As I flicked on the small hotel kettle, Mum got up and wandered into the bathroom. I heard a tap run and the toilet flush as I waited for the kettle to pop. Just as I was squeezing the bags and adding the milk she joined me, fully dressed.

'Christ, Mum, are we going now?'

'No, love, I just want to go for a walk. Get some air in my lungs.'

'Thank God. I've not prepared myself.'

'You take your time.'

'How did you do it, you know, with Dad?'

'Prepare myself for when I went to see him after he died? Honestly, I don't know.'

'Oh.'

'When I first visited your dad, it had only been a few days since we laid him to rest. And despite thinking I would handle it... I didn't, no one can.'

'What if I can't cope?'

'Then you lean on me and I'll hold you up.'

'And what if it's the other way around, what if it's too much for you?'

'Then I'll lean, and you'll hold me up. And if it's too much for both of us at once, we'll both crumble together.'

'You make it sound like it's OK to fall apart?'

'Sometimes, love, it's not OK... sometimes it's crucial.'

I knew what she was referring to. Over the years, I'd cried when the media storm became too much, I'd cried when I woke from the dreams. I'd cried at the frustration of being trapped in my life. But I'd never cried for him. Maybe it was because I wasn't there when they laid him to rest, and the evening of his death was just the flickers my subconscious would let me see. I was scared, both physically and emotionally, and yet it still wasn't entirely real.

'Do you fancy a walk, love?'

'No, Mum, you go ahead, I'd only slow you down.'

'I don't mind strolling.'

'Honestly, you go ahead, I'll wash and get ready.'

'You need me to stay?'

'Could you, just while I'm in the bathroom?' I asked quietly. Even after all this time, I felt embarrassed needing someone close by every time I shut a bathroom door.

Mum picked up her cup of tea and sat on the bed while I quickly washed and brushed my teeth. Once in the bedroom again she kissed me on the head and opened the bedroom door, told me she would only be half an hour at most and left, taking her mug of tea with her. I locked the door behind her.

I quickly dressed, trying to push my anxiety down for the day ahead. Finishing my tea, I stood by the closed window, looking out to the view of green meadows. I watched the trees swaying gently in the breeze and the clouds moving overhead at a much faster pace, some of them heavy and rain-laden, threatening to burst. I remembered how in this part of Ireland the sun and rain constantly butted their heads. Although the sun was winning right now, I knew I'd better take an umbrella.

In the field beyond the B&B I saw a golden Labrador running with a stick in its mouth. At first, I couldn't see the owner, but then, to my right and far away, there was a man with his back to me, and when he turned and our eyes met I felt the colour drain from my face. There was something about his way that said he knew me. I tried to see his face, hidden under the shadow of the peak of his hat, hoping he would smile or wave or look away embarrassed. But he didn't, he just stood there, staring, his shaded face expressionless. Then, he lifted his head, allowing the morning sun to illuminate his face and I could swear that he nodded ever so slightly, as if to say, 'Yes, Claire. It's me.'

Stumbling backwards, I fell onto the bed and fought with the icy hand to release my chest, so I could take a breath. I saw speckles in my vision and my lips tingled. Lowering my head between my knees I tried to stop myself passing out.

The bedroom door knob rattled and panicking, I fell off the bed onto the floor. I watched as the knob turned; someone was trying to get in. Looking around for something to defend myself with, the only thing to hand was the bedside lamp so I scrambled over to unplug it, ready to hurl at him.

'Claire? Could you let me in?'

Mum's voice calmed me enough to stumble towards the door, the lamp still in my fist, and unlock the door. As soon as she stepped in, I slammed it behind her, locking it again.

'Claire? What's wrong?'

'I saw him, I don't know how, but I saw him.'

'Who?'

'He's outside.' I could feel myself hyperventilating.

'Claire? Who's outside?'

'Him, I swear it was him. Tommy Kay, that man, he looked just like Tommy Kay.'

Chapter 14

The fifth and sixth

He couldn't see, the darkness was absolute, but he knew from experience that what was in front of him was breathtaking. If it were daytime, he would be looking down into the valley from the famous 'Ladies View' that overlooked the lakes of Killarney. He'd come here once with his mother as a child but hadn't appreciated it then. Instead, he'd moaned that the drive along the mountain roads took too long and that there was nothing to do. Usually his mother tended to his needs and complaints, but on that day, she sat on the car bonnet looking at the view for over an hour. He wished now he'd joined her on the car, held her hand and understood how much she needed it. That day was the last day he would spend with her alive. He didn't doubt that he had chosen his victims and this date because of it. Kilgaven was only a twenty-minute drive from Ladies View. Today's date, sixteen years after he was here with his mother.

It was colder now than in February 1992 when, just six weeks before his tenth birthday, he walked home from school to find her. He'd known something was wrong the moment he stepped through the front door. The TV was on, the news playing. Images from a helicopter filmed over somewhere in America after a tornado had swept through. People's belongings were scattered amongst the debris. They cut to a shot on ground level, homes like a stack of cards that had been knocked over. Children huddled to parents in their nightwear, their faces neutral, unable to absorb what had happened. The broadcaster said that the total dead was over forty, but likely to rise. His mother seldom watched the news, she said it was too depressing to know of the horrors in the world. The fact it was on, and she wasn't even in the room, had sent a shudder through his little body.

'Mummy? Mummy?'

She didn't respond and when he looked into the kitchen she wasn't there. Slowly he made his way upstairs, each step fueled by the fear he didn't understand. He checked her bedroom, then his, then slowly he opened the bathroom door.

His father should have been at home, but he was on one of his 'walkabouts', a phrase he had stolen from his favourite film, *Crocodile Dundee*. Even as a nine-year-old he could see his longing as he watched the character played by Paul Hogan, a man without responsibly or care. A man who would leave and go to the other side of the world, just because he wanted to. He knew, even then, that his father was a broken man, and 'walkabout' was his word for his binge-drinking days where he would be in a pub somewhere, or a ditch, or another woman's bed. He would then return home and feel like a caged animal. Pacing, shouting, hitting, trying to fight his way from the cage that was always unlocked. As an adult he suspected his father wanted his mother to throw him out, but she never did. She needed him despite his vile behaviour. Year after year she'd excused his actions, telling friends she was clumsy when a new bruise appeared, until her 'clumsiness' drove those close to her away. The more she lied and hid from the world, the easier it was for his father to control her until she was just as trapped as he felt.

In the end, she found a way out for herself, and it should have been his father who shouldered the responsibility to find her.

He didn't know that blood could travel so far from the human body when spilt. He was shocked to see how much of the tiled walls it could cover, the white ceramic painted a dark colour. It was the first thing he thought about after finding her in the bathtub: the volume of paint that came from her small body. The blood must have sprayed out of her, arching like a rainbow across the room to hit the wall on the other side. It wasn't red like his when he cut his knee or grazed his elbow, but dark brown. Placing his hand on the wall it was sticky, and when he pulled back his handprint was perfectly positioned beside the towel rail. He looked at it for a moment, before looking at his palm, the dark stain tacky and cold. He closed his fist and opened it again, and cracks appeared like dry earth. It made him think of the summer before, with the little bird.

Wiping his hand on his trouser leg, he turned to face her. She was covered in the dark brown stains. Her torso, chest, arms, face, all spattered. Her eyes were open, looking at him. He tried not to blink as he looked back, but his eyes stung, and he had to. He felt like he had disappointed her. Stepping towards her he picked up a cloth from the edge of the bath beside her and, wetting it in the sink, he washed her face; her skin was cold and the texture of wax. Once her face was clean, he rinsed the cloth, observing the dark brown lightening to blood red as it mixed with the water and circled down the drain. Then, he closed the door behind him and made his way downstairs to watch the afternoon cartoons and wait for his father to come home.

Details of what happened next were hazy. He couldn't quite remember what his father did when he returned, unable to place if he had told him about his mother or led him to the bathroom or waited for him to find her for himself. What he did remember was the way the flashing lights from the police cars and ambulance bounced a brilliant blue colour off the tree outside his house. He remembered that they led him away in his slippers. The thick clouds keeping the frost away. He remembered how he tried to see his breath like dragon smoke, but it was even too warm for that. A woman with kind eyes wrapped him in a blanket and helped him climb into a car. His father, wearing just his vest, watched from the window.

Looking up to the night sky he breathed out, the memory of the night floating away as the air left his lungs. Tonight, he could see his breath was thick and heavy, even in the near pitch-black conditions. The moon, new in its cycle, gave no light which meant the world was lit by the stars themselves. Although he couldn't see the view now, he stood and looked at it anyway, waiting for his adrenaline to die down after the evening's kill.

The fifth and the sixth, Justin and Melanie Turner, had gone according to the plan. 'I Got You Babe' by Sonny and Cher was his soundtrack for the weeks leading up to it – he'd thought it seemed apt given their relationship. As he worked on the pair, he noticed his technique had been honed since the last time he killed: the electricity had been killed; the wife drugged; the husband placed in the bathtub. He had removed her toes and dropped her on her husband's body before setting him alight. He did it all without needing a second thought. It was seamless. Tomorrow's papers would have the same headline as before: THE BLACK-OUT KILLER STRIKES AGAIN. And fear would be the beating heart of Ireland once more.

When he began this journey, he hoped the media would play along, sensationalising the kills, driving panic into communities up and down the country. They hadn't disappointed. Unknowingly, they had made it easier for him to be in two or more places at once. They had made him omnipresent, like a god. Their name for him, the Black-Out Killer, meant that every time there was a power outage, his power grew. Six weeks before, the town of Mallow had a power cut caused by a transformer malfunctioning and the town panicked. As soon as it was known the power was out the media stormed. Helicopters flew overhead, their torches lighting the ground. The police were out in force and people huddled in their homes, terrified the killer would strike them dead. Even when the police tried to announce it was just a technical issue, people still lived in terror. He was at home that evening watching the football; he'd had a beer and when the chaos in Mallow was at its peak, he was sound asleep.

The only disappointment was that the media hadn't discovered what linked all of his victims. They portrayed every man whose life he'd taken to be an innocent, not worthy of the brutal manner of execution. He suspected, or at least hoped, that the police knew different. But they hadn't divulged the information. The wives he'd taken were also misrepresented as happy spouses, the perfect couples killed before their time. That would soon change, for he himself would leak to the press the link, pretending to be an officer working the case to give it enough credibility to be printable. Once the reason for his kills, the link between them all, was in the public domain, he was confident the change he was working towards would be brought about, and then he would stop, until he was needed again.

Chapter 15

17th May 2018
Cullen, Ireland

It took about an hour to feel like I could get up – the icy hand inside me telling me to make myself small, hide my body, like it did that night. For a long time, I couldn't hear anything other than the sound of blood rushing in my ears. This had happened before, and Mum knew what to do. When I eventually felt like myself again and opened my eyes, I was on the floor, looking at the ceiling, my head on her lap. My top had ridden up, exposing the bottom of my scar, the angry pink smile carved into my flesh. Slowly I covered it, hoping Mum didn't see.

'Mum?'

'It's all right, love.'

'It was him, I was sure of it. It was Tommy Kay,' I said, knowing how ridiculous I sounded. It couldn't have been Tommy Kay, he was long dead, and I didn't believe in ghosts.

'No, darling, it was just a man walking his dog.'

Slowly I raised myself to a sitting position, my head feeling heavier than it should. I quietly laughed at myself, a sad, deflated, hopeless noise.

'Mum, I'm a mess. Why did I convince myself I had seen a dead man?'

'Because of what we are doing today. Because we're home for the first time since it happened. Because you are thinking about him and what he did.'

Gingerly, I sat myself on the edge of the bed and rubbed my eyes. Mum got up and sat beside me.

'I feel so stupid.'

'Don't. These next few days will be tough.'

Mum smiled sheepishly and busied herself, giving me a moment to collect my thoughts. I was so sure I was looking at a ghost, but I knew it was impossible. Then I realised I might have seen someone I knew, and my tired, overwhelmed brain had altered the image.

'Mum, did you get a look at the man?'

She looked at me and waited for me to continue.

'Do you think it could have been Killian I saw?'

'Your friend from the Facebook group? No, love, I don't think it was him.'

'Are you sure?'

'Pretty sure, the man outside was older.'

'Was he?'

'Yes, I only glimpsed him, but I'd say he was in his fifties. Too old to be your friend. Besides, what would be the chances of him walking his dog outside the place we are staying in ten years after you left?'

I thought about that for a moment, and I knew the answer was higher than it should be. Killian knew I was here in Ireland, it wouldn't take much to find out where I was staying.

'How sure are you it wasn't him?'

'Love, it wasn't him.'

My messed-up head was making me see things that weren't

there, probably driven by my guilt. And I was thinking the longer I delayed doing what I came for, the harder it would be to stay here. Slowly getting up, making sure I was steady on my feet, I put on my jacket and smiled at Mum. She reciprocated, saying nothing, and we left the room. After a quick breakfast of some toast and a pot of tea we headed to the car and, as we climbed in, I looked back at the B&B to see if anything seemed out of place. But for the old building and fields beyond I couldn't see anything, or anyone. It was just another day. Fastening my seatbelt, I took a deep breath, and Mum fired up the car. It was time to see Owen.

Chapter 16

17th May 2018
Kanturk Cemetery

Five minutes into our journey, the heavens opened. It started as a light drizzle, but with each passing mile it intensified until even with the wipers on full speed, Mum and I could barely see more than a few feet in front of the car. She held the steering wheel firmly, her hands at ten to two. Above there was a crack of thunder and I jumped. I tried to hide the fact I was startled, thinking I'd gotten away with it for a moment until Mum shot me a worried glance. I gently touched her tensed arm, reassuring her I was OK. I felt far from it. There was a flash of lightning somewhere in the distance and the thunder clapped again; again, I jumped, this time swearing.

'Do you kiss your mother with that mouth?'

I forced myself to laugh, I wanted to sound light, calm, but it came out lined with sadness because it made me think of Owen even more. He used to say the same thing. We both knew why I was jumpy, and, we both knew it was an entirely valid reaction. I hoped the thunder wasn't some foreshadowing of what we were doing today. The last time I saw Owen we were dancing in the living room, a thunderstorm raging overhead, both of us drunk from the three bottles of red wine we had consumed between us.

We continued blindly until we drove through the entrance of Kanturk Cemetery and up the lane that ran through the centre of it. My breathing was shallow, like I had just run up a hill, and I couldn't stop myself fidgeting with my house keys which hung around my neck. I counted them and said my mantra in my head. Front door, back door, downstairs windows, upstairs windows.

I looked out at the graveyard. Row after row of beautifully kept headstones. Each one sectioned off with small concrete boarders. Some were single in width, some double, offering space for loved ones to rest beside one another. Some filled already, some waiting to be joined. Mum stopped the car and pulled up the handbrake. She turned and waited for me to say or do something. But the sound of the rain hitting the metal roof and the wipers powering back and forth was all I could think about. I knew what she was doing; she was wanting me to lead, to take ownership of the moment. She had done it the first time I went outside after I recovered enough to leave the hospital. The first time I shopped in the supermarket. The first time I drove. All three occasions she was there, patiently waiting for me to take the initial step.

Today, I couldn't. I just couldn't, and it wasn't because of my fear, or anxiety, but something else, something that made me feel intense guilt. I looked at my hands gripping the keys on my long necklace, my knuckles white.

'Mum?'

'There's no rush.'

'It's not that, I'm OK to see him, I am.'

'Then lead the way.'

'Mum, I can't.'

'Claire, you can do...'

I cut her off and looked at her, I tried to hold her eye, but failed and instead focused on the space between her ear and shoulder. My words barely audible.

'Mum, I don't know which one Owen is.'

'Oh, darling.'

Mum had been here on the day they laid him to rest. She had followed the hearse into the ground and joined the mourners, dressed in black, tears flowing. She had listened to the priest give his service and his friends talk about what a wonderful man he was. How he was the life and soul of the party. A good friend, a life cut short. Mum was there at the wake after, watching people close to Owen eat food and share stories and raise a glass in his honour. I wasn't – I was still in Cork Hospital in an induced coma as my body did all it could to recover. When I was well enough to leave, I wanted to come to him, to say goodbye, but the media were in full flight with the story, and that picture of me I would never forget. Mum and the doctors decided it was better for my recovery if I left. So, I didn't get to see him and was instead whisked to the airport, and out of Ireland.

Mum got out of the car and opened her umbrella before walking round to my side and helping me out. Tears pressed behind my eyes, trying to spill and I almost let them, but held on. I would cry for my husband when I could see him, not before. Mum led as we walked along a narrow gravel path between the graves, the umbrella only keeping my left side dry as I walked behind her.

We drifted in silence and I looked at the stones as I passed. Most were a dark grey marble that didn't show age. Engraved into them were gold letters naming people who had died. Husbands and wives sharing space, side by side, or sometimes, one on top of the other. I read their names. *June and Patrick, together. Maureen and Sean, resting in peace.* As much as they were beautiful, and moving, I felt terrible reading them. Soon I would find Owen's grave, and I knew there was no space for me. But there should have been, they should have dug a hole for two.

Mum stopped and turned to face me. Her expression was grave and serious.

'He's just there,' she said, gesturing with her head to her left, my right. Swapping places, I stepped from under the umbrella and a few paces from Mum who didn't follow. She nodded at me, the small movement, one I cherished for its ability to reassure me.

I turned and looked, and there he was. Quietly waiting for me, his wife. His stone not dissimilar to the others'. The same dark marble, the same gold letters. But Owen had no flowers around, no candles or teddies like the others. The words themselves, shorter than I expected them to be.

In loving memory of Owen Moore.
Devoted husband and son.
Taken too early.
1982-2008.

I looked back to Mum, the rain water sticking my hair to my cheek. She had wandered off back towards the car to give me a moment. Both her hands were on the umbrella, her gait calm and mindful. As I watched her, a flash of that night snapped into my mind. Me on the floor, dazed, drugged, searching for something I could focus on. And Owen's limp arm hanging over the bathtub.

Looking back to Owen's stone I knew I should say something, but I didn't know what – where did you start after ten years of only talking to him using the voice inside your head? I hesitated, hoping he would say something first, but that obviously wouldn't happen. I took a breath, the air snagging in my throat, my words coming out as a half cough, half sob. I managed to catch it before it could fully form into a cry. Just. I looked for Mum, but she was back in the car, looking straight ahead as if she was trying to discreetly watch me in her peripheral vision, and although I really wished she was standing beside me, holding my hand, both of us huddled under the umbrella, I knew what she was doing was for the best. She had an uncanny ability to always know. Even if I didn't.

I closed my eyes, and as I spoke, I pictured Owen stood in front of me, his hair wet and stuck to the side of his face, like mine. His smile, beaming in my direction. It almost felt like, if I reached for him, I could take his hand.

'Hey.' My voice cracked as I fought to keep it light. I waited for a response that didn't come. He just continued to smile. 'I'm sorry I've not been before, it's been, well, I'm guessing you know. And I know I should have come, but…'

I imagined him nodding knowingly, encouraging me to carry on. I did, but the words were sticky in my mouth.

'I guess I don't really have an excuse for not coming, not after so long.'

I had to pause, wiping a tear from my eye that I didn't try to hold back. 'Owen? Can you hear me? Are you there?'

More tears. This time I didn't catch them but let them fall, as they should have done ten years ago. Rain water ran off the end of my nose, dripped off my chin. My hair was heavy and soaked, and several beads of the ice-cold water escaped from my hairline down the back of my neck and slid between my shoulder blades. I was cold, my hands turned slightly blue and my body shook as my muscles fought to stay warm, but I didn't care. I could feel the rain, the cold, the water running down and under the back of my bra. Owen couldn't feel anything, and the last thing he felt, I couldn't bear thinking about.

'I miss you.' The words were heavy after a decade of waiting to be said. 'I think about you every day and it's weird, but I still, even after all this time, expect you to be beside me… I expect to hear your voice.' I lowered my head, ashamed of the fact I couldn't remember what he sounded like anymore. 'When I woke up, in the hospital after… and Mum told me you had died, that they had buried you, I tried to come. They told me I couldn't... I should have said *no*, I should have insisted I came to see you... but the media wouldn't leave me alone. I was the one who lived, and the world wanted to know about all of it. I wasn't strong enough to cope, and Mum took me to England to live with her and Geoff. I didn't know what else to do. I know that doesn't excuse ten years of not being here with you.'

I felt my chin wobble and the icy hand that permanently hovered relaxed, letting me breathe freely for the first time since landing in Ireland. When I spoke, the words came through sobs that hurt so much it almost brought me to my knees. 'I'm so sorry, Owen, can you hear me? I'm so sorry. I'm sorry I wasn't there when they buried you, I'm so sorry I've not been back in so long. I'm so sorry I couldn't save you. I'm sorry I escaped.' Looking at his golden name in the dark marble I blinked away the tears, so I could see the letters clearer. Owen Moore, my Owen Moore. I continued, my voice at barely a whisper. My words just for him and me. 'I should have died with you that night, I'm sorry I let you down.'

Leaning in, placing my left knee on the ground, aware his head was under it somewhere, I kissed his name and slowly rose to my feet.

'I'm going now. I hope you are somewhere better, my love,' I said, trying to sound more upbeat. It didn't last. 'I hope you can forgive me.'

I smiled a weak smile, wondering if he might see it somewhere, and walked towards the car, not able to look back. As I climbed in, Mum handed me a towel from the back seat and I dried my hair and face. She offered no sympathy, no platitudes about Owen, but just nodded and fired up the engine to leave. As she slowly pulled away, I looked back at Owen's stone, and already I had lost its place amongst the others. I felt so ashamed. So guilty.

Just as we were about to leave the cemetery Mum slammed on her brakes, and although we weren't going quickly, the seatbelt dug into my collarbone.

'Jesus!'

'What, Mum, are you OK?'

'Some idiot just ran across the entrance, I nearly hit him.'

'What? Where?' I looked in front and around, I couldn't see anyone.

'He went that way,' she said, pointing to our right. Again, I looked, but no one was there and as Mum pulled away and indicated to turn the way the man had run, I kept looking. It was probably just someone running to evade the rain, and he absentmindedly ran in front of the entrance, perhaps not expecting anyone to be in the cemetery in such horrid conditions – but I couldn't fight my heart rate rising.

As we turned into the flow of traffic and increased our speed, Mum pointed out the man she nearly hit. He wasn't running but stood under a bus shelter and I let out a sigh of relief. As we passed, he turned, and in his hand I noticed a camera which he held up to his eye, blocking out his face. I saw a bulb flash and as he lowered the camera, I gasped.

'Claire? Love, what is it?'

'It's him. I'm sure of it!'

'What? Who?'

'Killian. The man you nearly hit was Killian.'

'Are you sure?'

'Yes, no. I don't know, Mum.'

'If it was him, what's he doing here?

'I think he was taking photos of me.'

Hello, Claire,

I wonder if you somehow sense how close we have been to one another. How both you and I have stood in the same places, looked at the same things. I wish I could have seen your face when you visited the grave. I wish I could have examined up close the expression: I wish, Claire, I could have heard the words you no doubt said... I wonder how they would have sounded?

Of all the nights I worked in Ireland, of all the houses I visited, of all the lives I ended, I think about the night with you the most. Perhaps it was because you refused to die, when the others accepted their fate. Or perhaps, and here is the kicker, Claire, perhaps it's because I let you go.

That's right, Claire, I let you climb out of the bathroom window that night. And although I know you will not read these words for some time, I still feel excited writing them, knowing one day you will.

And the reason I let you climb out of that window? You fought back, you dictated you wouldn't die without trying, and I enjoyed that. I let you climb out, and I watched you drag yourself through the grass, wondering if you would survive. And you did, look at you! I find it entertaining that the world thinks you escaped from me. But I could have stopped you. I almost did, but as I watched you crawl through the mud, I knew you were meant to survive.

All I ever wanted was for people like you to learn, and in that moment I knew what a great asset you'd become. Your face wasn't just another face, another victim. You were something else, and as long as people remembered who you were they would think about me, and about what I stood for. But, now, ten years on, you are forgetting me. You are forgetting why I came.

You were never supposed to get over that night. You were supposed to stay trapped in the existence I created for you, for ever. But you have chosen another way, one you don't yet understand is the same way you once lived.

That night, our night, is the closest I have ever felt to anyone. Nothing has come close to that moment we shared. But knowing I mean less to you now means I need to act. Someone will die soon. A woman. My eighth, the eighth – the one that could have been you. And once she is gone, the journey that will bring us together again will begin, to relive our moment together.

*Until then, I'm never far away. **I'm closer than you think.***

Chapter 17

18th May 2018
Cullen, Ireland

After Kanturk we went straight back to the B&B. I was feeling too unsettled, too on edge to do the other thing we had planned for our trip. The only other thing we needed to do. I foolishly hoped that seeing Owen and talking with him would bring me peace, and allow me to sleep. It may well have done were it not for seeing Killian, or someone I thought was Killian, his camera raised, capturing my startled look. If it was him, I couldn't fathom how he knew we were seeing Owen at that exact moment. If it was the date of the ten-year anniversary, then I could understand, but us going the day before. There was no logical explanation other than he had been following us the entire time we were in Ireland. Thinking about him lurking around, watching, sent a shiver up my spine with such force I was sure it had frozen entirely. Thick ice spread across my ribs, sweeping around their curves, rendering my entire core solid and lifeless. Then again, I was certain I had seen Tommy Kay in a field with a Labrador when I knew Tommy Kay was dead. I was wondering if I was starting to properly lose my mind.

On the drive back, I told Mum about how Killian had once been someone I'd confided in. What she didn't know was how things between us had become weird. He'd sent gifts – not the ones that the Facebook group sent, via Mum, of food, books, and those cheques I couldn't bring myself to bank. Killian's gifts were personal, and without the group involvement. He sent chocolates, flowers, CDs he liked and thought I would like to, and when I asked him to stop, he became angry, calling me ungrateful. Pointing out the things he had done, the effort he went to for me, his words stinging and forceful. He later apologised, and I accepted it, but things hadn't felt right since. There was something in the way he spoke, an undertone that made me want to back away. That feeling had died down, but it had never left. His messages, although infrequent, still felt invasive. Until the cemetery, I'd tried to rationalise that how I felt about them said more about me than him.

Now, seeing him taking photographs and knowing he'd been following me made me realise that my instincts about him were right.

That is, if it was him at all.

Mum told me, reassured me, that if he bothered us on our final day here, she would 'sort him out'. I laughed, picturing my mum exercising her martial arts she took up in her early fifties – Killian wouldn't know where to turn.

After a fitful sleep, I was up, showered and sat in the breakfast room to force down a bowl of muesli I couldn't stomach. Paul had messaged late at night, but I didn't respond. I was too tired to work out what to say. Besides, Paul had the ability to see through me. I knew if I messaged saying things were fine, he'd know the reality, and worry. I didn't want to do that to him, not when I knew he would feel powerless to help. Over breakfast he messaged again, asking if I slept well, and again I couldn't reply. I didn't want to lie and say I slept fine but also didn't want to say that last night's dreams were horrible. In my sleeping state

I'd relived the moment I'd woken from what I was told later was a Rohypnol-induced unconsciousness, my body being dragged and dumped in the bathroom. In my peripheral vision was Owen's lifeless body, with his limp left arm hanging over the edge, somehow looking thinner than it should have done. The man stood over me with the bolt cutters. His face a blur, but for his mouth, wide-open and bloodied. A dark cavern that seemed too large to be human. I often dreamt of that moment, but seldom did I recall what happen next. Usually I woke up as he stepped towards me, my subconscious knowing what was to come. Last night, I hadn't. And in my sleep, I'd endured the agonising moment the cold, sharp metal pinched my toes. Then, with one swift movement, white hot pain shot up my leg as he removed them. I must have cried out, because when I came to, Mum had been by my side, stroking my hair.

It's been a long time since I did that.

Finishing our breakfast, we packed up the car, as after our final trip – the one thing still left to do – we were driving back to Shannon to fly home. Sat in the passenger seat, I read the messages from Paul again, guilty for not being able to respond. Knowing I wasn't in the mood to talk, Mum gently hummed to herself as the Irish countryside rolled by. As we passed a sign saying Newmarket was two kilometres away, the air in the car started to feel charged. Mum stopped humming, her nerves showing signs of fraying as the intensity built. She tried to hide it by chitchatting about the weather – right now it was sunny, but rain was only one cloud away – and I nodded politely. I was in no mood for small talk. If we were to speak, I needed it to be direct, and about why we were here.

'Mum, what if there is another house there now?'

'There won't be, the land is still ours.'

'What? You didn't sell it?'

'I couldn't let it go. That bungalow was the one you grew up in. You played hula-hoop, built dens. You and your father played hide and seek in the garden. And when he was unwell, it was the place your father would sit, listening to the wind in the trees – he made peace with dying because of that garden. I know I should have sold the land, I should have got rid of it after that night. But I was so focused on helping you through it, it hardly seemed a priority, then, time went by and it was less important.'

'Do you know what's there?'

'Some of the bungalow remains, but not a lot.'

'I see.'

The land was still ours, probably untouched in the past decade apart from what the forensics had done, and the media who seemed to enjoy reporting from the garden once the police has finished with it. But the home that had been built on it, the one we all loved so much, that was gone. In some ways, I wished the land was too.

As we hit Newmarket town centre, I felt the familiar stirring on my diaphragm. The hand didn't pluck but ran its nails across the muscles in my chest, like fingers on a chalkboard, scratching a noise that hurt my teeth. The town centre was quiet, and besides the occasional traffic light being red, we didn't stop as we drove down the arterial road, Church Street. It was in this town Owen and I would get a takeaway after a few drinks in the pub, him leaning on me, singing because he'd had one too many. It was in this town I first told him I loved him, and he said he loved me too. It had been here I could sense him hinting that he wanted to marry me. Being back on this road, I expected something to happen: a face I'd not seen in a long time to look up and catch my eye, a yearning from me to get out and walk around. But there was nothing. We passed through Newmarket like it was just a place, a small town, like any other. But it wasn't, and once the town centre was behind us, I knew it was less than three kilometres until we were back home. Back to the place that haunted my dreams.

Chapter 18

18th May 2018
Newmarket, Ireland

I slowly pulled myself from the car and took a few steps towards the shell that had once been my home. A section of roof above the bathroom and front bedroom was entirely missing. All of the windows had been blown out in the fire, or smashed since, by kids no doubt. On the walls of the side where the roof was missing, I could see the black smear of fire damage, even after all this time. I turned to tell Mum it was like it happened weeks ago, not years, not an entire decade, but she was still sat in the car, looking my way, and I couldn't work out if she was giving me space, like she did when visiting Owen, or if she could not face the house that nearly killed me.

Turning back to the ruin I could feel the walls trying to whisper to me, trying to tell me the secrets they held, and for a moment, I listened, unable to move, incapable of blinking. That night tried to force its way into my head with all of its horrid, violent detail, but I stopped it, I held it back. I didn't want to remember anymore. I wanted to let go, and I guess that was why Mum had insisted, rather forcefully, that we came here, not to reminisce, not to remember, but to say goodbye. I knew that what had happened that night would always hold on to me, it would always impact on how I saw the world, but maybe it would loosen its grip.

For years I thought if I ever came back here it would kill me, but so far it hadn't. I had been to see Owen's final resting place and survived. I had seen someone spying on me, taking photographs of me. Maybe it was Killian, maybe it wasn't, either way I survived, and I would survive this. I became someone who was getting by.

Without looking back again to Mum, I walked towards the ruin, taking measured steps, trying to minimise my limp. It felt important to step back into that moment as someone who was not a victim. I wanted the universe to know I was here through my own choice.

I made my way round to the back of the bungalow. Everything that happened to us occurred at the back. As I passed the front door and went down the side of the bungalow, the icy hand played its tune, the song that was about this place, that night. It tried to stop me, but I pushed it out and kept going. Kept breathing.

I waded through weeds that strangled the bushes I'd once pruned and stepped into the large back garden. The first thing I focused on was the small patch of fencing in the furthest corner, next to the compost heap where we threw out bush trimmings and grass cuttings. It was there they'd found me on that night, the helicopter lighting me from above. The place they shot that picture. The one they dug up every year. The three-foot chain link that bordered our land from the farmer's behind was still bent from the damage I'd caused when I tried to lift myself over to escape. The view behind it was beautiful in the late morning sun. I had forgotten how much I loved it. I heard footsteps behind me and panic shot though me until I realised it was Mum who had quietly come to stand by my side

'The view really is something special,' she said lightly.

'It rained that night,' I replied, surprising myself. She didn't respond but waited for me to continue.

'And you see the way the fence post is at an angle,' I continued, pointing to the corner I couldn't avoid, despite not wanting to look at it, 'that's from where I tried to climb over it and it bent under my weight.'

I didn't think I would ever talk about that moment; I thought it would be something Mum would never know about beyond what was printed in the papers, and yet, saying it out loud felt good. It felt needed, and now I had started I didn't want to stop. I looked towards the remains of the bathroom window. And from where I was standing, I was almost able to see inside.

'When I fell out of the window I landed there,' I said, pointing to patch of tall weeds below it. 'Then I crawled away as fast as I could. To that corner.' I walked towards the fence, feeling the weight of the past pressing down on me. Mum followed beside me, not offering any kind words, but allowing me to have the moment I didn't know I had needed for so long. It was weird, but as I continued it felt like the wind had stopped blowing so the trees could listen to my story.

'When I made it to the fence, I tried to climb over, but it snapped from the post beneath my weight, and I dropped to the ground,' I said, unable to look anywhere but at the fence.

I remembered snippets of that night, after I fell into the garden, and over the years, I had pieced it together. But I wasn't recalling it from my own perspective. I was outside, looking at me on the floor, like I was seeing my body through the eyes of the killer. Swallowing the saliva that had built up in my mouth I continued.

'I didn't have the strength to try again, so I curled up into a ball and hoped that in the darkness, and through the pouring rain, he couldn't see me. I remember I was so cold I couldn't stop my teeth from chattering. They snapped together so hard it hurt my entire face. Weirdly, that hurt more than my foot, more than

109

my stomach. I hadn't even realised that when I'd fallen out of the window I had cut my arm open.' I looked to my arm despite knowing the scar was covered with my long-sleeved top.

As my gaze met Mum's, she opened her mouth to say something, but I continued talking, stopping her before she could. 'I don't know how long I was there for either. I know that I felt heat coming from...' I hesitated, swallowed, I didn't want to cry. I needed to finish. 'Coming from the fire. It warmed my right side, making me feel colder on my left. The light coming from it made me notice I was almost naked. The flames threw light over the entire garden and beyond and I knew he would be able to see me. I tried to cover myself with the grass cuttings Owen had piled up that afternoon. But it was becoming harder to move. Blood loss, I guess.'

A single tear fell from my eye and I wiped it away with the back of my hand. Mum said nothing, but held my gaze and waited.

'I must have passed out, because the next thing I remember is someone coming towards me. I thought was him, I thought it was Kay, coming to finish me off and I tried to hide myself deeper in the pile of grass cuttings. I burrowed like a rabbit, digging to hide myself. Then I saw the light from above, and knew it was a helicopter. I remember thinking I had a choice, I could hide from Kay, or I could wave and hope they saw me from above in time to be saved. I should have hidden, but something in me couldn't. Maybe I wanted to be found, maybe I wanted to die? I don't know. I reached up into the air, the light from the helicopter making the blood that covered my hands glow, illuminating the grass cuttings stuck to my body. Then a voice, metallic and distant, said something I couldn't make out, and the helicopter closed in on me.' I paused for a moment, remembering how the light of the helicopter blinded me. 'As I slipped unconscious, I heard the metallic voice again. In that moment, I knew Kay was going to kill me. But of course, it wasn't Kay, it was a policeman there to save me.'

I focused on the ground where I'd bled exactly a decade before. The memory of that moment the strongest it had ever been. I could smell the blood on my skin, I could taste the grass cuttings in my mouth.

I looked at Mum, who smiled meekly. 'What was the metallic voice?'

'His police radio. The next thing I remember is waking up in hospital weeks later. They had buried Owen, you were asleep in the chair beside me, and the photographers were waiting to call me a hero.'

'You are a hero,' Mum said, touching my arm.

'I'm not, Mum. I'm a coward. I ran, I hid.'

'You survived!'

I turned to face her, my voice shaking as I spoke. 'I left Owen to die.'

'You had no choice. Owen was...' She paused and looked down at our feet, unable to finish her sentence.

'Owen was what, Mum? Owen was what?'

'Owen was going to die, regardless.'

'You don't know that! I could have saved him.'

'No, you couldn't.'

'You don't know...'

Mum grabbed me by the shoulders, squeezing them hard, forcing me to stop talking and look at her. When she spoke, her tone had softened, replaced with something calmer, more confident.

'Claire, listen. There was no way you could have saved Owen. He was more than likely already dead when you climbed out of the window, and what you did that night was what any other person would have done if they could. But, those people before, God rest their souls, they weren't as strong as you are, as tough. You did the impossible that night, you performed a miracle because somehow, in spite of everything, you escaped. And Kay...'

'It was just luck, Mum.'

'And Kay hurt no one else after that night.'

'I'm not the reason he…'

She cut me off again. 'You survived, and it spooked him. Maybe he thought you would know who he was, maybe he realised someone had beaten him at his own game. But after that night, he didn't exist anymore. The press hounding you as they did, it was gruelling, I know that, but them looking at you meant they stopped looking for him. He lost his power. People were no longer afraid of the Black-Out Killer, because they had Claire Moore. The one who lived. That's what finished Tommy Kay – knowing he failed. He didn't know how to win at his sick game anymore, because you'd beaten him.'

I had to walk away, so headed back towards the bungalow, towards the bathroom window. Mum followed, a pace behind. The window ledge was covered in a dark brown stain, one that had faded after a decade of sunshine and rain. I had to fight with some weeds to get close but I stuck my head inside. I could still smell the smoke clinging to its walls. Above, the sun beamed in through the hole in the roof. The toilet was still in place, as was the sink. The bath however was gone, a stain on the ground where it once sat.

I pictured the moment I was dropped on the floor, Owen in the bath, just his thin arm hanging over the rim. The smell of petrol hanging in the air. Kay removed my toes then, and my scream startled him. I think he was expecting me to be delirious, like when I awoke just before he dragged me into the bathroom. He stumbled backwards, dropping the bolt cutters, and somehow I stood, swinging them wildly at him.

'Sometimes, in my dreams, I'm hitting him with the bolt cutters, sometimes he opens the door and runs, and I don't know which one is true.'

'What's true is you fought him. You know this.'

I did know there was a fight, I had scars to prove it.

'Then, I escaped. And he set Owen on fire.'

Saying it out loud felt wrong, but I didn't see the point in dressing it up. The facts were the facts. My husband died horrifically. His body was burnt alive, the temperature of the fire had made it impossible to identify him by sight – instead they'd confirmed it was him by a few of his teeth that had survived the inferno. Teeth that had been knocked clean out by Kay. All we could hope was that the injuries he'd sustained had killed him before the flames touched his skin.

Looking in the window, I could almost hear Owen speaking his final words. But I didn't know what they would have been. Would he have told Kay to leave me alone? Would he have said he loved me? They were nice ideas, but the reality was, he probably begged for his life, like anyone else would have done. I wanted to look away, but I couldn't take my eyes from the marking on the floor where the tub once sat. It hypnotised me. Before this bathroom, that night, I was someone else, someone who ran most mornings, who slept with the windows open. Someone who enjoyed sitting outside in the dark, stargazing, losing myself in the universe. Now I was none of those things. I was a ghost.

'You know, Mum, I was drunk that night. Owen and I had shared a few bottles of wine before I fell asleep on the sofa. When I woke, I was dazed, unable to think; he must have already been attacked, he must have called out. He must have knocked things over in the struggle, and I was too drunk to wake up and do anything about it.'

'Claire? You're not blaming yourself for what happened, are you?'

'I could have done more.'

She raised her voice, making me jump, snapping me away from looking into the bathroom, looking back to that night. 'Have you not listened to a word I've said?'

'Mum, please don't shout, this is hard for me.'

'I know it's hard.' Her voice cracked, her face reddening. 'It's bloody hard. A serial killer tried to murder you, and he murdered

113

Owen. I don't think many things in life could be harder than that.'

'Mum, stop shouting at me.'

'But you bloody blaming yourself...'

'Mum!'

'No, Claire, no. I've wanted to shout and scream and stamp my feet for ten long years. Ten years of wanting to shake you, slap you if needed to get you to see just how amazing you are. And you stand here, blaming yourself for what happened? That man, that *monster* killed six people before he came to this home. Six people. And Owen was seven, and you were supposed to be number eight. All if this is *his* fault, all of it.'

'But...' I stammered, tears falling freely.

'There is no but about it.' Her tone had softened. It somehow forced me to look into her eyes. 'None whatsoever.'

'How do I forgive myself?'

'By knowing right here, right now, that that awful man Tommy Kay was an experienced killer. He left nothing behind, he was smarter than everyone – despite the world knowing he did those awful things, they could never prove it – and you were just Claire Moore.'

'Just Claire Moore.'

'You know what I mean. You couldn't have done anything differently that night, besides die.'

I thought about it for a moment. She was right. He was experienced in killing, I wasn't in surviving. For the first time I considered how the odds had been stacked against me. But still, I couldn't shake the inescapable truth – I could have saved Owen.

Without warning, I felt heat behind my eyes and before I could cool it, I burst into tears and fell against Mum's shoulder. She didn't talk, she didn't comfort. She just held me and squeezed me and let me cry. I stayed on her shoulder for what felt like for ever. Sobbing, remembering. Once I had calmed down, Mum guided me away from the bungalow and helped me back into the hire car. As I put on my seatbelt, I looked back at the remains of my past and quietly said goodbye as we drove away.

'I guess it's time to go home.' I hoped to feel cleansed by the visit. But somehow, I just thought of Owen's death even more.

'Yes, love. It's time to go home.'

'I don't think I'll ever be able to forget what happened.'

'You're not supposed to, darling, but you have to move forwards.'

'Where do I even start?'

'Maybe by messaging Paul? Telling him what time we are due to land?'

'I'll never not love Owen,' I said, looking to her as she drove away from our former home.

'Of course.'

'How could I ever think about replacing him?'

Mum sighed, drumming her fingers on the steering wheel.

'Claire, you know I loved Owen, too, right?'

'Yes, Mum.'

'And you know I don't like to speak ill of the dead.'

I didn't reply, knowing exactly what was coming next,

'Do I really need to say it?' she asked

She didn't, and I couldn't look at her anymore so lowered my head. My Owen hadn't always been the nicest man. He'd had a temper at times, he drank a little too much at times. Disappeared for a day or two sometimes.

'Mum…'

'And I think he sometimes had a heavy hand.'

Her words felt like a slap in the face. I thought I had been clever, I thought I'd hidden it well, but it was obvious now I hadn't been as careful as I thought. I didn't respond, but lowered my head, a fresh tear escaping.

'I'm right, aren't I?' she said, quietly. And all I could do was nod yes.

'I'm not saying, stop loving him, I'm not saying forget how

115

when he was wonderful, he *was* wonderful. All I'm saying is don't give him a sainthood, he had some major flaws.'

'We all do,' I replied quickly.

'Now and then, let yourself see that version of Owen.'

'Why would I want to do that?'

'So, you realise that he wasn't perfect, so you can understand it's all right to like someone, love someone with imperfections. Let yourself have a chance of finding happiness again one day.'

'With Paul?'

'Well, now you've said it.'

'What if Paul doesn't get it?'

'I've got a funny feeling he already does. Give yourself a break, Claire. Stop seeing your old life as this perfect thing, because we both know it wasn't. I'm sorry Owen died, I really am, but it's time to take him off that pedestal he's been placed on by the world, and by you, and remember him properly, good things and the bad. And for God's sake, let someone else in.'

Nodding, I almost said something that I had withheld for a long time, a guilt I couldn't shift, but didn't. I couldn't, it would have to be a secret I took with me to my grave. Because if I said it out loud, I wouldn't be the person I wanted to be. To stop myself thinking about it, I took my phone from my bag and saw Paul had messaged me two hours ago. His message was short.

I'm thinking of you. X

I couldn't believe it, but reading it made me want to smile and push down the old guilt. Maybe time does heal all? Maybe someone telling me I didn't have to see Owen as a perfect man finally allowed me to stop? Maybe it was because of that and the fact today was exactly ten years since, meant I was having a catharsis of sorts. I stopped myself questioning it, questioning everything for a change, and messaged back, my text equally short, hoping it wouldn't show the battle raging between past, present and future.

Mum and I are due to land just after 10 p.m. What have you got planned for your evening?

I was shocked that as soon as I hit send the three dots appeared telling me he was typing back. His message was once again brief, direct, and I had read the exact same message before, after I tried and failed to call it off with him.

Hopefully seeing you.

Those three words told me he knew, he understood, and I couldn't help but feel something stirring inside. A lightness that I'd not felt in a very long time. I was looking forward to something. Something I believed I would never experience again. As Mum drove, I sat quietly gazing out of the window, saying a silent goodbye to Ireland, to Owen, and hopefully, to that night with Tommy Kay.

Chapter 19

May 2008
Newmarket, Ireland

The seventh

Finally, after two years the world had, with his help, connected the dots. He had, as planned, leaked to the papers the connection between them all, the random killings no longer random. The Black-Out Killer was targeting bad men, men who hit their wives, controlled their bank balances, dictated who they could and couldn't see. Abusive men like his own father. They still hadn't worked out why he also took the wives of these bad men – there was speculation, discussion about his sexuality, and hypotheses about his relationship with his own mother. One psychologist, writing for a tabloid, even spoke of him killing the women in a hope to be stopped. None were right, but he relished them trying to work it out. And the toes, they spoke of him keeping them as trophies, though he couldn't think of anything more disgusting. But he did enjoy how convoluted it had all become. His message had been delivered as planned. The victims, the 'brilliant and caring men', now were seen in their true light. And in the pubs whilst researching the next, he could hear the fear in the voices of men who knew they could be next. There had even been talk of how he was a vigilante, a voice for the abused. A hero. That was until the unexpected happened.

His last kills, the fifth and sixth on his list, Justin Turner and his wife Melanie, were like all the others. He was controlling, she was reluctant to change. He felt no remorse in ending their lives. But, in the media storm after, it was discovered that Melanie was fifteen weeks pregnant. The parents-to-be knew, as did their closest friends, but they hadn't gone public with the news. Melanie had lost two babies before and they wanted to be confident it wouldn't happen again before they got too excited. So, despite him getting to know Justin well enough to know he needed to be next, he hadn't known that in planning their end he was about to become everything he hated. That baby was innocent, neither an abuser nor coward. There was a chance for it to grow and be good and bring light into the world. He had ended that chance, he had become a man who killed an innocent life. He had become a man like his own father, a person who took the light of another. His father had done it to his mother, to him. And now he had done it to an unborn person.

As he learned of what he had unknowingly done, he felt the last light in him fade. The man he was, gone. He would no longer let himself think of his father and his wickedness, he would never think of his mother and her light. Everything about himself had to die. In his mind, he no longer had a name, or a face. He would be a shadow. He knew, after he punished his final couple, the man being someone who needed punishing more than anyone else, he would vanish. He would mourn the man he had been before he took an innocent life, and he would become something else. Something not quite human.

Knowing what he had become changed his perspective, altered his plans. The seventh and eighth he originally picked were no longer suitable. He knew from his research that they were trying for a baby themselves. And he had to let an innocent life be born, even if it was into a life of control and fear. He hoped his endeavours over the past two years meant that the child would grow up into a world that was better than it had been for him when he was young. But he would never know, because, after tonight, his work would be done.

With the original match out, he had quickly found another. He knew his walk to and from the power substation would be tough. It was nearly a mile away over the farmer's land, two if he stuck to the roads. It meant this job would be more challenging as there was more chance of being seen. But it was worth it. This last kill, because of how hard it would be to execute, would embed fear into every bad man in Ireland. It wasn't a hard kill because of the walk. It was hard because of the demographic of the other houses around the one he targeted. There were only nine but they all looked at one another across the narrow single-track lane. The residents were all curtain-twitchers. Their location meant seldom a car or person on foot walked past, and if they did it drew attention. Once the power was out, these people weren't the type to hide in their locked houses – they would be on the streets, trying to look out for one another. And he would find a way past them all, kill right under their noses. Because of his taking an innocent life the last time, it meant that tonight, he had to pull off the impossible and become a thing of legend. And everyone, even the good, would fear him. And after, once he had completed his task, he knew he would never be found.

He walked away from the bungalow towards the generator which was close to, but not quite in, Newmarket. He had prepped already, forcing the casing around the generator open. The other things needed for this evening were laid in a ditch, behind the Moore household, waiting for him to return and collect and use, as he had done each time before. In ten minutes the close would be plunged into darkness.

Then, he would execute his meticulous plan.

Tomorrow, the news would report of the deaths of Claire and Owen More, the seventh and eighth murders.

And their Black-Out Killer would have vanished.

Knowing he would never be found, never be caught, would ensure his legacy. And keep him in the minds of people who knew to fear him.

Chapter 20

18th May 2018
Stansted Airport

The flight home was far less eventful than I thought it would be; we were the last one of the day. An hour and ten minutes after taking off we landed, and within half an hour we had our cases and were heading for the exit. I was glad to be home and couldn't wait to get in my own bed: doors locked, windows closed and trying to catch up on sleep. It wasn't until we were in the baggage collection area that I stopped looking over my shoulder for Killian. Another benefit of the quiet flight was I saw everyone boarding, and he wasn't among them. As we rounded the corner and walked into arrivals, I noticed it was quiet, apart from a handful of people, scattered, alone and tired-looking.

Geoff was waiting for us. Mum saw him first and laughed, but I didn't know what was funny until I too spotted him. He was stood in a suit jacket, sporting a bow tie, but still in his old, threadbare jeans. In his hand he was holding a handwritten sign with 'My beautiful missus (and her kid)'. Then I saw who stood beside him and stopped laughing. Paul was there, in a suit jacket also, smiling hesitantly.

Mum ran over and hugged Geoff tightly, kissing him on the lips and calling him a berk. He made a comment about how the jacket felt a little snug since he'd last worn it as he grabbed her bag and walked away with Mum, hand in hand. It left Paul and I stood opposite one another, separated by my suitcase and a thousand unspoken thoughts.

'Hey,' he whispered.

'Hey,' I replied nervously.

'How was your flight?'

'It was fine, thank you.'

'Good, good, I'm pleased.'

He hesitated, taking a breath, clearly wanting to say more, but stopped himself. I watched as he wiped his hands on his legs and then grabbed my suitcase.

'Shall we get you home?' he said as he lifted the handle to drag my belongings out of the airport towards the car park. Without having time to reconsider I stepped near to him and kissed him on the lips, his bottom lip pressed between my two. He let go of the case and placed both hands on my cheeks, and I wrapped my arms around his waist, enjoying our closeness more than I thought I could. As we parted, I pressed my forehead to his. Something I'd done with Owen, something I hadn't done with another person since. It took a few moments to form words.

'Thank you for coming.'

'I'm just glad you're back.'

Our heads came apart and I looked into his brown eyes. Eyes with the same flecks of amber as Owen's. The intensity passing between us felt like the air had been sucked out of the arrival lounge. Besides the bubble we stood in, the world was entirely silent and still. I knew then that, when we went home, I didn't want to sleep alone, as I had done for so many years. I wanted to feel him beside me. I wanted to try, really try, to make this work. I couldn't say any of that. Instead, I quietly whispered, 'I'm glad too.'

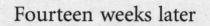

Fourteen weeks later

Chapter 21

29th August 2018
St Ives, Cambridgeshire

I roused myself and rolled onto my side to look at the clock – it was just after 5 a.m. I hadn't stirred early because of a dream, like I usually did, but because of birdsong filtering through the gap in the window and into my inner ear. I'd not had a dream that night, or the dark, cavernous mouth leaning over me, in nearly two weeks. I wouldn't tell anyone; with my luck, as soon as I did, it would come back in full force.

Paul lay sound asleep beside me. I didn't want to disturb him. I held my necklace so the keys wouldn't jangle and quietly I slipped out from under the covers placing my feet on the rough floor, before turning off my lamp. Paul hadn't been due to come to mine until later today, but instead of staying at the Travelodge his company paid for when he was away, he'd driven back late last night. I'd tried to talk him out of it, but he'd insisted, telling me he would rather be by my side with less sleep than not. I didn't protest too much – over the past few weeks, I had wanted Paul with me more often than not. I still had my days where I couldn't face anyone, even him, but thankfully they seemed to be less frequent. And when I had dark days, he was as good as ever. Paul didn't live with me, but perhaps he wasn't far from it. He had a few items of clothing here, as well as a few other bits, a spare car key, a phone charger, his Kindle and the all-important toothbrush. When he wasn't away with work, he stayed at mine about half the time. He never asked me to stay at his, knowing it would be difficult to do. Being comfortable in my own home was hard enough.

Paul mumbled something in his sleep and I held my breath, trying not to move as he rolled over, his brow furrowed like he was deep in concentration, or having a troubling dream. Twisting round, I leant in closer to him and watched as his left eyebrow twitched. Behind his eyelids I could see his eyes moving, flitting from side to side. I wondered what was going on in the darker corners of his subconscious mind. Most nights at some point Paul would dream of something that troubled him; he'd make indistinguishable sounds and his brow furrowed deeper. I always wanted to wake him, lean in further and wrap my arms around him, telling him it was OK, but didn't. He once said we all have a burden to carry, and I assumed he was working through his as he slept. His secret, something he wasn't ready to share. I leant away, leaving him to work through it on his own. As I stood, I hoped one day he would share whatever it was with me.

Padding to the bedroom window I took a deep breath of the fresh air coming from outside. I hadn't realised how much I missed the late-summer morning air in my home until a few weeks ago, when, with Paul here, I slept comfortably with the window on the latch for the first time since I moved to England. The birds that sang in the trees that lined the end of my garden sounded like they were singing just for me. I grabbed my dressing gown and limped out of the room, leaving Paul to catch up on some rest. I made my morning tea, stepped into the garden, and enjoyed the feeling of the sun kissing my collarbones.

Recently, following advice from Dr Porter, who I had started to see again once a week, I used my mornings to reflect – not on what happened ten years ago, but on the more recent past. The past since the trip to Ireland that I survived despite everything: visiting Owen's grave and the house; the lack of sleep; Killian. I spoke with Dr Porter about it all, and she helped me see that the visit, however tough it had been, did what I needed it to do. It helped me realise that although I could never let go of Owen, of what happened to us, I could have a life, something new. Owen still came to my daydreams, I knew it would never change. But now when I thought of him I remembered what Mum said. *I am Claire Moore, a woman inexperienced in surviving. Tommy Kay was a serial killer.* There was nothing I could have done differently, if I were to stay alive. Of course, I'd been told this countless times before, but knowing it for myself liberated me from the intense guilt I felt. With Dr Porter's help, the icy hand was still there inside me, and it still gripped my diaphragm, but now it held on a little lighter.

Paul had helped more than he would ever know. He had become an ear I could bend, a voice of reason, a man who I trusted – the only other man I could say the same for was Geoff. Paul made me feel like someone wanted me, made me feel less alone. I didn't think I could ever be intimate with another man when I recovered, and although we had to make love in the dark, we still made love. My scars, for now, were something only for me.

Putting my mug on the ground beside me, I tilted my head back into the sun and closed my eyes, allowing the heat to warm my neck and face. I sighed contentedly. The birds were singing in full voice, drowning out the sound of the cars on the A1. I sat there for nearly an hour before I heard noise coming from the kitchen.

'Morning.' He hummed as he landed a kiss on the top of my head.

'Morning.' I beamed back at him. 'Did you sleep all right?'

'Yes, did you?'

'Yes,' I replied, remembering I hadn't dreamt as I usually did.

'Want breakfast?' he said, not waiting for an answer, as he went back inside.

I picked up my mug and wandered back into the house, rubbing his shoulder as he cracked eggs next to the cooker. I went back upstairs to get my phone. I was seeing Penny later today and knew she'd texted late last night to confirm plans, and I hadn't replied.

I grabbed my phone and unlocked it with my thumb print to see I had eight new messages: four from Mum, two from Penny and two from numbers I didn't know. On the screen was also a notification telling me I had seven new voice messages, and another telling me there were several messages on Facebook, most coming from the support group set up in my name. Feeling a sudden wave of sickness, I tapped my voicemail icon and listened to the first message, left just after 3 a.m.

'Mrs Moore, my name is Guy Blakemore, calling from the *Mail*, I was wondering if you could call me back regarding recent events. You can reach me on…'

I deleted the message, before it went into the next one.

'Hi, Claire. It's Kyle calling from *Nation's Choice* magazine. I'd love to…'

I hit delete again, panic rising. The next message had come just after 5 a.m., and probably had woken me unknowingly. The voice that spoke was one I knew well, and her tone sounded scared, unsure. It roused the familiar hand inside my chest which had recently lain dormant, its cold fingers chilling me from within.

'Love, it's Mum. Call me, OK?'

Clutching my phone in my hand so tightly it hurt, I had to hold on to the wall with the other as I made my way back down the stairs and into the kitchen. Paul had his back to me, stirring a saucepan.

'I've gone for scrambled this morning, I hope that's OK?'

I didn't reply but held onto the doorframe for dear life, trying to work out why I had a newspaper and magazine contacting me. Sensing something was wrong. Paul turned, his smile replaced with that deep furrow of worry I'd noticed as he'd slept.

'Claire?'

'Something's going on.'

'What?' he said, coming over and taking my arm gently, probably sure I would fall if he didn't.

'I don't know,' I babbled as my feet moved towards the kitchen table, guided by Paul.

'I don't understand: what's happened, Claire?' he said, his voice high and stressed, as he sat me down and perched on the chair beside me.

'My voicemails,' was all I could say in explanation. I felt my body close itself off, the nerve endings in my extremities shutting down, to protect me from whatever was coming. I watched, unable to speak, unable to move, as Paul took the phone from my hand. The screen was locked, so he asked me for the code, but I couldn't remember. As I mumbled, trying to find some words to say, he took my hand and placed my thumb on the home button to unlock it with my thumb print. Then he lifted the phone to his ear to listen to my voicemails, and I saw the colour drain from his face.

Without offering an explanation, he moved quickly into the living room and swore loudly when he couldn't find the television buttons. Eventually I heard a voice: female, a news reporter. I couldn't make out what she was saying. Paul had turned the volume down, and I didn't want to know either. Whatever it was, it was bad. And yet, I felt the blood rushing back to my limbs, the nerve endings refiring, and before I could stop myself, I stood and walked into the lounge. Paul was frozen to the spot, the remote he had used to turn down the TV still held at a ninety-degree angle. His mouth was agape.

131

I looked from him to the TV mounted on the wall and at first couldn't see what had caused him to stand deathly still. The reporter, holding an umbrella but still damp from the rain, spoke, and I felt sick. Her words flashed on the screen as bullet points.

WHAT WE KNOW SO FAR...
- *POWER CUT TO A REMOTE VILLAGE, NEAR BETHESDA, WALES. LOCALS SAY IT WAS JUST AFTER 11 P.M.*
- *A HOUSE FIRE STARTED JUST AFTER 12 A.M.*
- *THE BODY OF A WOMAN HAS BEEN FOUND.*

The world spun, and before I could try to move to the sofa, I was already falling.

Chapter 22

29th August 2018
St Ives, Cambridgeshire

I don't remember hitting the floor, or Paul lifting me and placing me on the sofa. The first thought was that my left hand stung as pins and needles shot through my fingers, suggesting I had been out for some time. As I sat, I thought what I had seen on the TV screen was just some weird hallucination, brought on by my own fractured mind. It had tricked me into thinking that I'd finally turned a corner in my life. But as my eyes refocused on my surroundings I saw Paul staring at me, the TV behind him off now, and images from the news came back to me in full high definition.

There was no mention of a male victim, so it was different – in every other killing, there had always been a man. Ending with Owen. Perhaps this was a domestic situation, the husband or boyfriend trying to get away with it by making it look like the serial killer from a decade ago. Or maybe it was just a tragic accident. Perhaps she fell asleep with a cigarette burning, or the oven on, and the power cut was a complete coincidence. Both situations were more plausible than a killer copying someone from ten years before, weren't they?

Paul said something, but I didn't catch it. I focused on his face, concern etched into the lines around his eyes and across his forehead, and tried to speak, but the words only came out as a choke. Paul tried to hold me, no doubt about to tell me everything was all right. But as he leant towards me, I held up my hand, stopping him. He seemed to understand and instead sat on the chair opposite. He smiled weakly, but I couldn't return it. Behind me I heard the back door open, and I jumped, my flight mechanism ready to work, the shot of adrenaline hitting my bloodstream so fast I felt like I would faint again.

'Claire, it's OK, it's all right,' Paul whispered, his hands outstretched towards me, palms showing. 'I called your mum.'

She soon came bounding into the room, and dropping to her knees, wrapped her arms around me, pulling me into her familiar embrace. I buried my head against her shoulder, just for a moment, just long enough to take a few breaths in, have her comfort flood over me. It was my transparent shield that kept my guilt and loss and fear and grief and rage contained. I gently moved her away and stood. I was being ridiculous; I knew how the media sensationalised everything they could. And from what I'd seen, there were no real facts about it. Nothing to suggest it was anything but a house fire. Something similar happened only four years ago. I'd assumed the worst then too; I'd assumed what the media suggested was actually the facts and didn't sleep for weeks, thinking someone was out to kill me. I slept with a pair of scissors under my pillow, until they revealed that the fire was just a fire, and tragically, an elderly man and woman died. Husband and wife for forty-seven years. The smoke inhalation meant that when they went to bed that night, they didn't wake. No pain, no suffering. Side by side. Nothing sinister about it – in fact, a part of me was jealous when I learned the facts. If only all things were as simple as that. Regardless, it set me back to square one. I had to relearn how to unlock a front door and step outside. I couldn't go back to being that, not now. Not ever.

Grabbing the remote I switched the TV on, I wanted to see for myself that it was all some horrible coincidence, enhanced to gain ratings.

'Claire, love,' Mum started, but her gentle protest was shot down with a look.

'I'm not being a victim every time there is a house fire, Mum.'

'I really don't think you should watch the news.'

'I need to know.'

I turned my attention to the screen and the same images were there for me to see. The more I looked, the more I could see the obvious inconsistency. There was no dead man. This wasn't a serial killer, this was a bitter husband or boyfriend. I felt myself relaxing a little. This had nothing to do with me, and although the media had assumed I would want to talk, I knew I had to keep quiet. If I kept myself to myself it would go away as soon as they realised they had it wrong. On the screen was mobile phone footage shot by a neighbour of the house on fire. Black smoke billowed from the broken upstairs windows and some of the roof had fallen through; tall flames licked the sky in a terrifying but hypnotic way. Then the screen went blank, snapping away from my transfixed stare. I turned to Mum, the remote in her hand. She told me to sit down.

'Claire.'

'I'm OK, Mum, I know this is just—'

'The police called late last night.'

'Why?'

'They assumed you still lived with me.'

'What did they say?'

'They want to come and talk to you.'

'What? Why?'

'They didn't say, but I think they think it's a copycat. I think they think someone might be re-enacting what happened in Ireland.'

'Why would someone do that?' Paul said, rising to his feet. Mum said something else, directed towards Paul, but I didn't hear her words. The world around me had been reduced to the sound of blood rushing in my ears. Muffled, her voice filtering through, but like she was talking underwater.

I didn't want to believe it. I shouldn't believe it. They had said time and time again that there was a copycat, and they had been wrong every time: surely, they had to be again, didn't they? The police had always reassured us it wasn't anything we needed to be concerned about. But now, they wanted to talk, they wanted to come over. That meant something, didn't it? My mind raced, but my body felt lifeless as I slowly staggered out of the living room, down the hall and up the stairs. I could vaguely hear Paul's voice, followed by Mum's, but I didn't understand what they were saying.

I counted the stairs, thirteen in all, and then walked into the bedroom, closing the door behind me. Sitting on the edge of the bed I lowered my head into my hands, my whole body shaking so hard it hurt. I couldn't stop it, and I didn't want to. I shook until my stomach muscles ached and then I let the tears come. I had lived through the attack a decade ago, and the few occasions since where the world thought someone was copying the Black-Out Killer. But this time was different. Something about that house, that poor woman who died, was different. Knowing the police wanted to talk face-to-face told me as much.

Mum quietly knocked on the door, asking if I was OK. I wiped my eyes and said I was fine, that I just needed a minute. She agreed and went back downstairs to put on the kettle and wait for the police to come. Standing up, I looked in the mirror above the chest of drawers. My eyes were puffy and my skin blotchy. I took a deep breath, and my bottom lip quivered as I started to cry once more, but I forced myself to stop.

If this was a copycat killing, I knew the media would be like pack animals once again, hunting en masse, stalking for the kill.

I walked into the bathroom and splashed my face with cold water, the shock contracting my skin and snapping me back into focus. I had another look at my face, my bottom lip firmly under control once more.

Get a grip, Claire, get it under control.

As I walked down the stairs, Paul was standing at the bottom looking up, the worry furrows deeper than before. I told him I was OK, but really, I wasn't, and on a loop in my head were two questions:

If this was a copycat, would they want to finish what Tommy Kay started?

Would they come for me?

Hello, Claire,

It seems you have been on my mind more in the past few weeks than in the previous ten years. Everything I do, everywhere I go, I see things that remind me of our time together. I'm wondering if you think of me as much as I do you. I've tried to push reflections of you back into the dark spaces. But you are only half a thought away. I know it's because of the eighth, the woman from Bethesda and what I have done to her. I enjoyed it, as I always have, but I felt disloyal to you. You were my eighth, Claire, and I need you to know she wasn't a replacement. She was the first brick in the bridge that will bring us back together. When I was with her alone in her bathroom, I wanted her to fight like you. I even gave her the opportunity to strike but she didn't take it, or couldn't. There's no one else like you.

I wonder what you are thinking now? Are you frightened that I will come for you? I've asked myself, do you subconsciously know that the Wales incident was not the work of a copycat, that it was really me? I like to think that somewhere deep inside of you, a quiet place that only you and I know, there is a voice, as fragile as a bird wing that whispers the truth.

Claire, time is a wonderful thing, a gift, that cannot be taken for granted. And I feel you are wasting what time you have left. There is no time for secrets, for the unknown. Find the truth before I visit, Claire, so that when we meet, and you die, you do so enlightened.

I cannot wait for you to read these letters, and for us to be eye to eye after such a long time.

Until then, I am never far away. **Closer than you think.**

Chapter 23

29th August 2018
St Ives, Cambridgeshire

The police arrived an hour after Mum called back and said I was ready. When the doorbell rang I was in the living room, one hand clutching a cup of tea that had gone cold, the other fiddling with my keys around my neck. It was followed up with two loud knocks which made me jump. I got up to watch the front door from the doorway of the living room. Geoff answered. He had arrived half an hour before; staying at home initially, watching the news so he could get a more up-to-date account of what was happening, knowing I would be in meltdown and the TV would be off.

I don't know why, but when the door opened, I was expecting a team of police officers to come in and was surprised when I saw only one. A tall, rotund man with a thick red beard who introduced himself as Peter. As he stepped into the house, I could hear the unmistakable sound of camera shutters from the front lawn. I could see the flash of blubs. The press had arrived, wanting to get a photo. He saw me look beyond him to outside, and when our eyes met he smiled sympathetically. He came into the lounge and I retreated to the chair and sat, picking up my cold tea and staring at it for comfort. He removed his hat and said hello. His voice was soft, a lot softer than his somewhat forbidding presence would suggest, and looking up at him I saw he had kind eyes. I didn't say hello back, but gave him a nod. He took a seat opposite me, next to Paul who I could see wanted to be by my side but was respecting my need for space. Geoff emerged with a fresh tea for me, and also placed a cup next to Peter.

'Do you want sugar?' Geoff asked.

'No, thank you. It's perfect as it is,' he replied before turning his attention to me. 'How are you, Mrs Moore?'

'Surviving, and please, call me Claire.'

'Surviving. Good choice of words, Claire.' He smiled. 'You're probably wondering why I'm here with you and not telling you over the phone that last night's incident is nothing to be worried about.'

'Yes, we are,' Mum chipped in, her anxiety spilling over a little, manifesting as a polite aggression.

'Mum, let him speak,' I said, my eyes staying firmly on the police officer opposite.

'Sorry,' she said, leaning into Geoff who rubbed her back.

'I'll come straight to the point,' Peter continued, adjusting his sitting position. He leant forward in the chair to lower his gaze, and met my eyes. 'The fire last night, we believe it to be someone replicating the events in Ireland.'

'What has led you to believe that?' Mum exclaimed, her anxiety completely in the driving seat. 'Couldn't it be a domestic thing? An insurance scam or something – you hear about people killing partners for the money?' Geoff took her hand, pulling her closer.

'Love,' he said quietly, trying to reassure her. Again, she mumbled an apology.

'Don't say sorry, I understand this is a difficult time for you all.'

'Thank you,' I whispered, genuinely grateful for Peter's calm demeanour.

'Claire, there were many similarities between the incident last night and what happened to you in Ireland.'

'What similarities?' Mum asked, the aggression lost in her voice.

'The manner in which it was executed,' he said calmly. 'The killer knew Kay's methods and re-enacted them almost identically.'

'And are you sure it's a copycat?' asked Geoff.

'We believe it's possible.'

'So, are you telling me that last night, in Wales, that was someone connected to *him*?' I asked, my voice catching in my throat.

'Yes, Claire, we believe so.'

'Fuck.' I dropped my heads into my hands, trying desperately to catch my breath. Paul sat beside me, his hand going onto my back, as if he knew where the tightness came from.

'Claire, we think it's best you come with us. We can put you somewhere safe.'

'Are you suggesting she is in danger?' Mum asked again, her voice shrill. Geoff placed a calming hand on hers once more.

'No, there is nothing to suggest so, but you're easy enough to find, and once the media know for sure it is a copycat, it will be a difficult time for you.'

'Do the media know yet?'

'They are speculating, as always when there is a fire. But we will actively dismiss any hearsay or gossip. At this stage, this is all precautionary. Claire, what do you think?'

I almost spoke, the words on the tip of my tongue, but Mum interrupted. 'Where will she go?'

'To one of our safe houses.'

'Safe house? Is that even a thing? I thought that was just on the telly,' said Geoff.

'I assure you, we have them. And she would be perfectly safe there. No one will know where she is, and it'll be just until we catch him.'

'No,' I said in my head, my voice failing as my diaphragm felt like it was being crushed from the inside. Aloud I asked, 'How long will that take? I mean, you didn't catch Tommy Kay for the fires.'

'Yes, but we got lucky with him, prosecuting him for other crimes.'

Mum started again. 'So then how can we trust...'

'We will this time, Mrs O'Healy,' Peter said confidently.

'When will she have to go?'

'Today if possible, just to be safe.'

I'm not going, I thought, as I instinctively reached for my keys and counted them, my words still unable to form.

'OK, Geoff, get the suitcase out of her loft,' Mum said, her anxiety now replaced with purpose, direction, her voice drowning mine out.

'Yep.'

'Paul, can you make a start on a few things for her?'

'Of course.'

'Can I come with her?' he asked.

'Yes, of course. In fact, I recommend it. But you won't be able to talk to anyone. So, when we leave, you'll have to say goodbye for a while. We can let your employer know.'

'Fine, whatever it takes.'

'Great. We'll get a car ready. I've got my colleague outside who can make sure the press gives you space. My advice: don't say a word to them.'

I felt the icy hand melt; my chest was free, and my words erupted out of me like a volcanic explosion.

'I'm not going.'

'Claire, love? What do you mean, you're not going?' Mum said, worry etched on her face.

'I'm not going, Mum, I'm not leaving. I'm not running away again. If he...' I paused, shocked at the words coming out of my mouth, but immensely proud of myself for being able to say them. It didn't matter; in the moment, I meant them with every fibre in my being. And I felt victorious.

'If it is someone copying the Black-Out Killer, and if he is trying to find me, he will. Because if he is anything like Tommy Kay, he will be smarter than everyone else. I'm not hiding just to be found cowering in a corner. If he will find me, he is going to find me in my house, my space.'

'Claire, please, I think…'

'I know what you think, Mum, I do. And I understand…'

'Then, surely we need to move you?'

'I'm not leaving, Mum.'

'Why?'

As I spoke the next five words I felt utterly terrified, like I was sealing my fate by saying them. And yet, those words gave me power.

'Because *fuck him*, that's why. Tommy Kay tried to ruin my life, and he succeeded for a long time. I'm not letting his copycat do the same.'

Chapter 24

He ordered a black filter coffee from a pleasant-looking girl behind the till and smiled as he took it from her, noticing her blush. He couldn't help but feel taller. Stronger, more imposing. He hadn't felt this good in ten long years. He wasn't the little boy cowering from his father, waiting in a darkened room only allowed into the light to go to school. He was no longer forgotten, although the world didn't know it yet.

It wasn't the kill that made him feel like a giant. There had been others in the ten-year hiatus, people on the fringes of society who wouldn't be missed. It was their terror which made him grow.

He had forgotten just how good it felt to be feared, and the power that came with walking around, weaving in and out of people who were reading or watching or listening to something that was his doing, it made him feel invincible. He could see their shock, disbelief, curiosity. Best of all, he could engage with them, like he was just any other person. It fuelled him. He found a table in the corner of the coffee shop and sipped his hot drink, watching the world around him.

The kill was now four days old, and what he had done was still on the front of all the papers. They drew comparisons to the kills in Ireland, finding the connections in style and delivery which led them to state categorically it was someone known to Kay, continuing his work. It was compelling reading, and part of him could believe it. Of course, he knew Tommy Kay had nothing to do with what he had done in Ireland, and his arrest in the months after that night with Claire Moore came as a pleasant surprise. When he didn't kill again, the fingers started pointing and rumours started flying towards Kay being the Black-Out Killer. Kay weaved it into his tapestry to ensure immortality. One day they would know Tommy Kay had nothing to do with it, and therefore *he* had never been caught. When the time was right.

Beside him was an older man sat reading a tabloid, and as he glanced inside its pages he saw the eighth, Kath Brinck, staring back at him. It was the same picture that had been on every news report and splashed across the rest of the papers. She was dressed in a winter jumper and matching bobble hat, sometime near Christmas as decorations could be seen behind her. She was smiling at the camera, happy and full of life. He wondered for a moment about the person who took that picture, who they were, if they were still in her life. Looking away he saw another paper folded on the stand. Even with half the image obscured, he could see it was a photograph of the house on fire, the headline stating: *Is there a copycat BOK on our streets?*

Yes, and no, he thought. Enjoying the fact his 'brand' had become an acronym.

'Do you think it's a copycat? You know, that fire in Wales?' he asked politely of the older man, who he guessed was in his late fifties, maybe as old as sixty-five.

'Sorry?'

'The man who started that fire? Do you think he is copying

145

that killer, the Irish serial killer... oh, what was his name?' he said clicking his fingers and looking away, feigning forgetfulness.

'The Black-Out Killer,' the older man prompted.

'That's it, the Black-Out Killer. It was awful what he did.'

'Yes, it was.'

'I've not read a lot about this one, what have they said?'

'Not a great deal, but there's a source here that says it was done in a very similar way. Almost like Tommy Kay was there himself.'

'You know, they never proved it was him.'

'It had to be.'

'So, maybe it's someone who knew Kay?'

'That's what they think. Sick world we live in, isn't it?' the old man said.

'It certainly is. Let's hope they catch him this time,' he replied, as the old man got to his feet and made his way to the door.

'Yes, let's. Enjoy the rest of your morning.'

'And you,' he said as he sat back in his chair and watched the older man cross the road, blithely unaware that he had just conversed with a serial killer.

Taking out his mobile phone, he logged into his online dating account and saw he had three new messages. Michelle, Cath and Jennifer. All women living in the Wrexham area. The demographic was important for his plan. Their messages – light, chit-chatty, informal – didn't immediately suggest which one, if any, would be next. He would give it more time, allow the small talk to deepen. He wouldn't instigate any sexual relationships with them but would instead see what they would do, allow them to control their own fate. But he had to give it time, which meant the feeling of power that washed over him now would fade. He had to stay disciplined, like he did before when talking with the men in the pubs. The right one would separate themselves from the rest. She would be someone like the other women, like Claire Moore, too afraid to be someone new. They would try to fake that they had changed, and he would see right through them. They would be women who had left their husbands but who also ached to return. Or worse, they would want to find a man who was like the one they'd left, keeping them in the cycle that was his obligation to break.

His target would talk of evolving, like he had, but would be unable to.

He didn't respond to the messages; he'd do that later when he was alone. Instead, he planned and speculated. The heat from what he did four days before would cool, eventually going cold. People would assume, because of Kay being blamed for Ireland, that it was a copycat, and as shocking as that was, the fear would quickly fade. There was more than enough bad news to keep people occupied these days – that is, until he showed them how wrong they were and proved beyond doubt that he had returned. That he had never been caught. But only when the time was right.

As with Ireland, he had a justification, a plan, a final destination, and he hypothesised it would take four lives to complete it. The first, the woman from Bethcoda was dead. The last would be Claire. Then, after he had achieved his goal, he would disappear again. And they would never forget he was still out there, and he was watching.

147

Chapter 25

6th September 2018
St Ives, Cambridgeshire

The morning we found out there might be a copycat killer Mum, Geoff and Paul argued with me about wanting to stay at home for half an hour, and with each passing minute my conviction grew until one by one they quietened down, thinking of alternatives. Seeing I would not budge, Peter said he would arrange for an officer to watch the house, which I reluctantly agreed to. Being watched wasn't something I enjoyed. Mum insisted they had a key so they could get in quickly, just in case.

Once a plan of action we were all happy with had been agreed, Paul nipped into Huntingdon and bought a small camera and fixed it to the wall outside my house. He downloaded an app to my iPad which allowed me to see who was coming to the door. It also recorded the footage, just in case. He didn't need to – having a police officer stationed outside would be enough – and when I asked him why he was going to such expense he replied that he wanted me to have some control. And he was right – as soon as I could see onto my street whenever I wanted without having to be at the door, I felt more in control. And I knew, if Paul wasn't careful, I'd end up loving him.

Now, a week after I stamped my feet and refused to leave, I bitterly regretted my decision. I hadn't slept, I could barely eat and being in the bathroom freaked me out so much I had washed myself in the downstairs toilet sink, with the door left open so I didn't feel like I was being locked in. Worst of all, I had barely been able to take my eyes from my iPad screen. I felt the need to have it everywhere with me, constantly playing, and every time someone came close to my house, I felt a spike in my adrenaline. I didn't tell anyone; Geoff would insist I stopped and would suggest I got rid of the iPad, but it had become something akin to a security blanket. Paul, who had stayed with me since, knew I kept the iPad close but didn't know it was having negative effect on me. I couldn't say because he would feel guilty for installing it and Mum, well… Mum was angry with me still for not leaving with the police.

I didn't think anyone understood why I felt the need to dig my heels in about not leaving but Geoff told me last night over dinner that he understood, and that he would have done the same – much to Mum's annoyance. Paul was struggling and needed more convincing. He refused to go back to work. He said he would ask for some time off, so that he could stay by my side, but I said it would be ridiculous to let everything in his life grind to a halt because of me. The police were always nearby, and no one could get near the house anyway as there were reporters lurking around, wanting to take my photo and ask me questions. I'd not been outside yet, of course. But Mum, who was back and forth from hers, told me the journalists were mainly just wanting a statement from me, something about how I'm feeling, an insider account from 'one who lived'. They were persistent, and while invasive, they also meant I was safe – well, safer at least.

I also told Paul I needed space, time to process how I was feeling, so I could talk to him properly and continue to build on what we shared together. Reluctantly, just as the sun started to stir, a thin orange light breaking over the horizon, he showered and dressed to drive north to work on a site three hours away. I could see as he closed the door to leave how much he hated going. And, if I was honest, I did too. But I knew I needed to face being alone at some point. He locked the door behind him, got into his car and I watched through a gap in the curtains as he backed out of the drive. A lone photographer sprung to life to take a picture, the flash cutting through the darkness like a lightning strike. Paul drove away quickly, his tail lights fading in the distance. I watched the photographer look back at the house, peering into the windows – luckily, he couldn't see me.

Moving to the sofa, I wanted to sit down but instead stood paralysed, knowing that I was alone for the first time since waking up to the news of the killing in Wales. The house felt quieter than usual: still, as if the air in it had died. I knew I needed to do something, so I walked into the kitchen, my bare feet on the lino sounding like a drum beating against the silence of the house. Between Mum talking, the news playing, Geoff's heavy breathing, Paul reading aloud, I hadn't experienced quiet for a week. Now all this background noise was gone, I became acutely self-aware – and I didn't like it one bit. Worse still, the house seemed to notice me, and I couldn't help but think it was listening to my every move.

Turning on the tap to fill the kettle made me feel like I was making noise in a library. The boiling kettle came to a violent crescendo, and as I made my way into the living room to sit on the sofa, I thought the coffee in my hand would try to scald me.

I counted the seconds on the clock ticking by, resetting back to zero every time I hit sixty. And there I stayed for hours, counting each second of each minute and resetting at zero. I slowed my breathing, focused my mind on the small things, like I had been taught by Dr Porter. I had missed the last appointment and I was hopeful I would be able to go today. But I knew it wasn't going to happen. I was more afraid of stepping outside now than I had been in the past twelve months, and felt like a failure for it.

By the time I stopped counting the ticking clock, the sun was warming the sky and my coffee was stone cold. I drank it anyway, my swallowing loud and aggressive in the otherwise silent house. Sighing after I finished, I held the mug in my hands and noticed that the dregs of coffee in the bottom resembled the shape of a fire.

I heard movement from somewhere inside my home. My ears strained to listen around the corners of the room and work out where the noise was coming from, while my rational mind tried to dismiss it. It was just the house shifting in its foundations, or Baloo wandering around upstairs, although I wasn't sure if he was here or he was at Mum's – maybe it was a bird on the roof? I held my breath… waiting for the noise again.

There were three loud bangs, and I jumped, banging my knee on the coffee table and knocking the empty cup to the floor. Swearing, I stood, knowing it wouldn't be anything sinister, just the door. And yet, I was so terrified I couldn't control my body, which was now shaking. I grabbed the iPad from the corner of the sofa to look at the camera and see who it was. But the battery was flat and, putting it down, I cursed myself for not being careful with the one thing that provided me comfort. Outside, there was another knock and I clapped my hands together, trying to free myself from the fear. The copycat wouldn't come in the morning, with the papers nearby and a police officer parked outside. And even if he did, he was hardly likely to knock.

I told myself to get a grip.

But still, as I approached the front door, to find out who was there, I felt like I could throw up.

The person knocked again on the door, three loud bangs, each one vibrating through me, and I stumbled backwards, away from the door and into the archway into the living room.

More bangs, followed by someone calling my name. But I

151

couldn't respond, instead I sank to the floor. Made myself small. Then, there were no more bangs, no more voices. And the house was quiet again.

Without being able to stand, as if my legs belonged to someone else, I half-crawled, half-shuffled to the front door. I pressed my ear against the cool UPVC, straining to hear footsteps moving away. Nothing. Whoever it was had gone. I dragged myself over to the bottom of the stairs and buried my head into my hands telling myself to calm down, forcing myself to breathe. After a few minutes it worked, but just as I started to get up again a key went in the door and it quickly swung open, the suddenness of it terrifying me.

A police officer – Jenny, I think she said her name was – came in and my face flushed with the heat of the adrenaline coursing through my veins. She noticed me jump and raised her left hand apologetically. In her right, she had a box – there had been a courier trying to deliver a parcel.

'Sorry, Mrs Moore, I didn't mean to startle you.'

I wanted to say it was OK, but couldn't. Instead I sank back onto the step and cried. I didn't want to look weak, I didn't want her to pity me. But the sudden shock was unmanageable. As I cried I realised, when I truly believed I was in trouble, I had frozen like the proverbial rabbit in the headlights. Whereas once I could run, did run, I no longer could.

'I'm really sorry to burst in like that and scare you, but when you didn't answer the door I was concerned for you.'

'No, it's OK,' I said between sobs.

Outside I heard a commotion: a car pulling up quickly and the sound of cameras clicking, the freelance photographers hoping to get a cheque-worthy picture. Then I heard Mum's voice telling them to get out of her way. The police no doubt called her to see if I was at hers before letting themselves into my house. She bounded through the front door, in her gym wear. They must have interrupted her doing her daily yoga session at home.

'What's happened, love?'

'Nothing, Mum.'

'Then why…'

'I thought there as something wrong,' Jenny said. 'But I was mistaken.'

'You were mistaken? Could you perhaps be a little more sensitive?'

'Mum, she's just doing her job.'

'I'll leave you two to it. Sorry once again, Mrs Moore.'

I smiled to the officer as she put the box on the floor and backed out of the house, closing the door behind her. Once closed, Mum sat next to me on the stairs, her head resting on my shoulder. 'What happened?'

'Someone knocked on the door. Delivering that,' I said gesturing to the box. 'I panicked.'

'I see.'

'I'm a mess, Mum.'

'I know you are, darling. I know,' she replied in her teasing way, making me smile despite feeling I couldn't.

'Cheers, Mum. You could have dressed it up a little.'

'There's nothing wrong with calling it what it is.'

'It's shit.'

'Yes, it is.'

'It's fucking shit.'

'It's a massive, steaming pile of fucking shit.'

'Mum!' I said, shocked by her outburst.

'Well, you're allowed to swear.'

'Yes, but…'

'But nothing. Call it what it is!'

'You want me to call it exactly what it is?'

'Yes, let rip, love.'

'OK, it's exhausting.'

'Claire, you're safe…'

'I don't mean the copycat is exhausting. I mean living like this. I'm tired of living like this.'

Mum lifted her head from my shoulder, and I slipped into the safety of her embrace. Eventually, she released me, and I sat up, suddenly feeling the need to nap.

'Are you OK, love?' she asked.

'Not really, but thanks, Mum.'

'You're welcome. What's in the box?' she asked, gesturing towards the foot-square parcel I'd forgotten about.

'I don't know.'

Mum got up and moved towards it, examining the label on the top. 'Handwritten.'

She pinched the edge of tape and pulled, tearing it from the box. Unfolding the sides, I watched as she smiled at the contents. 'It's from that support group, a card from Wendy and Veronica. Are they people you know?'

'Yes,' I said, relieved it wasn't from Killian. 'They are two retired ladies who always send me Christmas and birthday cards. They say it's from the whole group. But it's always just them.'

'That's sweet.'

'What's the card say?'

Mum squinted, her glasses nowhere to be seen. After a few seconds of trying, she gave up and handed me the card to read.

To help relieve the stress you are no doubt feeling.
We are thinking of you, and only a message away.
Mary, Veronica and everyone else at CMSP

Mum slid the box open and looking inside I saw bath bombs, bubble bath, incense sticks and other things to help promote well-being. Their gift was sweet and thoughtful, but I slid the box back towards Mum.

'You have these, Mum. I won't use them.'

'What do you mean?' she said before looking in for herself. As soon as she did, she understood. As much as I missed them, I didn't take baths, couldn't take baths. Every time I tried, I'd feel worse after. In a bath all you can do is look at your body, and I had spent enough of my time looking at my scars.

'I see,' she said as she made her way back to the step, her shoulder and arm in contact with mine. 'Well, make sure you thank them, anyway.'

'I will.'

'Claire, as I'm doing something for you by taking away these *horrid* bath products…'

'They're hardly horrid.'

'… and I will have to suffer being Cleopatra tonight in the tub, Geoff doing my bidding…'

'Yuck, Mum, I don't want to know.'

'Tending to my every whim, feeding me grapes…'

'Mum, stop!' I nudged her gently. I didn't want to know what she and Geoff got up to in their private time.

'As I'm kindly doing all this for you, would you do something for me?'

It wasn't often Mum asked me to do anything for her, so I was taken aback; her expression had transformed from light to something serious. I didn't know what she would ask. Was it something to do with Geoff, or money? I had none of my own, but I still hadn't cashed the latest cheque from the group. I could give it to her rather than a charity.

'What is it, Mum?'

She took a deep breath, and just before she spoke, her lips curled into a teasing smile.

'Have a shower, love. You're beginning to pong.'

'You bugger, Mum, I was really worried.' I smelled my clothes. 'Oh God, I do, don't I? Sorry.'

'Don't say sorry to me, it's poor Paul I think about.'

'He's not said anything. He should have.'

'Perhaps he's just being kind.' She smiled at me, and I smiled back thinking just how kind he had actually been. He'd made sure I was eating, and massaged my shoulders when the tension was too much. He didn't feel the need to talk all the time, his stillness, his silence speaking to me instead. Making me feel safe. 'Either that or he's gone nose blind.'

Mum laughed too hard at her own joke and got to her feet. 'Come on upstairs, I'll put the shower on.'

Mum led, and I followed behind her. I didn't need to tell her that when I was feeling vulnerable, the bathroom was the most frightening place to be. She understood, probably more than I did, about the transference of trauma. And I didn't need to ask her to sit outside and chat loudly whilst I washed. Because she had done it a thousand times before.

Chapter 26

6th September 2018
St Ives, Cambridgeshire

I didn't want to be able to catch my reflection in the mirror, so I had to wait for the bathroom to fill with steam before I felt like I could step into the shower. Sitting on the edge of my bed I prepared myself to be in a bathroom, with the door shut, after a week of fearing it. I was grateful to Mum, who turned on the water, left the bathroom and without talking to me started to busy herself in the box room across the hall. She hummed as she pottered, giving me the space I needed but telling me she was not far away. Once I was satisfied the shower had steamed up, I slipped from my bedroom into the bathroom and shut the door. I undressed, thankful the mirror had completely fogged over. I turned the water up as hot as I could bear and scrubbed myself until all my skin was as pink as the scar tissue on my foot. As I washed myself, I could literally see the dead skin and dirt running from my body and down the plughole. Outside I listened as Mum sang to herself, loud enough to ensure I could hear her.

Getting out of the shower I wrapped the towel around my

body and with another I dried my hair quickly. Then, wiping the mirror glass, I looked at myself. Although still shaken, I looked all right. In fact, if I didn't know what I knew, if I didn't know who I was, I would have said I looked like anyone else. I was almost normal.

I never thought I would think that.

Looking at my feet, both still pink from the hot water, I focused on the right, looking at the patch of floor where two toes should have been, and then from my toes up my calf where the skin had melted when he'd set fire to me, just before I escaped. And I realised that was normal too. Not normal by anyone else's stand-ards, but it was *my* normal. I held out my arm and looked at the scar that had resulted from my fall out of the window. I wanted to drop my towel and look at my stomach, but was worried it would be too much, so stopped myself. Sometimes, the small victories are the most important.

I tried to understand why I suddenly felt OK with myself, and realised it was my self-preservation kicking in. I knew I still had the strength of the person who'd climbed out of that window, blood pouring from her body, trying to escape the clutches of a brutal killer. I was determined to survive, only this time, surviving wasn't running, hiding in grass cuttings. Surviving was stepping outside. Having a photo taken. Being a real person once more. Going outside felt like a more frightening prospect than trying to escape through that bathroom window. But, I needed to. Because if I didn't, I may as well be dead.

Mum looked up from a book she had come across in the box room as I stepped out of the bathroom. 'There, are you feeling better?'

'Yes, Mum. Fancy going out for cake and coffee?'

Mum's face lit up as a smile spread from ear to ear. 'Do I ever!'

Chapter 27

6th September 2018
St Ives, Cambridgeshire

As we left the house, the few photographers camped outside sprang to their feet. It was obvious when they heard the door open that they weren't expecting to see me coming out. The shutters clicked as we made our way towards Mum's car, which she had parked hastily on the drive. Mum walked in front of me and opened the passenger door for me to climb in. As she closed it my hand went up to my necklace. Front, back, upstairs, downstairs.

Mum started to back out of the drive and, still holding the keys, I looked out, catching the eye of a photographer, knowing a picture he had taken, or would take, could well end up in a paper or magazine somewhere. And he, the copycat would no doubt see it. Startled by me staring at him, he didn't take a photo, which allowed me a moment to wonder: if the copycat looked at a picture of me, what did I want him to see? A woman who was broken, sad and scared? Or a woman who held her head high, a woman defiantly not afraid of him? Knowing the answer straight away I smiled at the photographer through the glass. And he clicked his camera before smiling back. The world would see me, *he* would see me, happy, carefree. Unafraid. I wasn't just the one who lived. I was the one who lived and wouldn't hide. It was a small thing, but as we drove away towards the town centre, I couldn't help but feel like I had won a huge battle. Today was becoming a day of victories.

It only took five minutes to drive into town and park, and as we walked to the same café I always visited, I was expecting more eyes to be trained on me, asking more questions. But to my relief, no one cared. I hadn't watched the news in a week; I didn't dare. But I suspected that the picture from that night of me – bloodied, covered in grass cuttings and blinded by the helicopter lights – would have been revived. But I was hardly recognisable now and besides, people didn't expect to see someone like me in and around their lives. It wasn't a thing that happened to normal folk and I, from the outside at least, *was* normal. And I loved it.

I paid for our hot drinks and cakes. Mum had the coffee and walnut, while I had a blueberry muffin, and we made our way to the outside terrace that overlooked the river. Sitting in the corner, my back to the bridge, I sipped my coffee and wanted to allow myself to close my eyes, to try and enjoy the sun which shone proudly. I wanted to let myself melt into it and enjoy one of the few things I loved. But I couldn't quite do it, each car passing on the bridge snapped my attention back to my immediate surroundings, things that weren't nature: chatter, the clatter of cups on saucers, music from the speakers inside. It was exhausting to stop myself slipping into a panic. But I was glad I was out, glad I had said my silent 'fuck you' to my fear. Glad I'd smiled sweetly to the cameraman.

Glad as I was, however, I wanted to be back at home with the door locked and my curtains closed. I could feel the ever-present hand stroking my insides. I took several deep breaths and looked up, my sunglasses filtering the bright light, giving the sky a sepia hue, as the cloud hovered high above our heads. I tried to see a shape. But nothing. Mum didn't say much; she tried, but I couldn't focus on anything she said, so just agreed until she stopped talking. She closed her eyes, soaking up the sun, and for a while I just watched her, jealous of her ability to be so together.

Taking my phone out, I messaged Penny, telling her I was out in the world again and would she be like to come over later for a catch up? I then texted Paul saying I missed him. I waited for him to reply – he usually did quickly. But nothing came and eventually, the screen went black. He was busy. Sighing, I knew I should do one more thing on my phone before I put it away – I had to thank the Facebook group for the thoughtful gift. There were so many other things on my mind, but I knew I had to.

As soon as I opened the app, I wish I hadn't. The feed was busy with messages back and forth from some of the 8,027 members about what happened a week before. The latest part of the thread was a question raised by Killian.

Should we reopen the investigation?

There were 418 comments on the post and when I opened the feed I was surprised, and relieved, that most people were saying no. Some members commented that, as it was a fresh investigation, the police wouldn't want anyone getting in the way or interfering with their enquiries. Killian replied to a few comments, arguing his case about how if the copycat was as smart as Tommy Kay, then the police would be all but useless.

We all know he will go after Claire. We need to do what we can to protect her.

Nobody argued with him on that point. I looked at other comments in Killian's post. People were wishing me well. Sending their prayers. Offering support if I needed it. They meant well. But each message made me more of a victim, and I couldn't help but resent them. I needed to get out of the group as quickly as I could, so hastily posted my thank you for the box of bath treats and went to log out. Just before I did, a direct message popped up from Wendy Clarke. In the early days, before the group got out of control and behaved like a weird cult in my honour, I'd befriended a few of them. Wendy and Veronica, a retired police officer called Craig, and Killian. I should have deleted them from my friends list, but I didn't want to risk offending them. And mostly, they left me well enough alone.

Hi, Claire, I'm glad the box of goodies got to you all right. How are you? Can we do anything?

I looked at the little green dot beside her name. She was there, no doubt seeing my little green dot, telling her I was also online. I wanted to ignore her. But knew I shouldn't. She was just being kind.

Hi, Wendy. Thank you to you and Veronica, it was really thoughtful. And yes, I'm fine. I don't need anything else, thanks, not now I have my bathtime essentials.

I added a smiley emoji to the message, to keep it light. Her response was quick.

I'm really glad to hear it. If we can do anything, just let me know.

I paused for a moment and as I glanced up from my phone, Mum was looking back.

'You OK, love?'

'I'm on the group page, they want to start up their investigation again.'

'And how do you feel about it?'

'I don't want them to. It's too stressful.'

'Then tell them that.'

I nodded and typed the message to Wendy.

There is one thing. Could you ask the group, from me, not to start the investigation again? I find it quite upsetting.

Again, her response was quick.

Claire, I'm sorry to hear you find it upsetting. Yes, of course. I will speak to everyone, say we have talked and that you've requested we don't. I certainly don't think we should, anyway. We don't want to get the way of the police doing their job.

Thank you, Wendy.

Claire, just so you know, Killian is no longer part of CMSP.

Killian had founded the group ten years ago, and was the most active member on the page, rallying people, motivating them to do things for me (regardless of me wanting them to or not). I couldn't understand why he would leave. When I asked her why, her response made my blood run cold.

He didn't leave. We banned him from the group.

Chapter 28

6th September 2018
St Ives, Cambridgeshire

After discovering Killian had been kicked out of the group he created, I pushed Wendy for more details. She became evasive, but confided that he hadn't followed the group's rules. Maybe they found out he had followed me in Ireland, and that he had taken photographs of me in Kanturk, when I was visiting Owen. If it definitely had been him in Ireland, of course. Maybe that wasn't allowed. I had never wanted to know what their rules were as they were obviously a code of conduct outlining what they could and could not say to me. After finding out Killian had broken them, I felt I needed to know. I didn't tell Mum about Killian, as I knew she had enough to worry about at the moment. After we finished our drinks and cakes we left for home, the walk back to the car feeling much more oppressive than before. The world was once again staring at me with eyes that lived in the roofs, the trees and lampposts.

When we got home the photographers had gone. Satisfied with what they'd got, or perhaps bored by the lack of anything scandalous. I didn't care either way – I was just pleased that they had left. The police remained, for now, though I imagined they'd leave soon too. Mum offered to stay for the day, but as we made our way home Penny messaged back, saying she would love to come over for a takeaway and a glass of wine. The takeaway sounded good, but I knew I'd not be able to drink. It dulled my senses and although I knew I was perfectly safe as long as the police stayed close by, I couldn't take the risk. Not again. So, Mum came in, checked the house was as it should be and left, telling me to call if I needed her. I promised I would, before closing the door and watching her through the living room window as she got into her car and drove the short distance home.

Once she was out of sight, I felt very aware of being on my own again. To distract myself I made a list of things I needed to do, just in case someone came for me. I removed my necklace, feeling naked as soon as I did, and unlocked, then relocked all of the windows in the house. I did the same with the front and back door before placing my necklace back on. Flicking the keys in my fingers I counted them off, happy all four were in their rightful place. Still, I wasn't feeling entirely settled, perhaps because I had frozen like a rabbit earlier in the day. Something I couldn't afford to do if it came down to it. To combat it, I put an old tennis racquet near the front door, and a snooker cue that belonged to Geoff near the back. Just in case someone got in. I even placed a small pair of scissors in my bedside drawer. I almost put a knife there, but there was something too intimidating, too frightening about becoming a person who needed a blade beside her bed. After the checks, I paced around the house, cleaning and preparing, as Penny messaged telling me she would be at mine for 6 p.m. The iPad was never far away, the camera playing for me to see.

True to her word, at three minutes to, I heard two people talking outside. I glanced at the camera and could see the top of Penny's head and the helmet of a police officer. I watched as

Penny explained rather animatedly to the police officer who she was and why she was there. I could just make out the words 'why else would I have a bottle of wine?' filter through the front door.

Knowing my friend needed rescuing, I made my way to the door and unlocked the deadbolt before placing my hand on the Yale lock to open it. She was just outside, talking with a police officer, and yet I paused before opening the gateway between my safe little world, and the big wide one. As the door squeaked ajar, both sets of eyes turned from each other.

'It's OK, she's my friend.'

'I see, Mrs Moore. Sorry, we've only got your family on the list.'

'I am family!' Penny chimed in.

'It's OK, officer, thank you.'

He smiled, nodded and headed back to his car. Opposite my house and one door down.

'Have a nice evening,' Penny called, as he left. 'Jesus, what's that all about?'

'They wanted me to go somewhere else, you know, with what's happened. I said no.'

'You said no?'

'Yep,' I replied, unable to hide the pride in my voice.

'Good for you,' she said, punching me in the arm. 'You gonna let me in?'

'Yeah. Come on in.'

Penny stepped past me and made a beeline for the kitchen to open the rosé she clutched in her arms. I stepped in after her, looking down the street in both directions just before closing and locking the door. With both glasses full to the brim, she gingerly made her way into the lounge, placed the drinks on the Ikea coffee table Geoff had bought me despite my protests, and plonked herself on the sofa, kicking her shoes off like it was any other day.

'I'm bloody starving, please tell me you're ready to order a Chinese?'

'Yes, let's do it.'

'Marvellous, the usual?'

'Please, I'll get cash.'

'Nah, it's my turn to pay. You got it last time.'

Technically, it was her turn to pay. However, she must have paid eighty per cent of the time so really, I should have got the takeaways for the next six months. But I didn't argue, because she was like Mum in that respect – once she had made up her mind, that was that. Perhaps that's why she was my only friend. She and Mum were so similar in so many ways: strong, independent, unfettered. Everything I wished I was. As she ordered the food I couldn't help but smile. Penny really was a great friend because instead of fussing over me, asking if I was coping, tiptoeing around the fact I was a complete mess, she acted like it was just another takeaway on a normal Thursday evening.

The food came at just after seven and as I opened the foil lids, releasing the aroma of my chow mein, I suddenly felt famished and Penny and I ate in silence, apart from the odd grunt of satisfaction.

She talked about her husband, how he was doing and said he sent his love. She updated me on her job being typically impossible to do well. She had been a social worker for eight years, and I had no idea how she coped with the stress and volatility she was exposed to daily. Eventually, she asked about me and how I was holding up. I told her I was OK, but that I didn't want to go into any details because I needed a break from my head – of course she understood and changed the subject. Future holidays. A potential career change within social services. All things normal. In fact, it was the first time in a long time I'd felt normal around another person, and although I didn't talk much, it wasn't uncomfortable or awkward. It was nice to hear about all things in Penny's life; it reassured me the world went on spinning, regardless.

167

Penny left about eleven and I watched through the living room curtain as she zigzagged down my drive, waving to the police officer before disappearing from sight. I couldn't remember what it felt like to be that carefree, and that drunk. I'd poured most of my wine back into the bottle when she went to the loo, topping my glass up with lemonade to make a very weak spritzer. She'd happily consumed the rest, and I could almost hear the phone call tomorrow telling me she was never drinking again, until the next time.

I went into the kitchen to have a cup of tea before bed and felt jubilant that this was the first night sleeping on my own since the news came through about Wales. Even though I felt OK, I didn't have the strength to open the windows, letting the hot, still air of the house escape. But I didn't feel like I would have a fretful night either, thanks to some time with Penny. I made my tea and switched off all the downstairs lights, bar the hallway, and made my way upstairs. The house felt silent, pensive, but not oppressive. As I climbed into bed, I had a message ping through from Penny telling me she was home OK, and that she – rather predictably – was never drinking again. I also messaged Paul. Again, he didn't message back. But that was OK. He wasn't mine to dictate to, and I knew I'd wake up to a message from him in the morning.

I wanted to sleep, but the compulsive part of me needed to check the windows again, wondered whether I'd left my hair straighteners on despite not using them for months, or if I'd left the fridge open. I knew I wouldn't settle until I'd checked, so I rolled out of bed and padded to the window. Pulling back the curtain slightly, I looked and sure enough they were both closed. As I already knew. I saw that in the last half an hour a mist had descended on the road. Weird for the end of summer, but not that weird. This was England, after all, and on the edge of the fens the weather was different to any other part of the country. The tiny water droplets hanging on the air made the street lamp light outside my house look otherworldly, the light refracting around the moisture, illuminating the air. It reminded me of winter, and I missed the days when wrapping up in layers and stepping out for my morning coffee at my usual time meant I could watch the sunrise. I looked from the lamppost to the car on the other side of the road; the police officer inside looked like he was asleep. Then, just before stepping away, I scanned right. A man dressed entirely in black was standing further down the road, looking back through the lens of a camera. The photographers hadn't gone. Bastards. I was in my nightwear, about to go to sleep. Had they no compassion?

I wanted to flip him a middle finger but thought better of it, and as soon as the photographer saw I had seen him, he walked away, probably concerned I would notify the sleeping policeman and tell him I was being harassed. He was right to worry because that was exactly what I would do.

I didn't get a good look at his face to help with that, so opening my iPad I went through the security-camera footage to see if I could get a glimpse, enough to point him out to the police officer, anyway. First, I went back too far and when I slowed the footage down, I watched Penny walking away, wave to the police officer in the car and then stumble home. I hit fast forward again, and the night moved on at three times the normal speed. I saw the photographer and slowed the footage down. I watched as he made his way towards the police car first, peering inside to make sure the officer was asleep before walking away more confidently. Frustratingly, his back was to the camera. Then he stopped in the place I had seen him, and I saw him take his camera out and turn, showing me his face.

Even with the image grainy, and the man shrouded in the mist, I thought I knew who it was. I couldn't be completely sure but the man in the image looked a lot like Killian.

Chapter 29

6th September 2018
Wrexham, Wales

Sipping his wine, he smiled when he thought he should and made agreeable noises now and then to feign listening to the woman sat opposite him. He held her gaze when she looked his way. When she wasn't, which was often as her eyes wandered when she rambled about her work, he surveyed the dimly lit restaurant that was still taking food orders, despite it being so late into the night.

As he looked, he saw an attractive woman sat opposite a considerably older and fatter man who sat upright like a lord at his table. He assumed she was probably with him for the money. He couldn't see the face of the man as his back was to him, but the woman looked bored and didn't try to hide it. She looked as bored as he felt listening to his date drone on.

There was an older couple to his left, neither talking, sitting in companionable silence. They knew how each other worked, how the other one thought, and so speech became unnecessary. It was a nice thought, although truthfully, they were probably bored as well. In fact, looking around the rest of the restaurant, he felt the room was suffused with boredom. The only person who seemed content was a man sitting by himself, a man in his late twenties perhaps, completely at peace with the fact he was alone in a restaurant which was set up for romance. The man was reading a novel entitled *Play Dead*. He smiled at the title.

Taking another sip of wine, he noticed that his date, Jennifer, was looking at him intently. She was waiting for a response, but he did not understand what he was responding to. The last time he'd actually been listening to her, she was talking about her friend Sam at work, and just before that, she was wittering on about her dog. He couldn't even begin to guess what she had asked.

'Sorry, I was miles away.'

'I'd noticed,' she said, sweeping her hair behind her left ear. 'Is everything all right?'

He didn't know when it was acceptable to ask personal questions with someone you had only recently met. But he knew it wasn't on the second dinner date.

'Yes, I'm fine, just a bit preoccupied with work.'

'Do you want to talk about it?'

He smiled to himself, a smile that she would interpret as him being touched that she cared. But that wasn't it. He was smiling because for a moment he imagined telling her his work troubles. How he would have to kill again in a matter of weeks, but he still didn't have the right woman to kill, and that she was lucky because this evening he had concluded that despite her being at the top of his shortlist, it wouldn't be her life he would take. She was too keen, too chatty, too self-sufficient. It was what he wanted all women to be, able to stand on their own two feet and leave their shit lives behind them. And because she was doing just that, she wouldn't be the ninth.

He wondered what she would do if he told her everything about his work. He assumed she would run, call the police and

171

have him arrested. But then again, she was a pleaser. She wanted to keep the peace, be polite. So perhaps she would feel uneasy and want to leave but instead she would laugh it off. Thinking he was being funny, even though it would be anything but.

'No, it's OK. Just boring paperwork stuff.'

'I hate paperwork, that's why I do what I do.'

She worked as a veterinarian nurse, a job that presumably involved ample paperwork. Again, she was trying so hard to please him, even when he was offhand with her. Seemingly unoffended by him not listening, she began talking again, saying how she liked to fill silences. *No shit.* As she waffled on, he became acutely aware of the clock on the wall behind her animated head. He was wasting time, sitting here with the final woman on his current shortlist, who had seemed perfect until now. His instincts told him it was right to be giving her his precious time; but it seemed, unusually, his instincts had failed him.

After incessantly talking for another ten minutes, Jennifer excused herself and walked to the bathroom a little artificially, knowing he was watching her move. She wasn't unattractive, and he knew she was interested in sleeping with him. She'd made comments about his physique, his perfect teeth and smile, to use her words. But he wasn't interested in anything other than the task at hand. For him, the thrill of a perfectly executed kill far exceeded the thrill of sex with someone new.

Once she was out of sight, he turned his attention back to the other couples who were eating, mostly in silence. The old couple had moved on to their desserts, the man on his own had paid and was putting away his book, ready to leave. The man and his trophy woman were still on their main, her knife and fork down, him shoveling food into his mouth. As he watched, the woman went to pick up her wineglass and knocked her knife from the plate, sending it crashing to the tiled floor, drawing people's attention. She apologised quietly and picked it up, returning it to the table. Then, she locked eyes on him.

At first, he thought she was apologising directly to him, although he didn't know why. He didn't care about her dropping her cutlery. But, as she turned her attention away from him, back to the man across from her, he watched as her shoulders rose towards her chin, just slightly. And he knew that it wasn't an apologetic look she had shown him, but one laced with fear. She rubbed the side of her neck before raising her head a little too high, her chin protruding a little too much. Faking confidence. It made her interesting. He settled his attention on her companion, his back still turned, as he continued to shovel food into his fat mouth, but his body language had altered. He sat proudly as before, only now his right hand rested on the table, and was curled into a fist. He must have been staring too intently, because the woman looked again, prompting her companion to turn in his chair and stare back, trying to intimidate. It didn't work.

He muttered *prick* under his breath before he continued to eat. Jennifer approached from behind their table and smiled towards him. Just as she sat down and sipped her wine, he looked over her shoulder and the fearful woman caught his eye once more, a desperation, a need on her face. And he knew why his instincts had told him to come to this restaurant tonight.

'What are you smiling about?' asked Jennifer, and he replied by saying *you*, making her blush and tuck her hair behind her ear. But he wasn't smiling because of the woman directly in front of him; he was smiling because of the one twenty feet away.

He needed confirmation, but he felt in his gut that he may have just found his ninth.

Chapter 30

7th September 2018
St Ives, Cambridgeshire

I looked at the footage recorded on my security camera for hours. Watching and watching again the moment the man approached and took photos. Each time I viewed it, I became less and less sure that it was Killian until, just after two in the morning, I finally concluded it couldn't have been him, just like it couldn't have been him in Ireland. But, if it wasn't him, who was looking into my house?

Unable to sleep I tried to read, but couldn't focus, and didn't dare turn the TV on for fear of not hearing something, or someone, in the house. So I watched the live feed from the camera and observed the world outside my front door, a world that was mostly quiet. I saw a young couple walking arm in arm; the woman holding her evening shoes and wearing the man's coat on her shoulders, both unsteady after a few too many drinks. Ten minutes after they wobbled out of sight. I saw a group of young men, boys really, running and climbing on one another in the middle of the road without a care in the world. I saw in the grainy image the police officer parked outside look at them, then quickly turn his attention back to the inside of his eyelids. Shortly after, another young man, hands in his pockets, head low, walking as if he carried the other boys' troubles for them. And then later, I saw a fox cross the road in front of the police car before disappearing into the mist which had staked its claim over the night. And at some point, after that fox and before the sun was strong enough to burn away the fog, I had fallen asleep, fully clothed.

When I woke, feeling like it was still yesterday, I gingerly made my way down for a cup of coffee which I cupped in my hands, the steam rising and the aroma tricking my brain into feeling more awake than I was. I looked at my back door, wanting to open it to let the sunny morning in, but I couldn't. The unease about the man outside my house stopped me. With my head feeling slightly clearer I listed who it could have been. The obvious answer was it was just another reporter – they had been around since the fire in Wales – and yet my gut told me it wasn't a reporter. There was something in the way he was standing, the clothes he was wearing, that meant it was someone else, someone taking pictures for a different reason.

I knew I should tell Mum and Geoff about what I had seen; I knew I should show them the footage, so they could cast their slightly more objective eye over the image and tell me categorically if it was or wasn't Killian, but I couldn't put them through it, not again. I had always felt like I was being watched; I guess that's just something I had to live with, something that made up who I was, and most of the time I managed it the best I could. But once, about four years ago, I didn't manage, couldn't manage. I was so convinced a murderer was watching me, I ended up being so sleep-deprived, and so malnourished that I collapsed one morning and woke in a hospital bed, where I stayed for two weeks and had to undergo rigorous psychological assessments.

I didn't want to go back to that place, not now, not after so long after fighting to win the battles I faced each morning. So, for now, I would keep quiet about the footage, and my paranoia, and I would push forwards with my day.

I would call Penny or put on the TV or listen to music. I would also allow the air to move around my house freely. I would look like I was coping. Setting my coffee cup down on the kitchen counter, I took off my necklace and put the back door key in the lock. As I turned it I heard the sound of the mechanism freeing itself, the snap of the lock disengaging from the door frame. I told myself it was just another morning, just like any other, and there was nothing to fear: there was no reason I couldn't step outside if I wanted. It was a hard-fought battle in my head, but eventually I made myself tentatively opened the door. The bracing morning air felt like another small victory, notched.

Leaving the back door open I picked up my coffee and walked into the lounge where the air was circulating pleasantly, and curled up on the sofa. I wanted to relieve the silence, so grabbed my phone from my trouser pocket to put my music on shuffle. It was hard, almost impossible to not have an ear on my back door, another listening to sounds above my head. So much so, I couldn't say what the previous song was. Then, the phone played a song I hadn't heard in a long time. A song that reminded me of that night. As I heard the first piano chord, the sound of rain behind it, the icy hand tried to play along on my diaphragm. Jumping up I skipped the track, and as the next song played, I sat back down and focused on stopping my hands from shaking. I was amazed that after all this time that song would still make me feel so sick.

The next song, an old one by Maroon 5, reminded me of a holiday I'd taken when I was about twenty. I forced myself to listen to it, just to stop my thoughts from going back to where the previous song tried to take me. As Adam Levine, an old crush of mine, sang, a memory from that time in my life surfaced. And I fought to hold on to the pictures in my mind from a girls' trip. Back then, Owen and I were officially boyfriend and girlfriend and I knew it would probably be the last time I'd have a holiday with just the girls. I went with three friends – Michelle, Cassy and Molly – for a week of sun and drinking and dancing in Corfu. I let myself imagine I was back on that beach. Lying in the sun, nursing a hangover without a care in the world. I wondered what had happened to those friends I'd loved so dearly back then.

What do they say – youth is wasted on the young? Thinking about those days was momentarily blissful, but then I got to thinking about what my life might have been were it not for the events of one night. I had to get up, stop the music and shut the back door again, my victory short-lived.

I couldn't listen to music, I couldn't go outside, I couldn't watch TV, but I needed to do something to keep my sanity. Then a thought entered my head, one I'd been trying to block out ever since Paul turned on the TV last week. It had been nine days since someone killed that poor woman in Wales, and I didn't even know her name. I had to know more about who the eighth was, out of respect, because I knew all too well that the number was supposed to be mine. I grabbed my phone and Googled 'murder in Wales' to find out as much as I could.

Chapter 31

7th September 2018
St Ives, Cambridgeshire

The woman killed in Bethesda was named Kath Brinck, and was just twenty-six when she died. The same age I had been when he almost killed me. She had no children, just like me. She was also married, but that was where the similarities ended. Until that night, I'd lived a relatively quiet and sheltered existence, hers was anything but. From what I had seen scrolling through her public Facebook feed, she had lived a rich, full life. In every one of her pictures she looked happy, content, smiling without restraint. She was in lots of pictures with friends on nights out, but in most, she was with her husband. A man whose name I learned to be Neil when I hovered over one of their many pictures together. You could clearly see the love in her eyes.

Her most recent pictures were from a holiday, the album on Facebook entitled 'Zakynthos 2017'. Her sun-kissed skin was enviable, as was the obvious affection her husband had for her. One image that was particularly touching showed the pair standing in the calm sea, an island the shape of a turtle behind them. Their smiles, their eyes – they were living in bliss. I knew social media always showed the best versions of ourselves, the filters heightening our joy, glossing over the cracks. But still, I really believed she was as happy as she looked. Although I couldn't help but notice Neil wasn't in any of the recent pictures.

Her timeline was full of messages from friends expressing their grief, their shock. Telling her that she was loved and missed and would never be forgotten. I scrolled down, reading the outpouring of love and kindness for hours, their words touching me but also making me feel more uncomfortable as I went on, like I was invading her privacy. Friends relived their best memories with her on her page, memories they would hold on to for ever. Reading them, I learnt she was a woman who was fiercely protective of the people she loved, standing up for several of them when they needed someone to do so. She was funny, daring, at times wild. Her friends reshared photos of her in the timeline of younger years, before she was married, she was mischievous and bold. I couldn't help but like her, while feeling guilty at the same time.

It took me a long time to scroll down far enough to find a post from Neil. It was short, four days after she had died and reading it, I couldn't stop a tear escaping.

Kath. I don't know how I'll go on without you. Please, please come back. I should have tried harder to show you how much I love you, I should have done more.

I'm so sorry, my love.

I knew what I was doing wasn't healthy, I shouldn't be looking into someone's life, someone I didn't know, someone whose death was tangentially connected to me. But for my own sanity, I had to try to work out why she had been targeted. Why her? Why now? I hoped that by looking at her life I would see some tragic connection. However, Kath Brinck was nothing like me: bright, engaging, in the world. She was not a ghost.

I learnt she studied at Cardiff University and had been employed as a care worker on the Isle of Anglesey, near Bethesda, where she lived. She worked with people who needed support and care, which made me feel selfish – she was clearly a far better human being than I was, and that compacted my guilt even more. I couldn't help but wonder, despite being a decade apart, if I'd been the eighth as intended – would she have lived? Would the path have been altered to let her live to be old and grey and content with her life? It seemed unfair that she should die and I, who had done nothing but waste the last ten years of my life, should continue to breathe.

I felt the need to say something so, I typed on her page two words.

I'm sorry.

And for a while, I really believed she would read it.

Baloo, who had been at Mum's but sauntered over and wandered in whilst the back door was open this morning, purred at my feet. I looked at the clock and saw it was nearly 11 a.m. The cat was probably starving. So, I pulled myself away from the laptop to feed him. When I returned, I saw there had been traction on my post. People knew I was *the* Claire Moore. They told me it wasn't my fault; that there was nothing I could have done and for a moment, I felt comforted. Then, scrolling, I saw her husband had left a message and the feeling of comfort was gone. He said I was being inappropriate, and even though he was grieving he was polite and respectful. I realised I'd crossed a line and hastily deleted my post. A new message popped into my inbox, I thought it was someone else from Kath's page telling me I was being inconsiderate, but it wasn't. It was Killian, and I felt my heart rate start to increase.

Hey, I see you're online, can we talk?

If I ignored him, he would message again, or worse, he might turn up at my front door. I still wasn't sure if it had been him I'd seen on the camera feed. I didn't want to, but I knew I needed to talk to him. I needed him to back off.

I've been meaning to message you, Killian.

You have? What do you want to talk about? Are you all right?

Why were you outside the cemetery in Kanturk?

There was a pause.

Yes, I didn't think you saw me.

I knew it. It was him, which meant it had also been him outside my house taking photos.

Yes, saw you. Why were you there?

I wanted to make sure you were OK. You didn't reply to my messages; I was worried.

That's very kind, Killian, but you shouldn't worry about me.

Well, we have known each other a long time, it's my job to care.

It's not.

But you're all on your own, Claire, I want to be there for you.

This was it, if I told him about Paul, he would back away. I took the plunge.

Killian, I'm not alone.

There was another pause. This one longer.

Oh, you've met someone?

I knew I had to be delicate. But, worded right, I would protect his feelings, and make him leave me alone. *If* I worded it right.

Yes, and I'm happy. You don't need to worry about me anymore. I know you were outside my house last night. If you really cared, you'd give me some space. As you know, I don't like being watched. I need you to respect my wishes, please.

I waited for him to respond, but the green icon that indicted he was online had gone. I just hoped it would be a permanent thing. I'd wanted him to leave me alone for such a long time, and now I had finally said it out loud. I knew I'd upset him, but I couldn't feel responsible for that – I knew that it was best for us both in the long run. Without me to obsess over, he might find someone else to care for him who had the capacity to care back.

Closing the lid of the laptop I felt a rope being pulled, an internal tug of war. On the one hand, I was relieved that Killian might now leave me alone, on the other I felt deep shame at posting on a dead woman's Facebook wall. I shouldn't have done it, it was a mistake, but I knew I had to say something – whether other people liked it or not, we were now connected.

Standing up I stretched, uncurling my fingers towards the ceiling, feeling the scar tissue in my stomach pull as I did. I realised I hadn't eaten yet, and although I wasn't hungry I forced myself to have a slice of toast. Hardly a filling breakfast but it was a slippery slope if I didn't encourage myself to eat. After finishing my meal, if you could call it that, I did my checks. Because of Killian, the uneasy feeling was back.

When I was happy I was secure inside, I allowed myself to sit by my back door, and look through the glass at the sky, cloud hunting. I hoped I would see a shape on them, as I once could. But they were just clouds.

Chapter 32

8th September 2018
St Ives, Cambridgeshire

I dreamt I was back at the bungalow, standing in the back garden, looking towards the kitchen window. I was wearing dark clothes that I understood didn't belong to me and I was carrying something heavy in my right hand. The night was thick and heavy. The wind brought the lashing rain sideways, my wet hair sticking to my face. Stalking like a panther before it killed, I moved sideways to the bathroom window and looking in, I saw Owen's dead, limp, bone-thin arm hanging over the edge of the tub. I strolled away, turning past the kitchen to approach the main bedroom. I pressed my hands to the glass and looked in. In bed was a woman, young and petite. She rolled over in her sleep, and I could see, even in the low light, that it was my head on the pillow.

Above me came a rumble of thunder. I stepped back and counted: *one, two, three, four, five, six, seven, eight...* the lightning lit up the sky and for a moment I could see my reflection in the glass. But it wasn't my reflection at all. I was him; I was Tommy Kay. I couldn't make out the details of his face, but I knew. I turned and walked towards the back door and paused, looking up at a deep purple sheet of heavy, foreboding cloud that stretched in all directions. At any moment it looked like it would crash on my head, smothering me. I looked at my feet, in heavy work boots, and taking a few steps back I readied myself. I would kick the door down, run inside. Subdue Owen, drug me, then kill us both. Above came another rumble of thunder. Three large steps and I planted my foot on the door. The crash it made as it burst open was deafening.

Then I woke. The crash somehow lingered from the dream world into the real world.

My bedroom was pitch black. The lamp beside my bed was off and reaching over I flicked the switch to turn it back on. I tried several times, but nothing happened. I listened out to see if there was anything strange. But all I could hear was rain water running off the broken gutter outside. In the darkness, I made my way to the main light switch on the wall by the door. Trying to fight the panic at being in the dark for the first time in over a decade, I told myself, with each measured step, the bulb had blown, that was all it was. The bedside lamp wasn't designed to be on all night every night, and bulbs didn't last for ever. The filament eventually died, and I couldn't remember the last time I replaced it. Something easily fixed. I didn't know how many steps it was to the doorway, and I bumped into the corner of my bedframe and the chest of drawers as I approached it. I realised that I couldn't navigate my bedroom in the dark, because I had never needed to.

I reached the door and fumbled on the wall until I found the light switch. As I flicked it I expected to be blinded by light.

But nothing happened.

I tried again and again but the darkness held, and the icy hand tapped like fingers on a piano inside my chest. Soon it would play its symphony, and I would be rendered useless. I ran from my doorway to the window, and as I pulled back the curtain I felt the air escape from my lungs in a whimper. The rain was coming down in torrents, covering the roads in water that, when the wind whipped up, made the tarmac look like an ocean. But that wasn't what terrified me. The houses on the other side of the road were also in darkness, and I could see one or two lit from within with torches or phone lights. The street lamps as far as I could see were also out.

I was in a power cut.

I knew I needed to move, to grab my phone and turn on the light. But as much as my head told me to, my legs wouldn't budge. Before I could correct myself I slid down the wall to the floor. I wanted to make myself as small as I could, to try and become invisible. I tried to find my mobile, but I fumbled in the dark – it wasn't in its usual place on the bedside table. I must have left it downstairs, by my laptop perhaps? The noise I made as I knocked the lamp was amplified in the silence. I was declaring in the dark exactly where I was. Fearful I would be found, I decided to forget my phone and I dragged myself from my bedroom, trying to get downstairs, closer to the ground, ready to escape.

From somewhere in the house I heard a crash, like the sound in my dream as I kicked the door open. I thought someone had come in; I thought someone was coming to finish off what Tommy Kay started a decade before. And as I pulled myself on to unsteady feet and tried to descend the stairs, I slipped and fell down half the flight before righting myself and coming to a painful stop midway down. During the fall I had hit my face on something, the bannister perhaps, or a step. I could taste blood in my mouth. My right hip was also hurt, but not enough to stop me moving.

There was a flash, a camera taking a photo, and I covered my face. At least that's what I thought for a moment until I realised it was the lightning outside, illuminating the house as it streaked through the darkness. And the crashing sound I'd heard wasn't a door being kicked in, or a window being smashed, but the reverberation of the thunder. But that didn't mean someone wasn't coming, using the storm to hide their approach, wash away evidence like Tommy Kay did before, and so I fortified myself and prepared to move.

I slid down the rest of the stairs as quietly as I could and made my way to the kitchen. I knew from researching, that the kitchen was the best room to be in if there was a home invasion. My phone was in the lounge, it had to be, and I almost went for it. But didn't. I needed to be somewhere I could defend myself. In the kitchen drawers and cupboards there were plentiful potential weapons to throw and thrust to make an escape. I crawled towards it, fighting to control my breathing, to silence myself. The noise coming from my mouth seemed to be louder than the sound of the rain lashing against the window.

Pressing my back into the cooker, I reached up and opened the knife drawer, grabbing the biggest I could find. I wanted to bolt out the front door, but knew he could be waiting for me there. And I couldn't go for the back because he might assume I would and be waiting. It was fifty-fifty as to which entrance he would cover, and I couldn't decide which one to risk. I felt trapped, and all I could do was pray the power came back on soon. I prayed it was just the storm causing the outage. I prayed he wouldn't find me.

There was a noise, something that wasn't rain or my breathing or the song I fought to forget and never could. Something that my subconscious knew I needed to focus on. It stopped me breathing; it paused the tune the icy hand played. Then, there was silence. I heard the noise again, a creak, a snap, a footstep. Then another. And another. I saw a light on the floor, a weak beam that ebbed after a few seconds. A dim light, helping him get his bearings inside my pitch-black house.

Staring ahead of me, towards the kitchen doorway I couldn't see, I waited. Unable to blink. Unable to breathe, unable to run. Another footstep. Then a voice.

'Claire?'

I wanted to scream for help. I wanted to run, to hide. But I couldn't. All I could do was raise my hands, the knife held firmly in both, like a child with a toy sword.

'Hello? Claire?'

The small torch came on again, this time a lot closer, this time with me being able to see the hand that held it. They pointed the light into my face, and I turned my head instinctively as it blinded me, the knife lowered, my guard down. The light hit the floor; it focused on the washing machine beside me and I saw the rush of black cut across it. I wanted to thrust the knife, but I was too slow, and I felt arms around me, trapping the knife down to the ground. The steel of the blade caught torchlight and refracted it onto my body. His grip was firm, and I tried to fight but it was no use, he was too strong. His wet clothes stuck to my skin like death itself was wrapping around me.

'Claire, stop! Claire, it's me.'

'Get off me, let me go.'

'Claire it's me, it's Paul, calm down. It's OK, everything's OK.'

As soon as he said his name, I placed his voice and turned my head to make out his face in the dark.

'It's OK, everything is all right. I'm here.'

'Paul?'

'Yes, darling, it's me.'

Knowing for sure it was him was such a relief I burst into tears, sobbing long and hard into his chest. I breathed in his smell as he whispered everything was OK, everything was all right, and after a few minutes I calmed down enough to speak.

'I thought you were him. I thought you were the copycat.'

'I'm so sorry. I didn't mean to scare you.'

'I thought you were him, and I did nothing.'

'Claire, everything is OK. I've got you. Everything is OK.'

Paul stayed on the floor with me for over an hour, until the power came back on. The small lamp in the hallway lit the

187

downstairs of my house enough for me to feel like I could move once more. Exhausted, more so than usual, I didn't argue when he said we were going back to his. He led me upstairs and while I sat on the edge of the bed he packed a few things into an overnight bag. Then, taking me by the hand, he led me to the front door, and covering my head with his jacket, he guided me to his car.

As we drove in silence I felt exhausted from the adrenaline crash. There was nothing I wanted to do more than to close my eyes and sleep, but as exhausted as I felt, I knew I couldn't. I looked at the car's dashboard clock, the time saying it was just before 1 a.m. I didn't know why Paul was here. But I was so glad that he was. A few miles from his house, the storm still hadn't relented, and I watched as a fork of lightning shot across, startling me.

'Don't worry, in a storm, a car is one of the safest places to be,' Paul said tenderly, and reaching over, I placed my hand on his leg. The flash reminded me of the thought I had when I fell down the stairs, how I'd thought that the lightning was a camera bulb, and then I had remembered this had happened before. It happened on that night, and I must have suppressed the memory.

The night Owen was killed, the killer had taken our photo.

Chapter 33

8th September 2018
Ely, Cambridgeshire

It was just after 1.30 a.m. when we got back to Paul's house. He quietly led me to the sofa before disappearing into his kitchen and returning moments later, a glass in his hand.

'Here, I got you some water.'

'Thanks, Paul.'

I drank it quickly, not realising how thirsty I was until the liquid touched my lips. As I finished the glass and sighed in relief, Paul smiled softly.

'Have you got anything stronger?' I asked.

Paul touched my shoulder and left again for the kitchen, giving me a moment to look around. I hadn't been in Paul's home before, despite us having been a couple now for a few months. He always came to mine, to make it easier on me, but I felt guilty – his house was far nicer. The sofa was inviting and comfortable, and the rest of the living room was furnished to a much higher standard than mine. In front of me stood a real working fireplace, and I could picture him sat looking at the flames, a hot drink in one hand, a book in the other, the flames mesmerising and terrifying all at once. Above the fireplace were pictures of his girls; I was drawn to a thick silver frame that contained both of their graduation pictures. I'd not met them, and I suspected it would be a long time before I would. They looked like him. The same smile, and same mischievous glint in their eyes.

Paul returned with a whiskey or brandy, I wasn't sure which, and although I didn't like either, I thanked him and drank. The liquid heated my throat and stomach and warmed up the icy hand.

'Do you want another one?'

'No, thank you, one is enough. This is the first time I've been in your house.'

'Yes, it is,' he said without passing judgement as he sat beside me. I rested my head on his shoulder, both of us looking at the unused fireplace.

'I'm sorry.'

'For what?'

'For dragging you away from it so often. You have a lovely home.'

He kissed me on the top of the head. 'Don't be sorry, ever.'

For a while we sat looking into the fireplace. My head on his shoulder, his hand clasped between both of mine.

'I used to love fires,' I said. Paul didn't reply but nodded his head as if to say he understood. 'The crackle as wood split. The smell that came from them. I used to love watching them, feeling the heat on my face. When I was younger, I used to sit in the garden most evenings, regardless of how cold it was, with a fire pit burning away. No TV, no phones. Nothing but the fire that seemed to be alive, and the stars above my head.'

'That sounds perfect,' Paul whispered as he kissed me gently on the top of my head.

'Now, the idea of sitting by a fire in the dark, terrifies me.' I turned and looked to him and for a moment, his eyes weren't on mine, but looking at my burnt foot and leg. 'Paul, what if I never recover from what happened?'

'You will, in time.'

'It's been a long time already, and I still end up in such a state because of a power cut. This thing keeps beating me.'

Paul pulled his hand from mine and turned to face me, his eyes only inches away.

'No, Claire, you're winning. You're still moving, still being. That's more than most of us, more than I could do if I'd been through what you've been through.'

'Paul…'

Placing one hand on each shoulder he held me firmly. 'And every day you do it, every day you get up, keep moving, do your shopping, water your flowers. You are beating it. Every time you see me or go for a coffee with your mum, you are beating it.'

'It only seems that way because you or Mum are with me. I'm not beating it when I'm alone.'

'You will.'

'I hope so,' I said, at barely a whisper.

Taking my hand Paul led me upstairs, grabbing my overnight bag that was by the front door, and showed me the rest of his house. Two good-sized bedrooms, one of them decorated ready for visits from his girls. His bedroom was clean and tidy, but needed a feminine touch. There were no pictures, no ornaments. Just the bed, a wardrobe and a bookshelf, mostly housing crime and thriller novels. I sat on the edge of his bed and he left the room, returning with two large, thick towels.

'I figured you might want a hot shower?'

'You read my mind,' I smiled, enjoying the fact Paul was starting to know who I was, beyond the obvious facts about me and my 'quirks'.

'The bathroom is just here.' He pointed to his left, before he lifted my bag onto the bed and unzipped it. On the top were my pyjamas which he took out and handed to me, knowing I couldn't dress into them in front of him. Knowing that I still needed to hide.

'Thanks, Paul.'

'It's OK. I'll wait outside the bathroom door.'

'Why?' I asked as it was an odd thing to do, for anyone other than me. He didn't respond but gave me a look that told me he understood. I thanked him, feeling incredibly grateful for his ability to know. If I had any doubt that I was falling in love with Paul, that doubt was gone. 'Thank you, Paul,' was all I could say despite wanting to say so much more.

'It's OK.'

'No, I mean, for everything. For understanding.'

He smiled, and I kissed him before picking up the towels along with my pyjamas and disappearing into the bathroom.

Chapter 34

8th September 2018
Ely, Cambridgeshire

Resting my hands on the warm tiled wall I lowered my head beneath the shower and tried to enjoy the hot water as it hit the back of my neck and ran between my shoulders. I hoped it might release the tension. But I couldn't stop thinking about how I'd reacted to the power cut. I knew the day would come, everyone had them from time to time. I thought I would be more prepared when it happened to me. I thought I'd be more rational. I couldn't even leave my bedroom without hitting into things, and the way I sat paralyzed on the kitchen floor… I was disappointed with myself.

I was equally shocked that I was still learning new things about that night. Remembering the fact he'd taken my picture made it feel much more recent. Somewhere out there was a picture of me in my underwear, bleeding and no doubt looking terrified. And beside me, my dead husband. I couldn't help feeling jealous that Kay could see my husband's face that night, and I couldn't. The only image I had of Owen was his left arm hanging out of the bathtub, a visual I couldn't bring myself to dwell on. I had hundreds, thousands of other pictures of Owen. I didn't need that one. I didn't need to be back there like it was yesterday. Looking at my feet, the right turning pink as the hot water hit the scar tissue, I focused on it – scars cannot lie about how old they are, and their age comforted me, reminded me that that night had been a long time ago.

After washing myself with Paul's shower gel, his masculine smell shrouding me, I wrapped myself in the soft towels and looked at myself in the bathroom mirror. I saw a look I had seen in myself recently – just before I'd gone out with Mum for a coffee after the panic of having a parcel delivered. There was someone else who needed me to try. To be brave. There was a man sat in a room only ten feet away, someone who hadn't pushed me to do anything I didn't want to. Someone who, I knew, wanted to understand who I was, and the past that created me, but had never asked.

Leaving the bathroom, I walked back into the bedroom to see Paul sitting on the bed, still fully clothed, waiting. He couldn't hide the surprise in his eyes that I was still wrapped in a towel and not dressed.

'Claire, everything all right?' he asked softly as he stood.

'Yes.'

'Do you want me to leave so you can get dressed?'

'No.'

'Oh,' he said, confused. He didn't move, but held my gaze, and the intensity between us grew.

'Do you still want to know what happened?' I whispered.

'Yes. I do.' He paused. 'But only when you're ready.'

'You know about the bolt cutters and what he did with them?' I said, to which he nodded and looked at my foot. 'They printed in the papers that I was unconscious when it happened. I wasn't. I lied because I didn't want pity.'

'You were awake?'

'I was groggy, but yes, I remember every second of that moment.'

'Oh, Claire.'

'He took my toes and dropped them into the bath, on Owen, and then poured petrol on him. I wish I'd had the foresight to lean over and look at him one last time. All I have of him that night is the image of his limp arm. But even that's as if I'm seeing it through fog. He put down the bolt cutters afterwards, and that was when I grabbed them. These...' I turned so my right side faced him and nudged down my towel, to expose the scars on my ribs, 'are from the struggle with him. I don't remember all the details, but I think I hit him with the bolt cutters, and then as I tried to flee, he hit me back. He broke three of my ribs. I also had cuts and bruises on my face.'

'You fought him?'

'I guess so. That's what they say. They say that after I hit him, he panicked and fled, setting the fire first, of course. Apparently, I had some of the petrol on me, and when he lit the bathtub, my foot caught alight. And this—' I said, holding out my forearm '—is where I fell from the bathroom window as I escaped.'

I could see Paul was horrified by what I was telling him; I wouldn't have expected anything less. But it felt good for me to say it. I was expecting him to talk, to want more details, but instead he gently touched my back, my scars. My reaction was to pull away. I stopped myself, reminded myself that I wanted this. I wanted to finally bare all. Taking the tucked-in edge of the towel in my hand I pulled on the fold. As the towel dropped to the floor, he stepped back. Our eyes locked. I reached for his hand and placed it on my stomach, running it along the scar tissue. Paul looked at what he was touching, seeing the angry smile carved into me for the first time.

'When I woke up after being drugged, this had already happened. I didn't know then, but this would be the injury that would stop me being able to have any children of my own.'

He looked back at me, trying to remain neutral, but I saw sadness in his eyes.

Paul then did something I wasn't ready for. He lowered his head and kissed along the scar that ran up my forearm. His touch was gentle, tender and one that sent electricity flooding though my body. It was the first time I had let anyone touch there that wasn't my mum or a doctor. It felt weird, like I was doing something illicit, and part of me wanted to stop him, to turn off the lights, to hide. But that part of me had already notched a victory against the rest of me this evening in the power cut when it rendered me useless. I couldn't let it win again. I had to show I was in charge.

I closed my eyes and allowed Paul to continue. He kissed the pink tear in my skin and up my arm before sitting on the bed, his head now level with the scars on my ribs. As he ran his thumb over them, I felt goose bumps rise across my entire body. What we were doing felt dangerous, wild. He placed a kiss on my ribs and kissed down my stomach to the pink, fractured mass of tissue that made me feel ugly, and I felt my body tense. I was naked, in a bright room. I was with the man I was fond of – no, in love with – and I was being as brave as I had ever been. But still, the part of me that wanted to cower in the corner, a knife clenched between my shaking hands, wanted to push forward. He must have sensed it because he stopped looking at my stomach and instead looked up at me, his gaze intense and passionate. My body didn't horrify him; I could see in his eyes he wanted to stay. He wanted me, and I wanted him to want me. I wanted him to want it all, the scars I carried, the past I held onto, the secrets I had.

I smiled at him and ran my fingers through his hair, gently pushing his face against my body. He kissed my stomach, first around the scar, then on it. His warm lips soothed me. Without speaking he stood and kissed me on the lips fervently, and while doing so I undid his belt and wrestled with the buttons of his jeans, laughing when I couldn't undo them. He laughed too before unfastening them and taking them off. Then, I lifted his T-shirt over his head and looked at him in the same way he had looked at me. I realised then that I hadn't seen his body in the light either – he hadn't stepped from the shower with a towel around his waist; he hadn't changed in front of me.

As I kissed him once more, he slid down his underwear and I couldn't help but look. This was the first time either of us had seen the other undressed and I had to have him. I pushed him on the bed and climbed on top of him, my legs either side of his naked torso. I watched as his eyes moved from mine to my body all the way down past my stomach and between my thighs. I waited to see his expression change to one that was repulsed.

'What are you thinking?' I dared to ask, expecting him to say he was thinking my scars were hideous or that he wanted to turn the lights off again. But he didn't.

'That you are beautiful.'

Leaning in, I kissed him again, and I could feel him pressing into the inside of my thigh, close to where he would slip inside. As we kissed, he touched my body, my breasts, my scars, and it was terrifying and sexy as hell in equal measure.

I was naked; I was in the light, for the first time in a long time. I felt attractive. Not because of him telling me he found me beautiful, but because I volunteered to be seen. I instigated it. I let myself show all, and I felt empowered. From this moment, I knew I could never go back.

Leaning close to his ear, I told him I needed him and reaching down I took him in my hand, slipping him inside.

Chapter 35

27th September 2018
Wrexham, Wales

As he pushed his pound coin into the lock of the trolley, ready to buy food he didn't need, he thought about how he knew she – the new potential ninth – would be in the same supermarket shopping. He concluded, based on his observations of humanity, that as people got older, they became more predictable. It was as if their subconscious tried to fight the fact they knew they were ageing, their lives getting shorter day by day, and they hung onto the security of menial tasks to slow the process down. The more bored, the more routine they became, the more time they thought they had. It was sad, really – but he could use it to his advantage.

The potential did her weekly shop at the same Waitrose, at the same time every Thursday morning, after her Pilates class. It hadn't taken long, only two weeks, to see the trend. This was the third Thursday since their eyes locked in that restaurant, and he was ninety-nine per cent sure she would not let him down. Monday's she saw her mother, Saturdays she shopped in nearby

Wrexham, meeting with friends at the same time for coffee. He mused she was slightly older and slightly wealthier than his usual target, but of all of them thus far, she had been the easiest to follow. That night at the restaurant, he faked a message, telling the persistent talker he was dining with, Jennifer, that the daughter he'd made up was poorly and he had to leave. He apologised to her profusely, and she told him not to say sorry, that they could catch up another time? Perhaps another dinner? He agreed, knowing full well he would toss the pay-as-you-go mobile with the number she had. She would no doubt feel aggrieved when she discovered he wouldn't ever call. What Jennifer wouldn't know is that him not calling would in fact save her life.

As he'd stepped out into the September rain, already forgetting about his date, he'd watched as a black Range Rover sped past him, and the woman who stirred something primal inside him met his eye from her car window – her pale face wore a nervous expression. As they careered away he caught the registration plate, MR B1G. Naturally. After the taillights of the car had gone, he ran to his car, jumped in and drove quickly to catch up.

He drove for several minutes but couldn't see the Range Rover. It didn't worry him, his instincts were guiding him, telling him to join the southbound A483, and within half a mile along the main dual carriageway, the number plate came back into view. Keeping his distance, he followed for around ten minutes before coming off for a small place called Ruabon. He followed until they turned into a close, Paddock Row, the road sign stating it was a dead end. He didn't follow; he didn't even look as he passed. They lived somewhere on that road, and would be easy enough to find, he was sure of it.

Now, three weeks later, he was ready to speak to the woman he was so sure would be the ninth. He would find a way to intentionally 'bump' into her as they shopped. And when he did, one of three things would happen:

She would place him instantly from the restaurant.

She would think she knew his face, but not immediately recognise him.

She wouldn't recognise him at all.

It didn't matter really, he would manipulate her regardless because he knew she would judge as all people did. She would make assumptions based on what she saw before her, and then she would trust those assumptions.

Browsing the aisle, he loaded items into his trolley that told a disarming story. He picked up Petits Filous yoghurts, nappies, wet wipes and baby food pouches, as well as other sundries you'd gather during the weekly shop. He intentionally placed the things for a child on the top, so that when he bumped into her and she glanced at his shopping, it would tell the story he wanted it to. He was no threat. He was someone to trust.

It didn't take long to test his theory. For as he browsed, she walked past in the opposite direction. After carefully tracking her movement around the supermarket, he staged their meeting. As he turned the corner in the cereal aisle she was coming the other way, her eyes on the shelves. He made it look like his were too, and midway down, their trolleys collided. The impact pushed her trolley into her side and she dropped the box of granola she was holding.

Perfect.

'Oh gosh, I'm so sorry,' he said, his voice shocked and concerned, as he stepped around the trolley to pick up the box.

'No, no it's fine, it's my fault, I wasn't watching where I was going.'

'No, really, I should have been more careful,' he replied, dropping to one knee and picking up the cereal.

'Thank you.' She smiled as she looked at him, her eyes telling him she knew his face, but she couldn't place where from.

'I didn't hurt you, did I?' he said, his concern believable.

'No, I'm fine, thank you.' She smiled again, one that widened when she snapped a glance into his trolley.

'Are you sure? I feel terrible,' he said.

'No, honestly, I'm fine.'

'That's a relief. Once again, I'm very sorry.'

'No need to apologise.'

'OK, well, I hope you have a lovely day,' he said as he manoeuvred his trolley around her and away, knowing she was watching until he was gone.

The seed had been planted, and it would germinate quickly.

Half a trolley load later, he waited at the end of the freezer section for her to head towards the tills, her light grey leggings and bright red gym shoe combination making her easy to pick out in the mainly elderly mid-morning crowd. She stepped out four lanes from him and approached a till to pay. Keeping his head down he made his way towards one opposite her and queued.

For a moment he thought he would miss her as the old lady in front was taking too much time by querying the price of something on her receipt, insisting it should have been in a deal. Her raised voice drew subtle glances from those nearest, judgemental looks they were too polite to have anyone else see. The potential ninth also looked, then she saw him behind her and smiled. He made a face to suggest the old lady was crazy, and she had to look away. He wasn't being that funny, but she laughed, which meant the seed had taken hold. Eventually the old lady declared she would never shop there again before leaving, and he smiled politely as he bought the things he would later throw away.

As he walked towards the entrance she was standing outside. The heavens had opened, and she had stopped, no doubt hoping the rain would pass. He had established their connection, and now it was time to cement it. He knew she had to be the next. Everything was telling him so.

'Hello again,' he said as he parked his trolley close to hers.

'Rubbish weather.'

'The joys of living on a small island in the Atlantic.'

'Absolutely.'

Looking up at the clouds, he spoke, enjoying how easy it was becoming to talk to potential victims. When he knew he needed to return to his calling after a decade of abstinence, he thought he would struggle to talk with the opposite sex – he hadn't much engaged with them in his time off. But in fact, it was easier than when he had had to get to know the men he targeted in Ireland. 'It looks like it will blow over quickly.'

'That's what I'm hoping for. So, that woman in front of you, what was that about?'

'I think she was bent out of shape because of two quid on her bill.'

'Wow, some people. Life's too short.'

Perhaps shorter than you think.

'Sorry, this sounds weird,' she continued, 'but do I know you from somewhere?'

'I've had exactly the same thought.' He smiled.

'Oh, thank God. Makes you sound like a weirdo doesn't it?'

He laughed, enjoying her comment. 'No, not at all. I've been wracking my brain to think where we might have met? Do you have kids?' he asked, knowing the answer already.

'No.'

'Oh, I thought I might have seen you at a soft play or something.'

'I see you do,' she said, looking into the trolley full of nappies and baby food.

He lied. 'Yes, one.'

'How old?'

'Nearly two. She's a handful, but a lot of fun.'

'I bet.'

'I was so sure I recognised you from somewhere to do with kids?'

'Nope, sadly. What gym do you go to?' she asked.

'Do I look like someone who goes to the gym?' He laughed, even though since his metamorphosis he visited the gym regularly, and she laughed too. He couldn't believe how easy this was. All because of a few nappies in a trolley and a disarming nature.

'Then I have no idea.'

'Me neither. I'm Jason.'

'Lauren.'

'Nice name.'

'Thanks.'

He could see her blushing, her smile coy, enjoying the attention. He suspected this was the first positive attention she'd had in a while. Although all the signs pointed to her being the next one, he needed it confirmed, and that would take time. So, for now, he would let the seed that was sprouting grow stronger.

'Right, well, I'd better dash. Gotta pick up Charlotte, my daughter, from the childminder. Maybe I'll bump into you next week shopping. I'm such a creature of habit.' He smiled, realizing the name he had just given to his made-up daughter was also the name of his first female victim.

'Me too.' She smiled back, for entirely different reasons.

'Ahhh,' he said, triumphantly pointing his finger into the air. 'I bet that's why we recognise each other. I bet we've seen one another shopping.'

'Yes, I bet that's it.'

'Well, if I see you next week, I promise not to run you over.'

She laughed again. 'OK. Nice meeting you, Jason.'

'You too, Lauren.'

He walked towards his car, the rain soaking his neck, and as he loaded his bags he glanced back to see Lauren looking towards him. He offered a friendly wave before climbing behind the steering wheel and driving away.

He would confirm one way or the other in seven days' time. And then, once he knew for sure she was who he needed her to be, he would move in for the kill.

As he merged with the A483 he smiled to himself, enjoying the fact it was so easy.

Chapter 36

27th September 2018
Ely, Cambridgeshire

A few nights at Paul's had turned into a few weeks, and as much as I had loved being there, I was missing my own bed, my own things, my own space. After a decade of having only those things for comfort, to suddenly be without them was harder than I thought. The power cut and my subsequent meltdown was now something I was just about able to laugh about, and that told me it was time to go home. I needed some time to myself, not because I didn't want to be around Paul. I did, I wanted him around always. His company was both liberating and made me feel secure all at once. I needed a night by myself for a much more fundamental reason. I needed to know I could be alone without having a panic attack and regressing to the woman I once was. I knew that if I didn't do this, I would end up back at Mum's, unable to do anything or go anywhere like the first few years after Ireland. One night, just me, without having the protection I felt with Paul beside me in bed. I hoped I could explain it to Paul the same way I justified it in my head. I knew I needed to be just me for a night – not Claire the survivor, or Claire the victim, not even Claire Moore, but just Claire.

I told Paul, moments before he had to leave for his long drive up north for work. He made it clear he wasn't happy and wanted to come back with me, told me he wouldn't be able to sleep unless I was there. Hearing him say it, I almost conceded and agreed he could. But I knew I had to be strong and so I said no and watched as he seemed hurt by my decisiveness. I tried as best I could to explain my reasons, and his demeanour changed. He tried to understand, but he still didn't think it was a good idea for me, he said that the idea made him nervous, and as I firmly told him I needed to do it he paced the lounge, his brow furrowed in concentration.

'Paul, I will be fine.'

'I'm just worried, that's all. What if what the police told us is right, that the murder in Wales was someone copying Tommy Kay? What if he's planning something else?'

'Paul.'

'Or what about that creepy bloke, Killian?'

'He's harmless.'

'But you said you thought he was outside your house, taking photos.'

'You don't have to worry about him. I told him about you last time he messaged and that I didn't want any contact again, and I've not heard anything in weeks now.'

Paul stopped pacing. 'You told him about me?'

'Yes.'

'What did you say?' he said smiling, clearly enjoying the fact I was starting to turn beetroot.

'Just, well… Paul!'

He laughed and sat beside me, taking my hand and squeezing it gently.

'I still don't think it's a good idea,' he said quietly.

'I can't be controlled anymore, I can't. Killian isn't a threat and if the copycat is planning something, then he is planning something, and there isn't anything anyone can do about it.'

'But if you stay with me…' he continued, his voice tight and desperate. I cut him off.

'If I stay with you, it wouldn't stop him, anyway.'

'Claire…'

'No, Paul, please listen,' I said turning to face him. 'I lost everything ten years ago. I watched my house burn with my husband in it. I nearly died myself, and when I didn't I was sure I would never feel happy again. Now I do, I am, because I have my independence.' I paused, realising I was sounding like my mother when she was stressed. 'And you,' I continued, more softly. 'But I have to fight for my happiness. It doesn't come easy to someone who has been through something like I have. I love being around you. But if I stop being able to be around me, then there is no point. It's just one night. Just so I know in my head that I can be alone.'

'But what happens if…'

'Paul,' I said firmly. 'I'm doing this. I get you don't understand why, but you need to accept it.'

'All right,' he said, defeated.

'Thank you.' I leant over and kissed him gently.

'Just leave your phone on. I'll be back tonight, it'll be late, but if you need anything just say.'

'You should stay over at work.'

'But what if you need me?'

'Mum is around the corner, I'll call her. You've been driving to and from work every day for weeks, you look exhausted.'

'I don't mind. I like being with you at night.'

'And I'm grateful, I really am. But tonight, stay. Catch up on some sleep. I'll be fine.'

Putting down my coffee I took both his hands in mine. 'You joked a while ago that you had a life that wasn't about me. You need to not neglect it. I'll be fine for a night or two, you should stay close to the site. Have some beers with your colleagues. Read. Catch up with your girls. Do whatever it is you do when you're away.' I smiled, and he smiled back confirming I had sold the idea of some space on him. He needed it as much as I did.

'All right, you win. I'll pack a bag.'

Chapter 37

27th September 2018
Ely, Cambridge

As Paul climbed into his car, I could see he was still reluctant to leave. I understood why. He was about to drive to the site he was inspecting near Chester – 160 miles, and about four hours away if you were in favour with the traffic gods, as he liked to call it. I had to remind him twice, as he threw a few things into a small bag, that I had survived for a decade without him, and Mum was only around the corner. Once he had reversed his car from the drive and then put it into first, he smiled at me nervously and I smiled back, trying not to look nervous myself. I hoped I appeared aloof, unfazed by his departure. Truth was, I was terrified. Just because I needed to be alone, didn't mean I wanted to be or wasn't frightened by the idea of it.

As he drove away I stood on the doorstep and waited, watching his taillights until they disappeared around a corner. When I could no longer see any part of him, I felt the need to be back inside. I had to pick the right battles if I would win the war, so I listened and went back into Paul's house, locking the door behind me. After a quick wash, I packed my things and rang a cab to take me home. I could have rung Mum, and she or Geoff would have happily come to get me. But I didn't. If I was to be independent today, I would go all in.

The cab arrived just before half eight, a text popping up on my phone announcing it, as well as giving the number plate of the car. I left Paul's, locking the door with the spare set of keys he gave me. I noticed that I was feeling OK about going home on my own. The icy hand was still there, but only resting on my diaphragm.

The driver climbed out of the car and was walking towards me, his hands extended to help me with my suitcase.

'Morning, love.'

'Morning.'

'Let me get that for you,' he said taking the case from me and loading it into the back of his cab before mentioning something about how Indian summers weren't a thing when he was growing up.

I got into the back and told him my address. The whole journey he chatted like I was any other person. And I chatted back in the same manner. Light. Free. Liberated. The journey seemed to go by in a blink and before I knew it, I was home. I expected to see a police car outside, but there wasn't one, and I realized of course there wouldn't be. I'd not been home for weeks. I thanked the taxi driver for a lovely conversation and paid the fare. He thanked me also, saying most of the time people were too wrapped up in themselves to talk politely. And it felt like I had notched another victory. He offered to help me with my suitcase but I told him it wasn't necessary. As I walked up to my front porch he beeped a goodbye at me and I turned and waved before unlocking my front door and stepping inside.

The air was still, and stale. I could see dust particles floating, caught in a beam of light that filtered through the small window high above my front door. Dumping my case, I stooped and picked up my post that lay in a small pile near my feet, and sifted through it. There were the usual bills, a bank statement I daren't read and two handwritten envelopes. Just looking at them awoke the icy fingers and before they could start to play I put the pile on the radiator shelf, making sure the handwritten ones were on the bottom.

I walked into my front room, opening the curtains that had been shut since I left, and the light flooded in, highlighting the dust that hung like fog. I needed to open some windows. I did the same in the kitchen and my bedroom and it felt better, having clean air circulate through the house.

Feeling empowered by my decision to have time alone, I decided to have the spring clean I'd needed for the past few years. I started in my living room. I hoovered the floors and couch, fluffed the pillows, dropped old magazines into the recycling bin. I moved my sofa to the opposite wall and dusted the pictures that hung above it. In the kitchen I threw out old food, cleaned the insides of my cupboards that had never been cleaned. I even opened the back door, picked some Japanese anemone from the plant pot close to the house and put them in a vase on the breakfast bar before I felt I needed to shut and lock the door again. Leaving windows open was one thing: the door, however, was an entirely different battle.

After a break for a cup of tea, I started in my bedroom, then the box room, before finally I cleaned my bathroom. I scrubbed the tub, sprayed and wiped the sink and loo. And at no point did I feel nervous about doing it. Maybe I had learnt to manage my fear of such an innocuous space in the house. But I didn't let myself get too excited. Relapses happened.

Once I had finished, my bedroom felt loved, the box room was now free from junk and the bed could actually be slept in, if Penny ever again had one too many after our monthly takeaway, and my bathroom felt brand new. It had taken me five hours and I had worked up quite a sweat, my hair dishevelled and stuck to my forehead, and the exertion made my right foot throb. But I felt fantastic for it, almost how I used to feel after going for a run. I should have showered, but, as I was on my own, I couldn't. Instead I climbed into my comfies, a pair of jogging bottoms and a vest top, and flaked on the sofa, kneading the pink tissue where my toes used to be.

I remembered the two handwritten envelopes in my hallway and went to collect them. I put them on the arm of the sofa beside me and looked at them, unsure which one I should open first. One of them had a stamp in the corner, one didn't. Opening the stamped envelope, I my heart sank when I realised what it was. An invitation from *Nation's Choice*, the trashy national magazine who wanted my side of the story about the copycat killer. I didn't want to do an interview with anyone, but even less so with the people who still hounded me long after I was forgotten by everyone else all those years ago.

Throwing the letter on the coffee table, I grabbed the second envelope. This one made me feel more nervous, only because it had been hand delivered. Which meant someone had been to my front door. The letter felt heavy in my palm as I turned it over, trying to work out who it might be from. I held it up towards the window, so the sunlight filtered through, but I couldn't see any distinguishable words. Digging my fingernail under the sealed flap I hesitated. Before I opened it, I wanted to know who it was from. Grabbing my iPad, I logged on and looked at the footage of the past few weeks. Someone had been to my front door and posted it. I wanted to know who.

I went back to the night Paul saved me from myself and realised as the power was out there had been nothing recorded. The first image came just before 1 a.m. when the power came back on. Fast-forwarding through the footage, I watched night become day then became night again, slowing only when the shape of a person came close to my door. The postman, my usual, came several times. And on two occasions people I didn't know approached and knocked before looking thought the letter-box – their invasive nature telling me they were opportunist journalists, perhaps.

Then, just three days ago, the time stamp saying it was a little before four in the morning, I saw someone I know come to my door. In his hand, the letter.

It was Killian.

I watched as he left my front door and went around the back of my house, the camera losing him as he turned the corner. A few minutes later, he was back, and I could see he was shaking. He looked up and down the street and wiped his hands on his trousers, a dark smear transferring onto his thighs, before putting his head down and walking away quickly.

What was he doing in my back garden? I needed to know so I went to my back door, unlocking it with trembling hands. I stepped onto the patio to see what he was doing in my garden. At first it wasn't obvious. It was when I inspected the side wall and looked down the side alley that led to the front, that I saw what he had done, and sick flooded into my mouth. Running back into the house, the tears falling, I locked the doors and ran upstairs to close all the windows. Then, after searching in blind panic I found my mobile and called Mum who picked up after only two rings.

'Morning, Claire.'

'Mum, can you come over?'

'Claire, what's happened?'

'Just come over, please. He… killed our cat. He killed Baloo.'

Chapter 38

27th September 2018
St Ives, Cambridgeshire

As soon as Mum came over, we called the police and waited for them to arrive. She made me a cup of sweet tea and I held it in my shaking hands, unable to drink it. The image of Baloo burnt in my mind, and held me on the brink of either throwing up, crying hysterically or passing out. I didn't suppose the police would usually deal with incidents like this quickly, but given who I was they were at my door within the hour.

It surprised me to see it was the same red-bearded policeman, Peter, I had met before. As he saw me, he smiled sympathetically. He and his colleague Beth didn't stay long: they took my emotional statement, the camera footage and the unopened letter from Killian. Before leaving, Peter took it upon himself to ask for an old towel and after handing it to him I realised what it was for. When he asked if we wanted to keep Baloo to bury him ourselves, I said no. I couldn't see the poor cat again. Mum said Geoff would take him back to their house, and respectfully Peter lay the towel with our beloved cat inside in a plastic crate from the shed. At my front door he smiled and told me he would be in touch and asked if it would be all right. I told him not to worry. Mum was with me, Geoff was coming, and Paul would be back tomorrow. He nodded, understanding that I was too tired to care.

'Are you going to arrest Killian?' Mum asked, her anxiety coming aggressively to the fore.

'We will review what you have provided and if there is enough evidence, then yes. If not, we'll definitely be having a word with him, anyway,' he said.

I nodded and squeezed Mum to stop her saying any more. With one last kind smile, Peter left and Mum closed the front door. Silently Mum guided me to the sofa, and I curled up under a blanket. She switched on the TV and sat in the armchair to my right. *Mary Poppins* was on and I tried to transport myself to that world, a place where colour was softer, and smiles were wide. A place where songs floated on the air like the clouds above London and magic was real. I tried, but instead my vision blurred as my body succumbed to the numbness that was comforting and familiar. Mum didn't stay seated for long, and started to potter around me, complimenting me on how lovely my house looked, but I could tell she was just as upset as I was.

Death had once again returned to our little lives and the icy hand that usually lived in my chest had found a way out crawl up my throat, escaping every time I exhaled.

At some point, I must have fallen asleep because when I awoke it was dark once more. Mum was back in the armchair beside me, a blanket tucked up under her armpits. Even in the low light, I could see how haggard she looked. After a decade of having me so closely in her life, I understood why. Each wrinkle represented one of my meltdowns, each fine line, another panic attack. Her thinning lips were the work of my stints in hospital, her sunken eyes my sleepless nights. I wore my scars from that night, but so did she. I had to look away from the damage I had caused to such a beautiful woman.

Grabbing my phone, I saw two messages from Paul; I didn't message him amidst the trauma and shock that the day had brought. I replied, telling him I was fine, and I'd been asleep most of the day. He would understand, he knew how I had to catch up on my sleep. I didn't tell him about Killian and what he had done. But I didn't know why.

Getting up quietly, I went into the kitchen and grabbed myself a glass of water. Knowing I wouldn't get back to sleep I turned on the TV on the kitchen side, my finger hovering over the volume button to turn it down as soon as it sprung to life. The news was on; I didn't pay attention at first, but then I noticed the text that scrolled along the bottom of the screen:

BREAKING NEWS: A MAN HAS BEEN ARRESTED IN CONNECTION WITH THE 'BLACK-OUT' KILLING IN NORTH WALES

I read and reread the message that scrolled slowly and deliberately from right to left. Someone had been arrested, someone who they were confident was connected to the murder of Kath Brinck, and I couldn't help but think someone might be Killian. He was a man who had been in my life since I'd begun recovering from the night Owen died. A man who knew my movements, even when others didn't. A man who knew so many details about what happened in Ireland, not just to me and Owen, but the six other people who died.

A man who, after what he had done to Baloo, I knew could kill.

Chapter 39

28th September 2018
St Ives, Cambridgeshire

All night I sat and watched the small TV in the kitchen, my eyes glued to the news to learn more. I didn't wake Mum, she needed her sleep. Details were sketchy but suggested a 'tip-off' got their man. When Mum awoke and noticed I was gone she called out, panic in her voice. I told her where I was and she came dashing into the kitchen to join me. I said good morning to her, unable to take my eyes off the screen. There had been no new information, but there would be at some point and I wanted to see it before anyone else did. It was like I was watching for security camera stream again, waiting for something to happen, hoping it wouldn't. Selfishly I felt I deserved to know before the world. Despite it being so early, I could hear the press arriving outside. Hoping for a photo, some words from me about how I must be feeling. I wouldn't speak to them, not because I wanted to avoid them, but rather – if the copycat was really Killian all along – I didn't know how to feel.

As the day went on, I barely strayed from the news. Mum had

become impatient and tried to ring Peter who had left his number, but each time it went to voicemail. Eventually he called me back on my mobile, and as I picked up I put it on loudspeaker so Mum, and Geoff who had come over, fighting his way through the gathering crowds, could hear. Sitting on the sofa with Mum beside me and Geoff stood next to her, we all stared down at the phone in my hand.

'Claire, it's PC Blackmore, Peter.'

'Peter, what's going on?'

'I'm sorry it's taken so long, I've needed to get the facts in line.'

'OK?'

Peter explained that yesterday they visited Killian at the hotel he was staying in and noticed he was being evasive. After securing a warrant, they discovered enough evidence to place him under arrest.

'What evidence?' Mum interjected, the pitch of her voice forced and tight.

'He had a lot of details about Tommy Kay. We also found proof of him being in North Wales shortly after they reported the fire on the news, and a file with the victim's details. We seized his computer and phone. There were a lot of pictures of you. In Ireland, in your house. We also found out that he visited Kay in prison on several occasions before his death in 2014.'

'Do you think it's him, I mean, do you think he is the copycat?'

'It's highly likely.'

'Why would he do it?' I asked, unable to comprehend that the man who had been so supportive in the months after Owen died could be capable of this.

'His letter to you, did you read it?'

'No.'

'It spoke of him needing you, him unable to see a life without you in it. Claire, Killian is obsessed with you. And from what we discovered, he has been for a very long time. We suspect he did what he did to keep you close.'

217

I thought about it and it made sense, horrific as it was. Back when I was recovering from what had happened Kilian and I were close, perhaps too close. And for a while, in my desperate need, I wondered if there was something more between us. I felt like I owed him for his kindness when I was learning to cope. I guess I'd chosen to ignore his more erratic behaviour in recent years, until a few months ago, when I met Paul. And when I told Killian I had met someone, he sounded shocked, but he must have known, he knew everything else about me. And then, just as Paul and I start to get serious, a woman dies.

Did he kill Kath Brinck to bring us closer? Was I responsible for an innocent person being murdered?

I tried to thank Peter for calling but the words caught in my throat. Instead, Geoff said he was grateful to Peter for keeping us in his mind during what must be a very precarious time. Peter then promised that he would keep me updated as best he could, before hanging up the phone.

For a moment the three of us were motionless, all still staring at the phone which was now a dark screen. I was trying to process the information, working backwards to see the signs that had always been there about Killian, and the more I thought about it, the more I was sure it was him. The realisation made me feel sick. Because of me, an innocent woman had died.

Mum broke the trance we were all in and declared she would make a tea for us all, her go-to response when she was trying to process something. Geoff came and sat beside me. I rested my head on his shoulder and he rubbed my back as I focused on the carpet.

'Are you OK, kid?'

'Not really.'

'Silly question, sorry.'

'I'm struggling to process it all, I mean… it sort of makes sense. There has always been something weird about him. But… he's the copycat?'

'It seems he is. It will probably take a while to wrap your head around it.'

I nodded, knowing it would take a lifetime to understand.

'Claire, look at me.'

I did, and his large brown eyes were focused intently on mine. He continued, and I believed every word he said. 'You will wrap your head around this, and until then, focus on the fact it's over. No more fear. No more looking over your shoulder. No more being stuck in the past you've battled so hard to escape. These past several weeks have been so hard on you... on all of us. But now you can get on with your life again.'

'Yeah,' was all I could say in reply, and sensing I needed time he kissed me on the head and walked into the kitchen to join Mum. At the doorway he paused, and I was sure he would turn back and say something, but he just tapped the wall twice and left. His last words echoed in my mind. No more looking over my shoulder. No more looking back. Once it was confirmed, once they had definitive proof, I would speak to the press and say my piece about how now he was caught, life would go on, and that was exactly what I would do. I would go on.

Chapter 40

28th September 2018
Wrexham, Wales

Standing in front of his hotel's bathroom mirror, he appraised himself, liking what he saw. His body wet from the shower caught the evening light and his naked skin shimmered, like gold. A decade ago he was fat around the middle, his eyes heavy, his teeth crooked. But now, the man before him was perfect. Strong, athletic, beautiful. The caterpillar had become the butterfly. He flexed his chest muscles, and the gold shimmered just before the sun slipped behind a cloud, one of the few that had hung around for the day, and was gone. His body became mortal once more. He'd noticed that age was taking over – fine lines splintered from the corner of his eye, the hair on his chest greying. Even the scar that flicked like a whiplash across his chin, the one gifted to him by Claire Moore, looked faded, as if it would one day turn to dust with the rest of him. But it didn't worry him, life was all just borrowed time.

Stepping into his bedroom, he turned on the TV and began thinking about the ninth. They had exchanged numbers in the same supermarket exactly a week after 'bumping' into one another, and she had messaged to ask if he was free this evening. He had lied, saying he was stuck at work. In reality, she would see him very soon. He was readying himself to visit her in her home. As the picture on the TV sprang to life, the news came into focus. He watched nothing else. They were talking of Killian Jones, a meek-looking man who they had arrested in connection with the eighth. He knew who he was; he was the friend of Claire Moore, and one they speculated was the copycat killer. Seeing them discuss their reasoning for suspecting Killian stopped him in his tracks. They were more stupid, more misguided than he thought.

Learning the wrong man had been arrested disappointed him. He expected more of the authorities, and someone else drawing attention for his work infuriated him. It had been the same with Tommy Kay, until he saw that with all eyes looking elsewhere, he'd been presented a wonderful opportunity to cement his legacy. Smiling to himself, he knew he could become even more infamous with his next kill. The nation's press were so caught up in pointing fingers at the poor man who had been arrested, so sure he was the copycat killer, that when they knew for certain he wasn't, and that, even worse, the killings were not a copycat at all, but the original come back to terrorise, he would become the stuff of legend. Fate had presented this opportunity, and he had to seize it. He almost felt sorry for the poor man, who was no doubt scared to death in some prison cell.

It was almost too perfect. The news of the arrest meant that he would delay his kill, and he could use that to confirm Lauren was the right choice. As he thought about it, he realised it would be to his benefit in more ways than one if Killian was charged. He hoped the speculation, the finger-pointing became their version of the facts. And when that happened, he would kill the ninth and pull the rug out from under everyone's feet. But if they released Killian without charge and then he claimed his ninth,

Killian would still be their prime suspect. And he didn't want that to happen. On paper, it seemed too risky, but his instincts told him it was a risk he needed to take.

In the short time he had known Lauren, he had seen that her life of routine extended to her heavy-handed husband, also a creature of routine, his schedule easy to follow. On Mondays and Fridays he told his wife he worked late, but when he'd followed him the previous week, he'd watched as the husband checked into a hotel with a younger woman, who he was no doubt sleeping with. It was abhorrent, disgusting, but it gave him a window to kill his wife. It wouldn't be tonight as he thought, but sometime very soon.

With more time before he killed her, he knew he should seize the moment and know for sure she was a perfect image for his grand design, so he messaged saying they had cancelled his meeting and was free, if she still wanted to do something. It didn't take long for her to reply saying she was still available and would love to go for a drink.

Available. He thought it was an interesting choice of word.

Grabbing his towel, he dried his hair and body before dressing in a pair of dark blue jeans and a black shirt, and left to meet her, leaving his ready-packed rucksack at the foot of his bed, as he wouldn't be needing it tonight

The drive to Wrexham took him, or as the ninth knew him, Jason, under fifteen minutes, and parking his car close to the town centre he walked in to meet her outside of the bar she had suggested. They had agreed to meet at eight and, checking his watch, he saw he was a few minutes early. He waited patiently outside for her to arrive, expecting her to be late. She wasn't. He saw her coming down the main road before she saw him and that gave him an opportunity to watch her, to step inside her head, to read her thoughts. She was nervous. That was good, nerves forced the mind to focus on surroundings, on moods, but usually at the cost of clouding over words. It meant that he could manipulate her and learn what he needed to. Once she spotted him, she smiled, and he watched as she straightened her back, fixed her expression and hid the emotions she was feeling, something she was used to from living with her disgusting husband. As they embraced and kissed on both cheeks, he wondered how much she had to hide. This evening he would find out.

'You look lovely,' he said.

'Thank you.'

She didn't compliment him back, even though he knew he looked impressive. Her nerves were in charge, the words lost.

'Shall we grab a drink?'

Opening the door, he let her step inside before him and finding a table, she sat while he ordered a white wine for her and an alcohol-free beer for him. Returning to the table he instigated small talk, asking about her day, discussing the warm weather that had lasted way into September. He told her about his work and talked about Charlotte starting pre-school. As he talked about his fake daughter, he noticed the ninth relax in her seat. The safety net of appearing to be a doting dad worked its charm; he would have to remember that, and use it again when grooming the tenth.

After an hour and another glass of wine, the conversation moved onto deeper, more personal things. She initiated the conversation, asking him if she should feel bad for enjoying his company, being married and all.

'That depends?' he said, his tone even, suggesting he wasn't judging.

'On what?'

'On whether he is good to you. If he is, and treats you as you deserve, then yes, feel bad. If he doesn't, then no. Besides, we aren't doing anything wrong, we're just two adults enjoying each other's company.'

'You've such a way with words, Jason. Thank you.'

'So, do you feel bad?'

She looked at him and said five words which were all the proof he needed. Five words sealed her fate.

'No. I don't at all.'

Chapter 41

30th September 2018
St Ives, Cambridgeshire

Paul smiled at me sympathetically through the bedroom mirror as I adjusted my hair, trying to make it more presentable. For a moment I wondered what I would have done with it if I'd kept it long. The thought of longer hair stopped me preparing for the thing I was about to do. And I went back there, to that night in Ireland, in the dark, being dragged by it, dazed, drugged, about to see Owen's arm hanging over the rim of a bath. Paul assumed my hesitation was because of what I was about to do.

'Claire, you look lovely.'

His voice snapped me back from there. 'I look frazzled, and my bloody hair...'

He cut me off, planting a kiss on my shoulder. 'Honestly. You look amazing.'

'Thanks. Sorry, I'm nervous.'

'You're allowed to be. It will all be over soon.'

'Really? When?'

'After tonight you can begin to go back to the way things were.'

225

'The way things were still feels a long way away.'

'I know honey,' he said, kneading a knot in my shoulder. 'But it isn't, it's closer than you...'

'Are you ready?' Geoff shouted upstairs, interrupting Paul, his voice steady and calm, as it always was.

'Almost,' I called back.

'OK, love. They'll wait for you, so take as much time as you need.'

Looking at myself in the mirror again, I took my necklace and tucked it into my top, where it wouldn't be seen. I took a deep breath. My expression was either courageous or terrified, or both. I couldn't be sure either way.

'You don't have to do this,' Paul whispered, as I turned to him, my head resting onto his chest bone.

'Yes, I do. And then it's done, isn't it? If I give them what they want, they will leave us alone.'

I waited for him to disagree, to say they wouldn't and give me my get-out clause I desperately wanted. But he didn't, he just stepped back, his hands on my shoulders and smiled, telling me I was right, and that meant I had to see it through.

'Claire?' This time it was Mum, sounding less controlled than Geoff. She was being badgered for me to come downstairs, step out of my front door to the lectern erected on my front lawn, to tell the world how I was feeling about Killian who, after three days of investigation, had been charged with the murder of Kath Brinck.

I made my way down the stairs fiddling with the chain around my neck through my top. Front, back, upstairs and down. With each step I tried to convince myself it would be all right. I would be all right. Paul came down behind me keeping a little distance, knowing I needed it. As I reached the bottom step Mum gave me a hug and Geoff nodded as our eyes met over her shoulder. Penny was also there, and though she smiled at me, I could see that she was just as nervous as I was.

226

'You've got this, Claire.'

'Thanks, Pen.' I offered a smile, but it felt weak.

As I walked to the front door, Paul stopped me and handed me my notes.

'You might need these.'

'Oh God, I almost forgot. Thanks, Paul.'

'It's going to be fine.'

'Paul, I know I said I wanted to do this alone. But will you come with me?'

I was expecting Paul to say yes, and he did, but there was a hesitation, a beat. Although it was only for a split second, it seemed to last longer and said so much.

'You don't have to, sorry, I shouldn't have asked.'

'No, it's OK.'

'No really. I'll be fine,' I replied, my voice tight and breathless.

'Claire, if you want me to come with you, I'll come with you.'

He took my hand and wrapped it in his. And although he smiled, I could see he was tense, just as tense as I felt.

'Are you ready?' he asked.

I shrugged my shoulders. 'No, but it's happening anyway.'

He squeezed my hand a little harder and opened the front door to the flashes from cameras that blinded me. I felt myself wanting to retreat into the house. If it wasn't for Paul, who with his spare hand in the small of my back gently guided me, I would never have made it to the lectern to speak. As I put my notes down, my front lawn fell silent, the flashes paused, and people waited. I hadn't noticed that the press were talking until they stopped. In the silence I heard a bird calling and for a moment I focused on that, noting how strange it was to hear it when it was dark. It seemed to distract me enough to open my mouth. I took an intake of breath which was amplified through the five microphones in front of me, and my gasp bounced off the houses opposite and back into my ears. I let out the same breath, again amplified, and then spoke. Forgetting to take another breath in, the first thing I said sounded forced, and out of control.

'Killian Jones was someone I knew.'

I inhaled sharply, my lungs out of air, and had to turn my head to cough. It was going wrong. I wanted to show that I was in control. The more control I had, the more likely I wouldn't be a good story, and therefore the stronger the chance was, after tonight, I would be left alone. So far, I was presenting as a broken woman. As I coughed the flashes started up again, the media capturing me in my fragile state. I wanted to go back into the house, but didn't. After the coughing had stopped, I stood as tall as I could. My fingers gripped the edge of the lectern until the tips went white. I continued. 'He… he supported me in the months after I was nearly killed ten years ago, the same night my husband, Owen Moore, became the seventh victim of Tommy Kay.'

Out of the corner of my eye I saw Mum leaning into Geoff with her eyes shut. He looked at me with such kind intensity that I felt myself gain some courage. Enough for me to look at the media before me; a sea of faces with Dictaphones and cameras acting as extensions of their bodies. Their faces were mostly in the shadow of lights that were focused on me. They became something unreal, something you couldn't quite make out.

'The killer himself died long ago, and although he never confessed to the killings, the authorities believed he was their man. Since then, I have tried to survive, tried to live my day to day life as best I can.'

Another pause to breathe, another look at Geoff and Mum. Beside me, Paul placed a hand on my back again, and I knew he was telling me I was doing all right.

'Learning of Kath Brinck's killing shook me to my core, and my heart goes out to her friends and family. From experience, I understand what a difficult time you are going through. To learn that she died at the hands of Killian Jones breaks my heart, and I cannot help but shoulder some responsibility for her death. His terrible, terrible act, his act of evil, was one to attract my attention and so to her family, if you are listening, I am so, so sorry.'

I welled up, so I stepped back from the lectern and lowered my head. It was the first time I had said out loud the reason Killian killed that poor woman, and hearing myself say it made it even more real. She had died because I had lived. Paul wrapped his arm around me, and leant in. He whispered I should keep going and the cameras flashed again. I felt his body tense. I couldn't help but think regardless of what I said and how I presented myself, they would make a story out of it. So, I steadied myself and pressed on. The sooner I said what I needed to say, the sooner I could go back inside. Turning over the notes that sat on the lectern I looked at Mum who looked back, sensing something had changed in me. I chose to ignore my cue cards, my prepared words and as I spoke, I made a point of looking at as many of the reporters as I could.

'I have struggled over the past ten years to feel like I can be all right. I'm still afraid of the dark, I still need my mother nearby.' I laughed sadly at myself, and Paul closed the gap between us. I would never say these things out loud again. So, I needed to finish it.

'I still have bad dreams most nights. I still struggle to be out of the house on my own. But all those things were getting easier to manage, with time, with space. Recently, because of what happened to Kath Brinck, things have become just as tough as they were in the months after, the years after, that night in Ireland. And to know the man who killed her is someone I have spoken with, someone who I once confided in, is hard for me to swallow.'

I paused, focusing on my fingertips.

'And I may never forgive myself for it. With Killian Jones behind bars where he belongs, I will recover, in time. Respectfully, I ask that after today my family are left alone. That I'm left alone. Surviving is hard, learning Mrs Brinck died at the hand of someone I know is hard. And I request the space to deal with what has happened privately. The news of Killian being charged with her murder shouldn't have been about me, it should be about that poor woman, and her family.'

As I stepped back, it being clear I had finished what I needed to say, the cameras flashed with more intensity and the press erupted as questions fired towards me. Their shouts like a wall of noise, pressing against my head. I felt my blood boil; I had just asked for peace and it was so quickly forgotten. Stepping back up I couldn't hide the anger in my voice as I addressed the reporter nearest me.

'What's your name?'

He seemed stunned I had addressed him directly.

'Rupert.'

'Rupert, have you ever had someone try to kill you?'

My question was greeted with a stunned silence, not just from him, but from everyone.

'What about you?' I addressed the woman next to him; she held my eye and shook her head.

'You?' I said again to the next along. He looked down.

'Any of you?'

My question was greeted with silence.

'No, I thought not. You're all very lucky. I know I am too, I survived. But it comes with a price none of you know how to pay.'

Again, my statement was received silently, and I walked away from the press back into the house, Penny wrapped her arms around me.

'Claire, that was so brave.'

I couldn't respond but nodded and walked into the lounge.

Mum, Geoff and finally Paul stepped inside, and the front door was closed. Mum sat beside me on the sofa and rubbed my back. I suddenly felt exhausted, and so flopped onto my side. Then, without knowing it was coming, I cried. I didn't know why exactly; I wasn't thinking of anything at all. But I cried regardless,

I cried unapologetically, with every fibre in every muscle, every atom. And, strangely, no one tried to comfort me, no one tried to quell the outburst. They gave me the space to express myself that I needed, and I couldn't have loved the people surrounding me more for granting it.

Chapter 42

1st October 2018
Wrexham, Wales

The ninth

Fate had once again delivered. After Claire Moore's emotional, if not desperate, press interview the previous night, he knew they had charged Killian with his crime. It was hard viewing, watching her struggle. The details were still sketchy, but they didn't matter. What mattered was the country believed they had their man. The best part was, the news of Killian being charged was released on a Sunday and therefore, his target's husband would be out the following night with his young mistress. Fate, or destiny once again, showing him how his plans were vitally important. After seeing Claire, he slept deeply and soundly, knowing he could end the ninth quickly, just over twenty-four hours after Killian was charged.

Oh, how they would crumble.

The day had gone according to his schedule, his rucksack was packed with all the tools he would need for the night. Each one had a place in the bag that was its own, like a seasoned traveller would pack a suitcase. He was ready, and, as with the eighth, the excitement, anticipation and adrenaline of another kill meant he left his house early. The extra week's wait fuelled his desire.

As he left the house he listened to 'Careless Whisper', the ninth's favourite song. The sun was filtering into nothing along the horizon. It was still too early to enact his plan. The houses on her road usually turned off their lights around 10.30 p.m., meaning he would have to be patient until near that time. The drive to her street took thirty minutes, but that still meant he was ninety minutes early. So, he parked his car in a layby around ten miles from her house and waited.

Looking out of his car window to the west, the sun just throwing the last of its light into the sky, bouncing off the clouds in the most beautiful colours. He wondered how anyone could doubt God with such a sight, and for a moment he forgot what he was doing, where he was, and let himself be wrapped up in it. And in that moment, he pictured his mother with him, watching the colours float in the sky.

Tonight, he would make her proud, tonight he would leave his message, and men would once again have to work to be kinder, and women would once again be brave enough to escape if they couldn't. Because tonight he would leave something undeniable for the police to find. A note, explaining it was never Tommy Kay. That there was no copycat. To prove it he would leave three Polaroid pictures outside the premises for the police to find. The first had Blair Patterson's mutilated body. The second Jamie Connell, and the third, Charlotte and Jack Merrill. Pictures taken moments before he set them on fire. Then, he would leak the information to the press and the police would think they had a leak from the inside. Someone selling the proof that the Black-Out Killer wasn't Tommy Kay, and it wasn't a copycat. The world would know that he had never been caught.

And it would be as beautiful as the setting sun.

It was at this point he knew he needed to walk through the

evening in his mind; the steps he would need to take to successfully complete his task. He closed his eyes and watched himself drive the ten miles to the green sub-generator behind the locked fence, only two hundred metres from her house. Then he saw himself cutting the lock before stepping inside and opening the housing to the substation, which supplied around four hundred homes. He visualised killing the power; the world plunging into consuming, absolute darkness. Then, he would walk, the fear leaking through the gaps under front doors and keyholes of the houses he passed tasting sweet on the tip of his tongue. He knew the route to the ninth's house and paced it in his mind. He saw himself climbing over the back fence, approaching the rear door and breaking in, knowing the husband would be out fucking his young mistress. He let himself visualise the moment he stepped into her lounge. The ninth lighting candles on the coffee table, fear leaking from every pore. But as he tried to visualise her face, it was Claire's in front of him instead. Seeing her pathetic and desperate on the news was like a thorn that kept catching. He expected more. He wanted the press to want to be around her. Hounding her, waiting outside her door to glimpse her. But now, after her plea, it worried him they would back off, like she wanted.

When he returned to kill her right under their noses, they would remember him for all time. She would be the eleventh, the same number as Jack the Ripper by a favorable coincidence. They would draw comparisons between him and the Ripper because of the number. They would assume there was a link, but there wasn't. It would result in them finding themselves even more in the dark as to who he truly was, ironically, just like old Jack himself. And Claire Moore would be the last, Claire Moore would be his swan song.

He tried to refocus on visualising the kill he would perform in an hour, but he couldn't shake the image of Claire. She'd presented herself first as desperate, then confrontational. He understood what she was trying to do; she was trying to appear brave, bold. But she had failed. Her desperation wasn't who she was, and he wanted no one to think that was the case. She presented the wrong version of herself, and he knew, from experience, that self-deception can eat away at who you are. That press conference on her lawn would have eaten her up inside.

The same way it had eaten at his mother.

When his mother died, his family told him she was funny, bright, a woman who lit up a room as soon as she stepped into it. He could just about remember that side of her. When they were out, on rare occasions, as a family, men would stand taller, attracted to her. Women would smile at her, unthreatened. Everyone liked her, and everyone wanted to be a little like her. In public, she had it all. And he often wondered, if she'd been allowed to show the truth, to show she was sad, scared, hurting, would someone have helped her? Would someone have been able to stop what happened? Would they have told her to leave her husband, take her son and start again? He would never know. And even if he could, he wouldn't want to anyway. Because the answer would have probably been yes, and then he wouldn't have found his mother dead that day.

After they buried her, his father wasn't the same man. Instead of shouting, he stopped talking. Stopped being visible. He came and went as he pleased, often staying out till after dark, wandering the streets, drinking himself into oblivion. On a cold night, exactly a year after she was gone, a year to the day, he tried to talk to his father for the final time. He told his dad he needed him; he told him he was sad and lonely, and his dad replied by telling him it was his fault he felt those things because he was the reason she was dead.

'Our life, before you, was good,' he slurred, a bottle of wine in his hand, half empty, sloshing around as he spoke. 'Your mum and I were happy until she gave birth to you. And you fucked it up.'

He ran out of the house and to Kanturk Castle, the ancient

bricks being his only safe refuge. Being there reminded him of the feeling he had when he had killed the injured bird. And without giving it much thought he hunted in the grounds of the castle for a nest in a tree. When he eventually found one he climbed, hearing the chirps of hungry chicks waiting for their next meal.

He knew he should think about what he was doing right now and the life he was about to end, but he couldn't stop himself recalling the moment he saw the seven raven chicks in the nest. He picked up the first chick, its feathers not fully formed, and held its little fragile body in his hands. He cradled it in his palms. The little animal was confused, but it wasn't afraid. He wondered if it could fly, if it could soar above the clouds, and for a moment, he wished he could himself. He would fly away somewhere where he was loved and cared for, somewhere he would be allowed a night-light after the sun had set. Holding the chick out, he opened his palms and watched as it tried to spread its wings and fly, its instincts teaching it to survive. But its little body was too small, and he watched as it somersaulted to the ground, its head hitting the stony path below with a dull thud.

The sound somehow made him feel better, stronger, like the actions and words of his father couldn't hurt him anymore. He picked up a second and tried again, and again it plummeted to the ground. He picked up the third, this time throwing it up in the air, so he could watch it fall past him, and again it hurtled to the ground. Thud. Grabbing the fourth roughly, he squeezed as he held and instead of dropping or throwing upwards, he threw it like a cricket ball and watched it arch away, disappearing from sight behind a small wall. The fifth he launched towards the tree beside the one he was in, and listened to it smash into the trunk. Thud. Seeing it tumble to the ground after made him laugh. Only two left in the nest. Eeny, meeny, miny, moe. The left one. Picking it up he squeezed, and the little animal didn't fight. He squeezed harder still, feeling its little body crush inside his hand. And still the little animal didn't struggle but stayed perfectly still as its ribs popped and broke. Opening his hand, he dropped the carcass, its blood staining his palm. He knew he should have felt bad about what he had just done, but he didn't, he felt in control, he felt safe. Leaving the last bird to chirp alone, perhaps chirp out his story, he climbed down from the tree. As he did, he couldn't help but wonder – if he squeezed his father in the same way, would he go pop too?

Then, he returned home to his father, who never spoke to him again, apart from when it was absolutely necessary. Lying in bed that night, he knew, if his mother had just presented the right, honest version of herself, none of it would have happened.

His watch alarm sounding snapped him away from his memories and he looked at the time on the car clock. Glancing to his left, the sun had died for another day. It was time to leave, and he fired up his car heading east, towards the darkness. Towards the ninth.

Chapter 43

2nd October 2018
St Ives, Cambridgeshire

As I opened my eyes to the light coming through my bedroom curtains, I could hear a noise, but feeling foggy, I couldn't place what it was. It was from somewhere in the house and after a moment I realised it was a TV playing, the voices indistinguishable. Weirdly, even with a groggy head, because of the sleeping tablets I had been taking for the last couple of nights, the world felt calm – speaking to the press had given them what they wanted. I wouldn't be the story anymore because, with Killian in jail, and my resulting press conference, there was no story left to tell.

Rolling out of bed I planted both feet, my right foot less sore than usual, on the floor. Slowly I made my way out to the window to look outside. I expected to see the quiet street, with maybe a car, or a bike pass by, or someone walking their dog in the sunshine, I couldn't hide my shock when the roads were still full of press, and once I was spotted, a fierce-looking woman pointing in my direction, they raised their cameras. Snapping the curtains shut I staggered back and fell onto the bed. I couldn't fathom why they were still there. I had said my piece; the story was over. They had charged Killian. My life should be back to what it was only a few weeks ago. I should have vanished back into the background.

I called out, first Mum, then Geoff and then Paul. But there was no response. My jeans, the ones I wore last night, were folded at the bottom of my bed and picking them up I rifled through the pockets until I found my mobile.

There were several missed calls.

Several messages.

Several Facebook notifications. All of which came from the support page.

The same thing happened when I found out about the death of Kath Brinck. I felt my heart drop into the stomach, the icy hand able to grab hold and squeeze.

It couldn't be...

I couldn't bring myself to open the messages, I didn't dare. I put on my clothes and moved towards the stairs, each step feeling heavy, like someone had poured lead into my thigh muscles. As I reached the top I called out again, and Geoff emerged from the lounge. I tried to smile, to appear calm, but it probably looked more like a grimace. When he didn't smile back, I knew. I knew Killian wasn't the copycat killer. And I knew whoever it was, had killed again.

My voice cracked. 'Where's Mum?'

'In the living room.'

'And Paul?'

'After you went to bed, he had a call from work and had to leave. I told him I would stay here, so you didn't wake up alone.'

'He went to work?'

'Yes.'

'When?'

'About nine, nine-thirty. He didn't want to, and insisted he would stay here, but I told him he should go. He called earlier, saying he would be back as soon as he could.'

'Geoff, has it happened again?' I asked, hoping I was just being paranoid.

He didn't reply and instead, lowered his head. Slowly and deliberately, I descended the stairs, trying to hang on to the warm feeling I'd had only minutes before. Geoff stood motionless, his eyes once more on me as I came down. When I reached the bottom, he said nothing but wrapped his arms around me.

'We should probably get you out of here,' he said.

'What's happened?' I asked, hoping my fears were wrong. But the look on Geoff's face told me they were right.

'There has been another power cut, another fire. They say a woman was in the house.'

'It's happened again?'

'Yes.'

'Oh God. It's not Killian!'

'No, no, it's not. Claire, I think you need to sit down,' Geoff mumbled as he let go and walked into the lounge. I followed and as I sat next to Mum, who offered me a tired and sad smile, he turned off the TV. Sitting on the chair opposite I could see he was tense, and that made the icy hand climb over my diaphragm and squeeze my heart. I glanced at Mum, who was on the verge of tears, and by the look of her, not for the first time this morning. She moved closer and hugged me.

'Mum, Geoff? What?'

'It's him,' Geoff whispered. Holding my eye. Trying to be strong.

'What?'

'It's not a copycat. It's him. it's the same person who was in Ireland.'

'What?' I said again, unable to process what Geoff was telling me. 'No, it can't be. Tommy Kay died in prison four years ago.'

'Claire, they got it wrong. Kay didn't do it,' Mum interjected, before breaking down in tears.

'How can you be sure?'

'It's on the news. They are saying the police have proof that suggests it's the same person as ten years ago.'

'But the news will say that,' I said, my voice raising, almost shouting at Geoff. 'They always try to make it something it's…'

'Claire.' Geoff cut me off. 'I've spoken with the police, with Peter. He confirmed that although they didn't want it to be public knowledge, they have had a leak from within the force. He said it's undeniable, he said it's the same man as in Ireland. It's the Black-Out Killer.'

'How – how can they be sure? They have been wrong about everything?'

'Photos were left for the police to find. Photos of his first four victims right before he killed them.'

Geoff's words echoed in my head as I tried to stand, my flight mechanism kicking in, but as I did, my vision blurred, and the world went black.

Hello, Claire,

So, now you know the truth, or some of it. I wish I could have seen your face when you discovered it. I wanted to be there, close by. I wanted to comfort you. But I was otherwise engaged. I'm sure you understand. But I wonder, Claire, did you know all along I was still out there? I like to think you did, and you are not letting yourself listen.

I came to your house recently, such is my curious nature. I wanted to see you, to watch you move around your home. I wanted to enjoy you clutch those keys around your neck. I like to think that when you hold those keys, you think of me. I intended to observe you, and then leave you be. But you were not there. It's interesting that you have cameras outside the front of your house, but not inside. I wonder if you have noticed I've been in? That I've sat on your sofa, I've looked in your cupboards. I took a few things from your home, small things. I wonder if you will notice they're gone. As I left, I saw your cat. It approached me so calm, so curious. You know what they say, Claire, about a curious cat.

I heard what Killian did to your cat. It must have been upsetting for you? And if I can tell you a secret, I am jealous that another man could instill fear in you. I had hoped that would be for me to do, and me alone.

Now I've told you a secret, will you tell me yours? Because I know you have one, Claire, but then, we all have our secrets, don't we? The things that are set apart from others. Things we keep quiet, things that we hope no one will ever notice. Even you do, Claire, the woman the whole world knows, still has something hiding in her shadows. But I can see in the dark, and I know what you hide there. Claire, I've known for a very long time.

One day we will talk face to face about the secrets we carry.

*Until then, I am never far away. **Closer than you think...***

Chapter 44

2nd October 2018
St Ives, Cambridgeshire

I've only passed out a handful of times I can remember, and two of them had been within the last month. Before I hit the floor, Geoff caught me and guided me to the sofa where I lay, looking at the ceiling and feeling confused. Slowly, I brought myself up to a sitting position and Mum, who was sat beside me, pulled me into her. She smiled at me and I burst into tears, the second time within twelve hours. Last night I cried because of relief, release, closure. I sobbed now because I was living in a nightmare once more. Twelve hours, what a difference it can make. Eventually I calmed down enough to ask for a cup of tea and springing up, Mum nipped into the kitchen. Geoff slipped into her space on the sofa as she left, and I felt him put his arm around my shoulders.

'You OK, kiddo?'

'How long was I out for?'

'Not even a second. By the time I caught you, you were coming around again.'

'It felt like I was out for ages.'

'That's shock. How are you feeling?'

'I don't know,' I replied, struggling to piece together what was happening. First it was a copycat, then that copycat was Killian, but now it wasn't him at all, nor was it Tommy Kay, but someone else, someone who had never been caught.

'Is it really him? I mean, is it really the same man who did...'

'That's what they say.'

'Shit.'

Dropping my head onto his shoulder, I sighed heavily, and he rubbed my back.

'Now we know this, love, what will you do with it?'

'What do you mean?'

'I mean, we have to leave here. Your house is obviously on the news, ours is too close. You need to go to Paul's. He knows exactly what's going on, and his work are doing what they can to help.'

'That's good.'

He repeated his strange question. 'But what are you going to do with it?'

'Geoff, I don't understand.'

'I've known you a long time, and in that time I've seen three versions of you. The first is the one before Owen died, the runner, the friend, the kid who didn't have a care in the world. The second is the girl who hid, scared to leave the house, scared to be seen, terrified because everyone became a killer in her eyes. The third, she evolved from the second, she's a woman who fights to do what she can to get by.'

'How do you know all this?'

'I know you, Claire, it's my job. I may not be your biological father, but that doesn't stop me being your dad.'

Geoff kissed me on the head and I closed my eyes – it was enough to keep the icy hand at bay for a moment.

'Claire, I guess what I'm saying is... which of these people are you going to be?'

'I don't know.'

'Because you can't go back to being the first. That person is gone.'

'So, it's either be the second, or the third.'

'And you can only pick one, kiddo,' he said as he heaved himself from the sofa. 'I'd better start on your suitcase, anything you want me to pack?'

'I can do it.'

'You stay with your mum, have a tea.'

'Thanks, Geoff, for everything.'

'You don't need to thank me. I love you, kiddo.'

Geoff didn't say he loved me often, in fact, the last time I can remember I was still in a hospital in Ireland. And that scared me and moved me in equal measure. Watching him head up the stairs slowly I almost called out. I almost told him something I had not been able to tell anyone, something about Owen. But the guilt of even considering saying it out loud crushed my voice before a sound could shape. Once he was out of sight, I thought about what he'd said. I could only be one version of me, and now I needed to choose.

Mum came back in with two teas and sat beside me once more. As she handed me my cup, I smelt the sugar. I usually have one but as I tasted it, it was sweeter than usual.

'I was sure it was Killian, Mum.'

'We all were.'

'What will happen to him now?'

'They've already released him.'

'But what about Baloo? The pictures he had? The letter?'

'They've assured us they're keeping an eye on him. He's not allowed within two hundred feet of this house, my house or Paul's. As for what he did to our cat... it'll go back to the courts. But for now, he goes home.'

'But how can they enforce the two hundred feet rule, what if...' I stopped myself. Geoff's speech about the versions of me echoed in my head. If I finished the sentence, I would become the second by default. I still might. I wasn't sure which way I would eventually go, but stopping myself meant in that moment, I had a choice.

Besides, Killian was the least of my worries. If he was alive, if they'd never caught him, if the Black-Out Killer was never Tommy Kay, I had much bigger things to worry about.

Chapter 45

2nd October 2018
Ely, Cambridgeshire

Geoff came downstairs with my case full of things, just five days after I had emptied it from my long stay at Paul's. Once we were ready, Geoff insisted we moved quickly, and said nothing. Mum and I were happy to agree. Throwing a coat over my head he and Mum led me to their car. The press pushed against us, tried to force a camera under the jacket to take a picture. They shouted questions at us and as we moved, I heard some of them. They asked how I was feeling about the Black-Out Killer being alive, if I felt remorseful for calling Killian a murderer. I didn't respond and as I climbed into the back, I tried not to answer them in my head.

The drive to Paul's took the best part of an hour as traffic seemed to be at a standstill everywhere in and out of St Ives. The journey was distinguished by an absolute silence as Mum, Geoff and I tried to independently process what had happened and what we had learnt. Geoff finally broke the silence by letting us know there was an unmarked police car behind us; Mum turned, I didn't.

247

As we pulled into the familiar road that led to Paul's, I was expecting to see press waiting, but they weren't. For now. It meant that we could slip into his house with the key he had given me when I was last here. As I stepped inside, I saw the unmarked car Geoff had spoken of, the officer in the passenger seat looking at me as they passed. He offered a weak smile, one I didn't return. I watched as they drove further down the road and parked, just before I closed the door.

Dumping my suitcase in the living room, I said I was going for a shower. Mum started to follow, as she always did, but I stopped her.

'I'm fine, Mum. I won't be long.'

As I headed towards the stairs and as I placed my foot on the first, I looked back at Geoff who nodded, smiling at me. He knew I had chosen to be the third version, for now at least.

Running the shower, I fought to keep myself calm. I reminded myself that I was safe, Mum and Geoff were here, the police were outside, and it was daylight. Besides, there was also a strong chance he wouldn't know where I was, anyway. I took my clothes off, opened the music app on my phone and pressed shuffle, and let the steam billow over the top of the shower screen before I stepped in. The hot water soothed my neck muscles and relieved the headache I didn't know I had.

Just when I was finally beginning to relax, I heard that song… our song. I was mesmerised by it, traumatised perhaps. The icy hand inside woke from its brief slumber and I could feel it tremor with excitement as it conducted across the base of my lungs. The rumble of drums built, its crescendo complete with a crash of a cymbal. A few more chords over the shower. The piano treble trilled, and continued to build and build…

Owen had loved The Who, and this song was one of his favourites. Hearing the song, letting it play, took me back to a moment from that night I hadn't recalled before. Prior to the power cut, Owen and I had been drinking, I knew that much, but I had lost the memory of us as we danced in the lounge to this song which played in a loop, over and over with Owen singing along out of tune. I let myself go back to that moment as the shower washed over my head. We danced and we laughed and spun and kissed. It was so hard to recall it, but I made myself. I wanted to, for once, be back there with my husband. And as I let myself succumb to the past, new things came into my mind. I remembered, for the first time, that Owen had told me he loved me that night. It wasn't often he said it so it was a special moment. He led me to the couch, and sat beside me, pushing my long hair out of my eyes before kissing me with the same intensity, the same lust as when we'd first met. We stripped down to our underwear and made love on the sofa. We made love like our lives depended on it. Although, perhaps it just felt that way now, because of what happened.

Then it was dark; the music had stopped, but I could still hear it on a loop in my head, and I couldn't see Owen anymore. I knew I should stop recalling it, I knew what was coming next, but I couldn't. I was lost in the memory of it, I was back there on that night.

I tried to call out for him, the sound that came from my mouth unrecognisable. Like an animal dying. I started to stand but I couldn't, my body wouldn't respond as I wanted it to. Instead, I slipped off the sofa onto the floor, my face pressed into the rug. I saw feet, at first, I thought there were several pairs, but then realised there weren't, I was just seeing multiple of the same pair. I tried to call for Owen again, and again, my words were unformed. Then I was being dragged by my hair. I could hear it tearing from my scalp. It should have hurt, but it didn't.

I was dragged into the bathroom, the song still looping in my head. I saw several arms, no, one arm, Owen's arm, hanging out of the tub, lifeless and thin. The last image of my husband I had. Then there was a man looming over me, a face I couldn't see a wide-open bloodied mouth, a dark cavern. Trying to swallow me whole…

'Claire?'

Hearing Mum call snapped me away from my thoughts, and I realised The Who song had finished.

'I'm OK, Mum.'

'OK, love.'

I listened as Mum made her way downstairs and I quickly washed my hair and body, fighting to stop myself reminiscing. I stepped out of the shower, stopped the music and dried my hair in silence, trying to force The Who song out of my head. But it had burrowed back in, made its nest. It would be there for a while.

Wiping the steam from the bathroom mirror with my hand, I saw myself, my short hair wet and limp, my eyes heavy and full of worry. I took a deep breath and told myself that I couldn't change the past, nor the present – the fact that the Black-Out Killer, the real killer, was back. But I could control how I dealt with it. I needed to be braver than ever; I needed to be able to go into my garden, to leave a window open. I needed to buy milk and bread when I ran out. I needed to control the icy hand.

Going into Paul's bedroom, I saw Mum had opened the suit-case on his bed and had removed a pair of leggings and a top for me to wear. I dressed before heading back downstairs to join Mum and Geoff. I knew I was safe, and that the Black-Out Killer wouldn't know where I was. No matter how many times I told myself this, though, I couldn't shake the feeling that he and I would meet again.

Chapter 46

2nd October 2018
Ely, Cambridgeshire

From outside the house I could hear voices – first someone I didn't know, then Paul's. He sounded irritated, angry even: 'Will you just get out of my way? It's my fucking house!'

I hadn't heard Paul turn aggressive before, it sounded alien coming from his mouth. Geoff leapt up and went to the front door to help, and I looked around the corner between the living room and hallway to see outside. I didn't dare go out, in case there were press. I wasn't ready. Paul eventually came into the house, slamming the door behind him, making me jump. He dropped his bag and then came into the front room, almost bumping into me in the doorway.

'Jesus, sorry, Claire.'

'Are you all right?'

He took a deep breath, clearly stressed by it all. 'Yes, sorry, I'm fine.'

Paul kissed me on the cheek and as he pulled back, I could tell he was as tired and overwhelmed as I was.

'How are you love?' he asked, the hardness in his voice gone.

'You know, surviving.'

'I'm glad you're here.'

'Me too,' I replied, meaning it. I knew this was where I was supposed to be.

'Do you want anything?'

'No, I'm fine now you're back.'

Paul smiled and went into the kitchen and I followed with my eyes. I saw him lean against the sink, his head heavy, shoulders rolling forward, as if they were too tired to hold him upright. It was only for a moment, but it said so much. He saw me looking and righted himself, beaming a smile my way.

'Do you want a tea?' he asked brightly.

'Please,' I replied, trying to mirror the lightness in his voice. He turned back to the sink to grab cups from the draining board. Catching his reflection in the window, I saw that the smile was gone, and the deep furrows in his brow had returned. The news had troubled him, and it broke my heart.

'Paul? Are you all right?'

He turned to me, opening his mouth, as if he was about to say something and stopped himself. 'I'm fine,' he said. I didn't believe it.

Mum and Geoff stayed for the rest of the afternoon, trying and failing to be as normal as they could. Mum, with Paul's help, cooked us all a lasagne, one of her comfort meals that was usually very well received. Most of it sat and congealed on the dining room table, none of us in the mood to eat. Geoff tried to lighten the mood by telling funny stories from when he was in the army, but none of us laughed either. None of us had the energy to. But I was grateful to them all for trying, and it made the day go faster than I thought it would.

As the sun set, Mum and Geoff reluctantly left, reassuring us they were only around the corner, despite that corner being seventeen miles away. Once the door was shut, the silence felt total and as I dropped onto the sofa, I watched Paul clean up glasses and mugs, his face beaten.

'Paul…'

'Don't worry, I'll clear up.'

'No, Paul, stop.'

He did as I asked and looked at me worried. 'What's wrong, Claire?'

'Nothing, well, nothing beyond what should be. Are you OK?'

'I'm fine,' he replied, a little too quickly.

'You don't look it.'

'Honestly, I'm OK, I'm just tired. I've not been sleeping well lately.'

'Why haven't you…'

'Claire, me losing a little sleep isn't what's important right now, is it?'

'Sorry, I just want to make sure you're all right.'

'I'm fine,' he said quietly, pinching the bridge of his nose.

'OK,' I whispered quietly, a strange sense of déjà vu sweeping over me. I got up to go into the kitchen and finish tidying, something to busy myself and shake off the strange feeling. As I passed Paul took my hand.

'Claire, I'm sorry. I am finding it tough, because I care so much. And I'm sorry if I've seemed a little off – a good night's sleep, next to you, and I'll be right as rain.'

I was worried about him, about us. There was something he clearly wanted to say but couldn't. I thought for a moment about his comment about us all having burdens from our past, and whether whatever was wrong was something to do with his. I dismissed it quickly. Something was wrong, and it had nothing to do with the past, and everything to do with the present right now, with me.

Standing, Paul kissed me on the forehead and went into the kitchen. As he continued to tidy, the sound of cups clattering together as he loaded them into the dishwasher swept through the whole house. The silence between us felt new, and the horrible feeling of déjà vu lingered. I need to do something. On the coffee table I saw the TV remote and felt the urge to pick it up. I knew I shouldn't; I knew I would only see reports on him. How it wasn't Tommy Kay, how they had gotten it wrong. I suspected they would pontificate about what the real Black-Out Killer had been doing for a decade, where he had been. I could almost hear them linking him to other unsolved murders. I knew it would upset me but, if I was to be the third version of me that Geoff spoke of, I couldn't hide from what was happening in the world. So, grabbing the remote I switched it on and turned to BBC News.

Nothing could have prepared me for what I saw. Staring back at me from the screen was Killian, standing behind a wall of microphones outside Huntingdon police station.

I turned the volume up and Paul came back into the lounge. 'Claire, I don't think…'

He was as shocked as me to see Killian and stopping mid-phrase, he slumped on the sofa beside me.

'… I'm not angry at Claire Moore for what she has said and done over the years, I pity her. My intention was always to help a desperate, sad and frightened person in the best way I knew how. I created the support page for her. We fundraised, we counselled, even investigated ourselves, trying to determine who the killer was and then questioned it when it was widely believed that Tommy Kay was the man behind those awful killings in Ireland…'

'That little fucker,' Paul said, before catching himself.

I couldn't believe what I was hearing, Killian wasn't lying, but the way he said it, the way he held himself… he made himself out to be my hero, my saviour. What about the letter, what about my poor cat? Before I could vocalise my outrage and shock, Killian was asked a question by an unseen voice behind the cameras. 'If

Claire Moore was here now, what would you say to her?'

As he answered, he looked directly at the lens, his eyes misting over. 'I would say I'm sorry that she thought I was trying to be anything more than a caring friend. I didn't mean you any harm, Claire, and the pictures found in my house were only to help with the investigation. To keep you safe.'

'Mr Jones, do you forgive her for calling you a murderer?'

'Of course, I do, but it means nothing, unless she first learns to forgive herself.'

Grabbing the remote control, I hurled it at the TV, cracking it diagonally across the middle. Killian's face was still there, answering a question about what he would do next, but his face was disproportionately shaped in the middle of the damaged screen. Paul jumped up and turned the TV off at the mains.

'What a fucking shit,' I said to the floor. 'What a fucking, fucking shit. How has he got away with what he has done?'

'I don't know,' Paul said as he picked up the remote and batteries which had broken loose on impact.

'He killed my cat. He's harassed me, taking pictures of me – why is he being made to look like a victim, my victim?'

I felt as if I might cry, but I had done so much of that lately I forced myself not to. Instead I stood, rage filling my veins, and stalked out of the living room. I needed to throw more things, hit something, so opening the back door, I stepped into Paul's garden: the usual fear was there as it always was when I stepped outside, especially after dark, but my rage pushed it down. Standing barefoot on the damp lawn I grabbed the first thing I found, a rake that was leaning up against the house, and smashed it into the ground until the forks were bent and broken. Dropping it on the floor, I grabbed a patio chair and swung it wildly at the garage wall, the shockwave that transferred into my hands was so forceful it hurt my fingers. But still, I wasn't satisfied, and moving to a pot plant I picked it up and threw it in the other direction. It bounced three times before rolling to a stop.

Unsatisfied I didn't manage to break it. Panting, I looked up to the night sky; the moonlight bounced off the clouds that floated in their carefree way, and I despised them for it. A noise escaped from my mouth – a deep, loud cry. The noise forming into two words. I screamed so loud the noise bounced off the clouds above me and came back as a *fuck you* to myself. And it was a *fuck you* at me. *Fuck you, Claire for surviving, fuck you for trying.* But also, it was a *fuck you* to the one who tried to kill me. *Fuck you, Killian for murdering my cat and fuck you to the press for making me believe it was over when he was arrested.*

I felt arms around me, Paul coming to rescue his garden from my attack. But I couldn't stop shouting. *Fuck you. Fuck you.* He held me tight, so tight I almost couldn't breathe, and it calmed me enough to realise what I had just done. Letting my legs buckle, Paul lowered me to the damp grass, and we both sat there, his arms around me. Keeping me close, keeping me safe. The rage quickly morphed into a tremble that slipped into a crushing sadness. As it faded, I could see the chaos I had caused.

'Paul, I'm so sorry.'

'Hey, don't be, it's OK.'

'I broke your TV.'

'Yeah, but it felt good, didn't it?' he said, smiling over my shoulder, I smiled too.

'Yeah, it did.'

'As for the garden – I'm just glad I don't have any gnomes.'

His comment caught me off-guard and I laughed, as did Paul. And for a moment, we were just two people, sat on a wet lawn, surrounded by mess, laughing. From the outside, it must have looked bizarre, and I loved that he didn't care. Feeling better, the outburst releasing me from the grip of both the icy hand, we went back into his house. Locking the door behind us, we headed upstairs.

Despite it being only around 8.30 p.m., I felt the need to sleep but wasn't sure if I would be able to and Paul, as if knowing my thoughts, left for the bathroom, re-emerging with some sleeping tablets. I took them without a second thought and lay down. Paul sat beside me, rubbing my back until I drifted into a medicated sleep.

Chapter 47

3rd October 2018
Daventry, Northamptonshire

Another restaurant, another town, another late night date. Her name was Esme Ormandy. The tenth. And after half a bottle of wine, the questions she asked were so predictable he could have scripted them for her.

'So, how long have you been single?'

'About a year.'

'Do you have any kids?'

'Yes, one, a girl.'

'Aww, that's sweet, what's her name?'

'Charlotte.'

'What are you looking for in a relationship?'

He found it dull. Easy. With the responses he gave he knew she would see him as a 'great guy', wondering why he hadn't been snapped up already.

He wasn't a great guy, of course. He was selfish. He didn't ask her about herself; he had no interest in who she was because he knew everything he needed to. She was married, but her husband was a controlling prick. He had recently moved out, but still visited her on a Wednesday evening to have 'his fix'. He supposed that was why she had asked to meet on Wednesday – she was hopeful, maybe for one night, she could sleep with him instead of her husband. He learnt, just from talking via the dating site that she'd left him, eventually, after a decade of him controlling what she wore, where she went, who she saw. He was the alpha, and she was just his little wife. And now here she was in the big bad world, and it scared her. Although she was interested in him sexually, he also knew she wanted to go back to what was safe. She was more like his mother than any of the others. He felt that she could do well on her own, the way she looked at him, he could see an intelligence he didn't see in the others. But she was also a coward. He could almost hear her say, as if to justify her husband's choices, 'He isn't perfect, but who is?' It was this weakness he could exploit. When the time was right, and he would wait for his instincts to tell him when that was. Regardless, he was ready, the route to her house mapped. The location of the substation determined.

With each kill it was getting easier and easier to prepare. It was almost a shame he would stop soon.

He and the tenth enjoyed a meal, a bottle and a half of wine between them, all but one glass she consumed, and just as he was about to wrap up the evening, before it wandered into the territory of her thinking they might go home together, she talked about Claire Moore.

'What do you think about what they're saying about her now?'

He wasn't aware of anything new. The last he heard, Killian had been released because they knew the real Black-Out Killer had never been never caught. Thanks to him and the photos he'd kept for so long.

'I don't watch the news often. Too depressing. What have they said?'

'That she used Killian to get back into the limelight.'

'What? Why would she do that?' he asked, confused, his blood stirring.

'You know how it is now for killers and victims and those types. Probably a book deal in it for her.'

'You think she is after money?'

'Maybe, that's what it says online, anyway.'

He nodded agreeably, passively, but a fire burnt inside. They were vultures, after his scraps of meat, and when there was none to have, they made up things about Claire Moore. She was only trying to survive, and people like Killian Jones were the ones trying to cash in. As he ordered dessert, the tenth allowing him to choose for her, the fire inside him raged. Just like the homes he had burnt.

As he said goodnight to the tenth, kissing her softly on her cheek, he could see the disappointment in her lonely eyes. He knew she would go home, and more than likely message her husband out of neediness. Although she was attractive to him, he couldn't indulge, even though he'd considered it.

Back at his car, he Googled Claire Moore, the first hits being familiar ones about their night. Scrolling down his Google search he saw a new article posted in one tabloid he hated dearly. Usually he didn't have time for anything printed by those morons – his preferred manner to learn how the world perceived him was through the BBC. But seeing Claire Moore on the front page of this trash piqued his curiosity, and he had to read.

The picture they used was one of her in a car beside her mother. Looking closely, he could see it had been altered. Her eyes had been darkened, and pushed deeper into their sockets, they had thinned her nose and her smile had been digitally widened. They had intentionally made her look malevolent. He read what they had printed about her, and he felt enraged by what they had said; the lies they told. They labelled her an attention-seeker, a Z-list celebrity, robbing people of their hard-earned money. They wrote about how she had been receiving gifts from a support group founded in her name for ten years by the now-vindicated Killian Jones. He read that she went on holidays using the money given to her from the support group, playing a victim to travel the world. But he knew it was nonsense. Besides being at her mother's, and that one trip to Ireland, Claire Moore had been nowhere. They quoted Killian Jones, misquoted probably, saying he hoped she could forgive herself for what she had done.

They painted her as a monster. They made her into something she wasn't, the liars. He needed to shift the focus from her once more; protect her once more, meaning he would have to kill the tenth sooner rather than later, sooner than he planned. He knew the tenth would go home and think about him, but possibly text her husband to come over, and that meant he wouldn't do it tonight. He could end both of them; it would be just like the old days in Ireland. But he wouldn't want to confuse his new message, his new reasoning.

Although some trashy magazines were talking about Claire, most were focusing on the connection between the latest victims. Now they knew it was really him. They had discovered that the women were separated from abusive husbands. The men themselves, publicly shamed. No heroes in the press. Only victims and villains. Just as he wanted. As for the few who were talking of Claire so venomously, he knew how to combat it – he would kill the tenth quickly after the ninth. With wide gaps between kills, people tricked themselves into feeling safe. He would take that last thread of comfort from them.

After driving back to his house he quietly checked the contents of his rucksack, knowing it was already packed and in order. As he lay on his bed he visualised his approach: first stop the sub-generator, then the mile-long walk to her house. He saw himself enter though the back door, see to her dog, if he needed to, and then end her life. He wouldn't do it tonight, he wanted to savour the moment a little, sleep soundly as he did before a kill, and tomorrow, he would claim his tenth.

And then the headlines wouldn't be about Claire Moore, their slanderous tones dulled by his work. The photos of the fourth, fifth and sixth victims from Ireland would be left behind for them to discover.

He would keep the last picture in his collection, the one he treasured the most. For now.

Chapter 48

4th October 2018
Ely, Cambridgeshire

Several days of self-medicating on Paul's sleeping tablets meant I was feeling more and more foggy each morning. But I didn't mind, I enjoyed the numbness that came with it. It did mean however, when I woke in his bed, it took me more than a moment to work out where I was, and why I wasn't at home in my bed. Then, as the questions slowly answered themselves, the icy hand awoke, and as groggy as I felt, it tried to play its tune. It sounded as distorted as the image of Killian after I smashed Paul's TV. Rolling onto my side took more effort than it should, and once I completed the gargantuan task, I was facing Paul's bedroom window. The sun was already high in the sky, and glancing to his beside clock I saw the time. I had been asleep for nearly twelve hours.

I swung myself up into a sitting position, and gingerly rose to my feet, my head swimming. I wasn't thinking properly and as I heaved myself upright, I placed most of my weight on my damaged foot, causing pain to shoot through me – I fell to the floor, banging my elbow on the radiator. Cursing myself, I got up, put my weight on my left, and walked slowly towards the bedroom door, feeling like I had the worst hangover in history. I called Paul's name as I descended to the kitchen, but I didn't need to. The house felt silent. The kind of silence where the air was noticeably still. I was alone. Making a cup of tea to hopefully settle my churning stomach I saw a note by the side of the mug tree.

I had to go back to work early. I'm sorry, I hate leaving you. I'll be back later tonight.

I don't know why, but for a second it disappointed me that he hadn't put me first. Then I metaphorically slapped myself for thinking it. I reminded myself that life must go on.

Putting on the radio, George Ezra played, and grabbing my coffee I walked to the back door, opened it and breathed in the morning air. I wanted to step outside, enjoy the cool ground under my feet, but I couldn't. The garden still bore the scars of my outburst two nights before, making me feel embarrassed. I almost plucked up the courage to step out and try fix the mess I had made, but was stopped as I heard the pulse of my phone vibrating. It wasn't in the kitchen but somewhere downstairs, and I moved into the lounge where the pulsing was louder. Before I could grab it from the coffee table, it went silent, and I saw I had four missed calls from Mum. I went to ring her back, but noticed I had several messages, voice and text, and lots of Facebook notifications. As I held the phone in my hand another message popped up from Facebook, then another. Something was going on. I panicked all over again, and the rising sickness returned – had he killed again, and so quickly?

My phone rang in my hand, the display telling me it was Mum. I couldn't pick up. I didn't dare. I didn't want to know. Whatever was happening, I couldn't change it and for once I wanted to remain ignorant to it all. I didn't want to know he had killed again, I didn't want to find out who the victim was or how similar we were. I couldn't shoulder the responsibility. Mum tried to call back again but again I couldn't answer. The third time I knew I needed to because she would worry if I didn't. As I picked up, the words caught in my throat.

'Claire? Have I woken you?'

'No, it's OK. What's happened?'

'You sound tired. Did you not sleep well?'

'Mum, what's happened?'

I heard her sign on the other end of the phone.

'Just stay offline, OK?'

'Has he done it again?'

'Oh, no, love, nothing like that.'

I brought my hand up to my face to clamp down the sob that tried to escape. I had to hold my breath for a moment.

'Claire? Are you there?'

'Yes, I'm here,' I said eventually. 'What is it? Why should I stay offline? Has Killian said something?'

'Nothing since his fifteen minutes of fame on TV. The little shit!'

'Paul said something similar. I can't believe it. If it isn't him, what is it about, what's happened?'

'It's...' She hesitated, trying to find the words. 'It's, well, the media are just being the media. It's nothing really, I don't want it upsetting you. Do you want me to come over?'

I wasn't sure why she would call me to tell me about staying offline because of the media. We were used to them hounding us. Her need to call me repeatedly meant something else was going on.

'Are you sure that's all it is, the media?'

'Yes. It's nothing really, I was just worrying, that's all.'

'OK?'

'Shall I come over later perhaps, for lunch?'

'Yeah, sure.'

'OK, see you later.'

Mum hung up, and I stood bewildered. It was unlike her to warn me about things, and to be so vague. Telling me to stay offline, when she knew I tried to anyway, seemed odd. What on earth had happened?

The phone pinged again, another Facebook notification, and ignoring my mother's warning I opened the app to see a string of messages posted in the CMSP group page. They started to flood in just after 9 p.m., when I was already in a medicated sleep.

Claire, don't worry about what they've said, who reads their crap anyway?

Claire. I think it's unfair what they have done. Just hang in there, kid.

Killian was out of order saying what he said. We know you aren't like he suggested, that's part of the reason we kicked him out of the group.

This makes me so angry. How dare they print that? Ignore them, Claire. They are just desperate to sell their magazines. Everyone knows they are full of shit.

Claire, I'm a solicitor. What they've said is slanderous. We will fight this, get a retraction and an apology. By the time we are done with them, they won't want to print another word about you ever again.

What the hell had happened? Going to Facebook Messenger I saw Wendy had been in touch. Reading her message, at first I felt shocked, then sick, then angry. I didn't message back but opened the Safari app and searched for the *Nation's Choice*, the magazine that had written to me. They were a trashy weekly that had headlines about people meeting aliens and marrying Elvis and other such nonsense. Their reputation wasn't exactly glowing, and I was fairly sure no one would take them seriously, and yet, as the page loaded, and I saw what was on the cover of this week's edition, I couldn't stop myself from crying. Because there I was, smiling at the camera: the picture taken of me weeks ago when I went out with Mum and wanted to appear like I was handling it. They had edited me to make me look like a ghoul, grinning maniacally at the camera. They wrote underneath: 'The Black-Out Killer is back, and Claire Moore is cashing in.' Beside the huge, altered picture was a smaller one of me, also taken when I was out with Mum. My sunglasses on, my head back, trying to relax for the first time in for ever. The two pictures depicted me as someone happy, at peace, when I was anything but, and that my happiness came from Killian's misfortune.

Although I knew I should ignore it, I couldn't, and for the first time since ten-year nightmare began, I was not the victim or hero. I was the villain.

I closed the Safari app and went into my recent calls list. I hoped Paul would answer. I needed to hear his voice, I needed him to tell me everything would be OK. It rang and rang, but he didn't pick up.

Chapter 49

4th October 2018
Ely, Cambridgeshire

I couldn't get hold of Paul all day, and left message after message. Whatever was happening at his work, it must have been big, and weirdly I hoped that meant he hadn't seen what I had seen, what the rest of the world had seen. Mum didn't come over for lunch, I told her not to. I lied, saying I was too tired and wanted to sleep. She was worried, as always, and I almost conceded until I reminded her that there was a police officer outside. I promised to call her after I had slept. And I tried, but I felt like I'd never sleep again.

Instead I paced and talked to myself, reassuring myself that it would be OK, and then, foolishly, I opened my news app on my phone and even though I knew I shouldn't, read about the ninth victim. The woman who was murdered when Killian was in custody was called Lauren Hegarty. Again, I felt a crushing guilt. I shouldn't have continued to read, but I couldn't take my eyes off the screen. There was a photo of her beside a tall, large man. Underneath was a description stating it was her husband, and the article went on to claim their relationship was volatile, that he ruled with a heavy hand. I read further down that they had made a similar link to the husband of the eighth victim.

Dropping my phone on the sofa, I forced myself away from the news, but for the next hour, I kept coming back to it, and the story of her life and what had happened in Ruabon – a place I'd never heard of until now. Her husband had been interviewed, not by the police, but by a tabloid, and I couldn't help but think he wasn't as sad as he should have been. Reading about her, on top of the few hateful reports about me, made me jumpy. Paul's house was a place I felt safe in, but I still didn't know the voices of the bricks and mortar like I did my own home. Each creak was a footstep on the landing floor, each bang from the noisy plumbing was a window being popped open at the hinge, and I knew I needed to distract myself, without reading anymore about *his* return.

I remembered how good I felt when I cleaned my house and I was sure Paul wouldn't mind – especially after I'd spent the last day smashing up his garden and damaging his TV. Besides, his place did need a feminine touch. I started in the kitchen, dusting the vases I'd never seen flowers in, and then realigned the pictures on the wall – photos Paul had taken when he travelled. I cleaned the glass of each one, intently focusing on the images, picturing Paul behind the camera. Some of them were so beautiful I struggled to believe he had been there once, taking that picture. As I left the kitchen to dust the hallway and go upstairs, I vowed I would travel one day.

I cleaned his bathroom, tidied the contents of the cabinet, avoiding my reflection in the door mirror and then moved onto the bedroom. I fluffed the pillows, stripped the bedding and put on fresh sheets. As I moved the bed to tuck the corners in, I saw a piece of paper on the floor, and picking it up I looked and saw it was one of Paul's fuel receipts. It was for seventy pounds and from a petrol station in Daventry. That must be where he was working. It was only about an hour away, but still I felt terrible for the time he was spending on the road because he felt he had to come home at night. Knowing he would need it to claim back on expenses, I put it in my pocket and carried on. With the bed perfectly made, I did the same in the guest room and then loaded all the old bedding into the washing machine. As the machine filled with water, I noticed the day was drifting to an end; the sun just hanging on, throwing the last of its light into the world. When I checked my phone I realised I had lost the last few hours to cleaning. And I felt grateful for it.

But the gratitude was short-lived as I still hadn't heard from Paul, and was getting worried. What could have happened at work which meant he couldn't reply to any of my messages? Because I had stopped being busy, or maybe because of the sound of the washing machine drowned out anything else I might hear, probably both, I felt a growing unease build inside me. Quietly and quickly, as if by moving fast it would quell the feeling, I meticulously checked and rechecked every window, every door to make sure I was safely locked in. I made sure the keys themselves were positioned in the locks, so I could leave quickly if I needed to. I wanted them around my neck, with my house keys, but felt I shouldn't. If I had to leave quickly, I wouldn't know which key was for which door. I counted mine, despite there being no point. Front, back, upstairs and down. I checked the garden; the security light was off and I hoped the sensor was working. And then I checked the front. The road was quiet, and I could see the police parked down the road, the officer behind the wheel looking at something on his phone which illuminated his car interior in an eerie glow.

I went upstairs to find the file or box where Paul put his receipts, so I could add the one he had dropped. If I kept myself busy, I could stop myself from calling Mum to come and rescue me. I knew he filed things in the spare room, and with it being small there weren't many places it could be.

I looked in the wardrobe, the top shelf rammed with thick jumpers and jogging bottoms. Paul also had a chin-up bar that looked barely used. The base of the wardrobe was stacked high with books, mostly work ones. Getting to my knees, I opened the drawers that were under the divan bed. There were four drawers in all, two on each side. The first was full of photo albums, and I fought the urge to leaf through the one containing photos of his ex-wife. It was surely in one of the other three. The second was full of junk, an old phone, some batteries, but still nowhere he'd store receipts. Climbing over, I opened the third and found a filing box, full of receipts. I put in the petrol receipt and closed the box before putting it back exactly where I found it. Then, with only one drawer I hadn't explored, my curiosity took over. Inside was another box identical to the one that held receipts, and wondering if I had put his petrol bill in the wrong place, I pulled it out and opened it.

What I saw inside pulled the air from my lungs.

It was a newspaper, one I knew the date of before I looked: 19 May 2008. The morning after Owen had died. The image covering the entire front page was the one I was familiar with. It was me, half-blinded, staring towards a light, unable to see what was behind it. My right hand stretched up, covered in grass and blood. My skin was ashen, my eyes hollow, desperately pleading to be saved. Underneath, where my legs were hidden in the grass cuttings, four words. *The One That Lived.*

Paul had a copy all along, he had followed what happened to me, and he had been lying about how much he knew.

Chapter 50

4th October 2018
Daventry, Northamptonshire

The tenth

Putting his tools back into his rucksack, he noticed he hadn't packed it with the same level of attention as he usually did – the items had been haphazardly thrown in and then zipped inside. Checking the surrounding floor, he was confident he had left nothing behind. He stood and calmly removed the white protective coverall. Taking his camera from the front pocket of his bag, he took her photo, the flash sharp on his eyes, before putting it away again. He was likely to keep that photo for a long time, maybe it would never be seen by anyone other than him. The final thing he had to do was usually the thing he most enjoyed, and yet, as he took the lighter from his trouser pocket, he felt nothing. Perhaps it was because the tenth had something about her, and he was sorry she couldn't save herself, like his mother hadn't been able to. Perhaps it was because he had killed twice in four short days, and his feeling of control, of self-worth, was diluted rather than concentrated. But really, he knew it was because the next time he did this, it would be Claire Moore's body doused in petrol.

Flicking the lighter, he touched the tenth's damaged foot, and then watched as it reacted with the petrol he had poured on her body, transforming her into an inferno. He watched her face, unable to look at the flames as they climbed up her leg, melting her pyjamas to her thighs before igniting her top. She was heavily sedated, more so than anyone before, due to her likeness to his mother. He didn't want her to wake. She couldn't know what was happening.

As he looked at her, he pictured his mother in the bath the day he found her, her face, just as peaceful as the tenth's. He stopped himself remembering and acted before a tear could escape from his eye. He didn't know why he wanted to cry. It wasn't for his mother, or the woman before him, but something else, something he couldn't find, something buried too deep within him. Focusing back on the fire engulfing her body, the only way he could tell she wasn't already dead was a slight tremble in her lip that flickered just before the flames, now three feet tall, blocked her face from him.

He swung his bag over his shoulder, with more effort needed than usual, fatigue setting in. And then he left the house the same way he had come in. He didn't look back until he was at his car parked close to the power substation. When he'd first turned off the power, he'd sensed movement coming from all of the houses. Like rats scurrying behind a wall; the fear leaking through the gaps in the curtains. People were hiding. He saw some jump into cars and drive away. Children crying in the arms of their parents because they had been woken with a start. But now there was just silence. The next breath would be one of relief, once those around the house of the tenth saw the fire and knew they were safe. He wondered, if people were less selfish, would he have been stopped? The answer was yes. If the streets suddenly filled with people, all looking his way, seeing him as a stranger in their community, it would be over.

But they never did.

As he climbed into his car, he felt exhausted. The adrenaline from the ninth still coursed through his body and with the tenth now dead as well, it was too much, even for him. Starting the car, he drove away silently. Knowing he should listen to the tenth's song, 'Sealed by a Kiss', but not wanting to. Strangely, he didn't want to remember this one with the same level of detail as the others. If he'd had more time between the ninth and tenth, he might have felt differently, but his instincts told him to move fast, and he didn't question them. Those same instincts now said to wait, to give it time, to fall silent, and he would do as they instructed. Then, when the time was right, he would go to Claire Moore.

The death of the tenth, the number that was one below Jack the Ripper's alleged total, wasn't his finest hour, and as he drove into the night, for the first time, he wanted to forget what he had just done, what he had done before, what had happened to him as a child.

He wanted to forget. He wanted to sleep uninterrupted. Just for one night.

But he had one more job to do, one more thing to accomplish before he could go home and sleep. His final job would sow the seed for his future visit with Claire. And it would immortalise him, as well as his message, for all time.

Chapter 51

4th October 2018
Ely, Cambridgeshire

I didn't know what to think. Paul had adamantly stated that he didn't know many details about what happened to me, that he didn't follow the news. And yet, under his bed was the first newspaper printed after that night. I put the newspaper on the bed and looked at the back of the drawer, hoping to find nothing else.

There was a hardback book. I lifted it out and opened it somewhere near the middle, finding a scrap of newspaper. A section about me. The date in the top right-hand corner said it was from three weeks after that night. The article was exploring the kind of person who could be a serial killer, with the tell-tale signs: broken home, trauma, neglect, propensity to kill animals, all highlighted. Glued to the adjacent page, they spoke in more detail of me, what had happened, and Paul had highlighted the details of my injuries in fluorescent orange. When I'd let Paul touch my scars, when I'd explained how I'd got them, he reacted like it was the first time knew. But now I knew he had lied.

As a wave of sickness flooded into my mouth, I swallowed hard, fighting to control my breathing, which was fleeting and sharp, like I had been running. I fought to get enough oxygen into me as I turned another page, hoping that would be it. It wasn't, of course, and stuck down was an article discussing the psychological impacts of trauma and surviving something terrible. Lots of articles of that nature had circulated once I was out of hospital. I wasn't shocked to see it, or I wouldn't have been if it was anywhere else but here. I read one of the highlighted paragraphs; it talked about how someone might struggle to adjust to the new reality; it talked of nightmares and phobias.

I flicked to the beginning of the book. On the first page was an article about the first death. The column was only short as it was assumed Blair Patterson had died in a tragic accident. I hated reading it, but the icy hand enjoyed itself and conducted its familiar song. I turned over the pages and found exactly the same level of information about the second, third and fourth victims. These articles were more detailed, and carried by more papers. Paul had highlighted one of the headlines that stated, 'Ireland is at the mercy of a serial killer.' As blind panic set in, I skipped forward again, not understanding why I wanted to find out more. I found the reports from the murder of Kath Brinck, and Lauren Hegarty. But she'd been killed only four days ago? At some point, whilst I was here, he had added her death to his journal.

Closing the book, I sat on the bed not knowing what to do. Part of me, most of me, wanted to ring Mum, for her to collect me and take me far away from him, or call for the police officer who was still hopefully outside. But that part was the second version of me, paranoid and accusing, the second version who was in the driving seat when talking about Killian to the press, and it had been wrong. I was so blinded by my fear, I couldn't see the truth.

I didn't want to jump to the same conclusions with Paul. He had only been supportive, loving, caring. There must be a logical explanation as to why Paul had so much information about the Black-Out Killer, his victims, and me. I forced myself to focus and think, and could just about hear the other version of me, the third person, quietly whispering that I would want to know if it was the other way around, if this had happened to someone I care about. That had to be it. Yes, that had to be it. Still, I needed to talk to Mum about it. Realising it was late, I assumed her phone would be off but tried anyway. Her voicemail message spoke to me without it ringing first. I could ring her house phone, and she would answer, but it seemed unfair to worry her over something that might be just like my reaction to Killian. I scrolled down my call list to Penny and called. Thankfully, she picked up.

'Claire!' she said brightly, but with the undertone of concern.

'Hey, Pen.'

'Are you all right?'

'Yes, yes, I'm fine.'

'Listen, I'm sorry I've not called, I figured you'd want a little space to deal with what that little shit said, and what happened, you know, the other day.'

'No, I get it, you don't have to apologise.'

'They're all a bunch of dickheads if you ask me.'

'Yeah. Listen, can I ask you something?'

'Yes, sure?'

'How much stuff have you got about me?'

'How do you mean?'

'Like, papers and things. Did you keep any of it?' There was a pause, a hesitation. 'Penny?'

'When we first met, I looked it all up. And yes, I had a few bits.'

'But you don't now?'

'No, I chucked it all a few years ago.'

'Why?'

'Because you were my friend, and I knew you better than those shitty papers.'

'No, I mean, why did you look it up?' I knew the answer before she said, but I needed to hear it anyway, because she would inadvertently defend Paul, and I needed someone to do that when I couldn't.

'I wanted to know, so I didn't do or say anything that would hurt you.'

'Penny, I know you wouldn't hurt me.'

'Not directly no, but, Claire, we both know you are a fragile person. It's not a bad thing, it makes you who you are. And I love you for it. I was so scared about saying or doing something that would either push you away, or make you want to run.'

'I'm not going anywhere,' I said, smiling.

'Well, not now, you're stuck with me.'

'Good.'

'Claire, why did you want to know about me researching?'

'Because…' I paused, feeling silly for calling in the first place, annoyed I didn't trust myself more. 'Because I'm at Paul's, and I've found a folder full of things, about me, about then.'

'I'm sure he's just doing what I did.'

'Yeah, I should have seen that. I feel stupid now.'

'Claire, you shouldn't think that way. There is a lot going on. If it were me, I would have freaked out! I'm so glad you called, shows you're much more together than I am.'

'I'm hardly together.'

'Give yourself some credit. You're doing better than you think.'

'Thanks, Pen.'

'Are you going to be all right?'

'Yeah, I'm gonna turn in, try to get to sleep.'

'If you need anything, just say, OK?'

'I will.'

Penny hung up, and I sighed with relief, before tidying the room to look as undisturbed as possible. The third version of me pushed itself to the front. It made me leave the room and get ready for bed. I checked my phone again: still nothing from Paul

278

and trying to call it went straight to voicemail. I didn't bother leaving a message. Climbing into his bed, I knew as soon as he came home, I would talk to him about what I'd found and wait for him to explain. Then I would tell him, if he wanted to know things, he just had to ask. I didn't like that he was keeping his knowledge about me a secret.

But then, I suppose we all have our secrets.

Chapter 52

5th October 2018
Ely, Cambridgeshire

I couldn't sleep. I wanted to, needed to, fought to. But despite my body being entirely depleted, to the point I could barely turn over in bed, my mind was still running hard and fast. Because of how overwhelming the past few days had been, I hadn't really had time to think about the fact that Owen's killer, my would-be killer, had never been caught and brought to justice. He had been free for the past ten years, and I couldn't help but wonder what he had been doing for all that time. Had he been living a normal life? Had he met someone he loved, did he have a family? Had he and I met? Had he made a point of saying hello? I wracked my brain. Could he have been the man who smiled at me once in the doctor's surgery when I was waiting to see Dr Porter? Was he the man who offered his umbrella in the rain? Had he delivered a parcel to my door? Could he have been the man who paid for my shopping only a few months ago?

I started to ask the bigger questions: what had brought him back? Why was he killing again? Would he come for me and finished what he started? The last question, although only whispered, meant that when Paul did eventually get home, I jumped at the sound of the door opening. I knew I shouldn't have pretended to be asleep, but I also knew that if I told him I found his folder, there might be an argument, and I didn't have the energy, and as he came into the bedroom and sighed, I thought that at that moment, he didn't either.

'Are you awake?' he whispered quietly, and I murmured, suggesting I was, but only because he had just stirred me.

'I'm so sorry it's so late. I didn't take my phone charger and my battery died, and my bloody car broke down.'

Again, I mumbled, and he rubbed my arm. 'Anyway, go back to sleep. We'll talk in the morning,' he said, sounding tired and low.

I listened as he left the room, going to the bathroom to brush his teeth and get ready for bed. When he climbed in beside me, I didn't respond. He kissed me on the shoulder and rolled onto his side, his back to me, and within a few minutes he was sound asleep, gently snoring.

I was still unsettled about finding the folder but pushed my feelings to one side and thought of what Penny had told me about not wanting to cause harm. Closing my eyes, I focused on my breathing, matching mine to Paul's steady rate. After a few minutes I felt my diaphragm release, and I knew that my exhausted body would soon concede. Just as I felt my mind drift towards oblivion, I was snapped from the peace by a light bouncing off the ceiling, and rolling onto my side, I grabbed its source: my phone. On the screen was a news update:

HOUSE FIRE IN DAVENTRY, A SINGLE FEMALE OCCUPANT FEARED DEAD.

He had struck again, quickly. His tenth kill. The third since this nightmare began in August. But that wasn't the most terrifying thing. What scared me more was the place. It wasn't the first time I'd read the word Daventry this evening.

Slowly I got out of bed, so as not to disturb Paul, and quickly made my way to the guest room. I grabbed the folder where he kept his receipts and work logs, and taking them downstairs I went into the kitchen and closed the door behind me. Turning on the under-counter lights, I opened the box beside the cooker.

I found the receipt I put in earlier and reread it. Daventry. I looked at the date and noticed that it was from two days ago. It had to be a coincidence, didn't it? I looked at other receipts for the past month and saw most of them were from services close to home. But some from other places, most of which I hadn't heard of and couldn't pronounce: their names looked Welsh.

Opening my phone, I Googled Kath Brinck and remembered she lived in a placed called Bethesda. Looking at the date of her death, 28th August, I searched for a receipt close to it. There was one on the same date from a service station near Betws-y-Coed. I put the town name into Google Maps and my heart skipped a beat when I found it was only fifteen miles from where she lived. Then I Googled Lauren Hegarty, the ninth, remembered that her address was in Ruabon. I found a receipt for a Tesco meal deal from Wrexham, on 26th September. She was killed five days later, and Wrexham was only seven miles away.

Paul had been in the same places, at similar times to when those women died. And tonight, he had been near Daventry. And now a woman was dead.

At first, I didn't let myself believe it, but I remembered how when I'd had a power cut weeks before, I hadn't heard him move through my house to find me. Most people, myself included, would stumble, hit things, but he didn't – he moved stealthily, like he was used to the dark. And I hadn't even considered how he'd got in. I hadn't given him a key, and yet he'd managed to enter without making a noise? Then I remembered the way he held me, so tight I thought I would pass out. He was strong, strong enough to drag someone by their hair. And the recent murders – Bethesda, Ruabon, Daventry. Each one getting closer to home, closer to me.

I didn't want to believe it. but the evidence was there. He had been within a few miles of each of the murders. Because of his work, he knew how to isolate power. To damage a generator. And the folder he kept, a record of his work. It was Paul; it was Paul all along. He was the Black-Out Killer. Ten years ago, it was him who came into my house, it was him who killed Owen. He had found me through the dating website. He had found me and worked his way into my life. To finish what he started.

I needed to get out, and fast. Grabbing the receipts, I dropped several on the floor, my hands shaking so much I knew I had to fight the sensation of wanting to be sick or pass out. I scooped them up and made my way for the front door, not caring about how quiet I was. As soon as the door was open I would scream with all of my might, alerting the police officer across the road.

But, as I opened the kitchen door to run, Paul was at the bottom of the stairs, staring at me with a look in his eyes I had never seen before.

Chapter 53

5th October 2018
Ely, Cambridgeshire

'Claire?' He stepped towards me, and as I spoke I was expecting my voice to sound desperate, weak. Instead, I was shocked to hear my tone was steady and low.

'Stay away from me.'

'Claire? I've just seen the news. He has done it again. He is getting closer. We need to get you somewhere safe.'

'I'm not going anywhere. Not with you.'

'Claire, we have to. We have to get you somewhere where no one can find you.' He took another step, and he looked confused. But then he looked down at the receipts in my hand and I watched as his expression changed into something else. When he spoke, it was more measured, a forced air of calm about him. 'What have you got in your hands?'

'You know fucking well what I have.'

'Claire, I need you to calm down.'

'You were there in North Wales. In Wrexham. You were there in Daventry.'

'Claire…'

'You were there in the same places as where those women died.'

'You need to let me explain. It's not what you think, it's all just a…'

Pressing down on my right foot hurt like hell, but I bit my lip and did so anyway, so I could spring forward, hoping, if I moved fast enough, it would catch him off-guard and I could push past him and make the front door. If I could get it open, I could shout, and the police officer parked outside would hear me, and they would come and save me. I moved as fast as I could, but Paul moved just as quickly and as I skimmed past him, I felt his hands in my hair, pulling me back. I fell, expecting him to drag me backwards like he had done all those years ago, but instead he wrapped an arm around my waist, his fingers digging into my scar on my stomach, and as he hauled off my feet, I cried out. With one arm encircling my torso he slapped the palm of the other across my mouth, trapping the sound of my pain.

His hand smelt of petrol.

He pulled me back into the kitchen his back slamming into the fridge, and my right foot ended up under his. He pressed his weight on my foot for a moment, but the pain was so much I was sure my scar tissue had split open. The sudden pain snapped a memory back from that night. The moments after he cut off my toes. I remembered hitting him with the bolt cutters. I remembered staggering towards the window. I looked at my foot, blood pumping out with each pulse from my heart, and knew I would bleed to death if I didn't act. He didn't set me on fire as I was told, but I had done it to myself. I had caused that much pain to my own body because doing so stemmed the bleeding and cauterised the wound. My scarred right leg wasn't that of a victim, but of a survivor, and knowing what lengths I went to in order to escape him then gave me fresh resolve. Even then, I was the third version. Perhaps I always had been?

I struggled to free myself but every time I did, his grip tight-

285

ened and his fingers dug into my stomach, hurting so much I thought I would be sick. I tried to kick, to hit out at him, but I was helpless, useless. But I wasn't frightened. My terror had been replaced with something else that moved like terror, sounded like terror, but I wasn't afraid. A decade of living in fear, living in the shadows and now my worst nightmare had come true, and I was less scared of this than I was a thunderstorm, or the dark.

I relaxed my body; I stopped fighting, and I felt his grip loosen. He thought I had given up, or was perhaps so terrified that I had passed out, and that was exactly what I wanted. With his hand still over my mouth I felt his other arm release my waist just enough for me to act. Dropping my weight, I twisted and pushed. Flinging myself away from him across the kitchen floor, struggling to my feet I grabbed a chair from around his dining table and as he came for me again, I swung it with all of my might. The sound of the wood hitting his skull was something I would never forget and as Paul fell to the ground, I fell too from the sheer effort of trying to knock him out.

I scrambled up as he moaned and rolled onto his back, blood from the wound on the right side of his head pooling underneath him. I had expected him to stay down, but he was already getting to his feet. Bolting for the kitchen door I opened it, sending it crashing into the work surface, and I hobbled as fast as I could with my right foot, which was searing with white hot pain. Grabbing the front door handle I turned to open it, and he was on me again, spinning me to face him. Blood soaked his face, framing his eyes, making the whites of them seem like they were glowing, monstrous, like the devil. I screamed for help and he covered my mouth again, pressing hard, pushing my skull into the door frame. I drove my right knee into his groin, buckling him in half.

As he hit the floor I opened the door and ran out into the night. Someone must have heard my scream because as I made the edge of the drive, the police officer was out of his car and running towards me. As I fell into his arms, I managed just seven words.

'It's him, he's the Black-Out Killer.'

Epilogue

29th December 2018
St Ives, Cambridgeshire

Opening my front door, I flicked on the hallway light and paused for a moment, listening to my house. It was quiet, as I knew it would be. I felt myself hesitate. Beside me Geoff placed his hand on my shoulder.

'Do you want me to come in?'

'No, I'm all right,' I replied smiling.

'Yes, you are,' he said smiling back. 'Your mum and I are really proud of you, love.'

'Thanks, Geoff. A lot of that is down to you, you know?'

'Because I walk you home?'

'Because you showed me the three versions of myself. Since then, it's always on my mind, and it's forced me to work harder to be the third one.'

'The second wasn't your best,' he conceded.

'And the first belongs to a girl who doesn't exist anymore,' I said, finishing his sentence.

He smiled again. 'I'm glad I could do something for you.'

'More than something, Geoff, you are the reason I fought Paul. You're the reason I got out. Paul… I still can't believe it.'

'Nor can I but it's done now,' he said as he hugged me. ''Night, kid.'

''Night, Geoff.'

'Try to get some sleep, you've got an early shift tomorrow.'

'I will, thanks for a lovely evening.'

'Even though I burnt dinner?'

'It was lovely all the same. As long as you haven't poisoned my mum and me.'

I kissed him on the cheek and he turned and walked away, his hands in his pockets, back towards his house. Closing the front door, I held my breath for a moment longer than I should have before dumping my bag on the floor and headed for the kitchen.

Looking at the cooker clock, I saw it was just before 10 p.m. And knowing I would need to be up at five to get ready and be at work for six, I told myself I'd have a quick cup of tea and then turn in. My job was hardly taxing – I cleaned at the local children's centre in Huntingdon, not working with young ones directly like I'd wanted to, like I used to when I was young, but that didn't matter. It was a job, my job, my first here in England, only my second ever, and I loved it. I cherished it.

Paul was in prison. He was first charged, and then prosecuted, for the murders of Kath Brinck, Lauren Hegarty and Esme Ormandy. After he was arrested, and the press got involved, things from Paul's past started to come out, including his ex-wife speaking of how he'd hit her. Her story of 'how I survived a serial killer' hit all the tabloids. Apparently, as a young man he drank and then ruled with an iron fist. Just like the men he'd targeted in Ireland and the wives of the men he'd targeted recently.

I was so angry at myself for not seeing it. The critical evidence to charge him was found in the boot of his car. He had foolishly left the bolt cutters, the blood of all three victims found on them. The physical evidence and the file of details around the murders, and the proof he was near each town around the time of the murders, meant the trial was short, and a jury unanimously elected to give him three life sentences. He wasn't charged for Ireland, for the seven, including Owen who died there. But they knew, the whole world knew it was him. Knowing he would never leave jail was enough for me – it had to be. I wished he would confess and help me, and the other families, find the closure we all lacked, but of course he protested his innocence. Regardless, it was over, really over. And knowing I had survived not one, but two attempts on my life changed something within me. I was a survivor. And, for the first time, I was OK with that. I could move on. I could be alone. I hadn't conquered all of my fears. I still had to leave a lamp on at night. I still carried keys on me, but now I kept them in my pocket.

With my tea in my hand, I made sure the front door was locked, and went up to my bedroom, brushed my teeth, readied my work clothes for the morning and before I climbed into bed I looked out of my window. The moon was full and bright, so bright I could make out the light wintry clouds. In them, I could see shapes of various things. A dragon, a castle, a train. Smiling, I climbed into bed. Flicking on the TV, *News at 10* was just starting and still they were talking about Paul. I had no interest anymore. The third version of me was done with it. Changing the channel, the screen went black momentarily before some home makeover show lit it again. I loved these programmes; they made me think of my own plans for my house, to start building a life I knew I deserved. But I couldn't lose myself in dreams anymore, and so went to change the channel. Again, the screen went black and then a children's cartoon was on. I wondered who on earth would be watching it this late. I changed the channel again. And the screen went dark, along with the rest of my room. For a moment I thought I was imagining it, but there was no light from anywhere. I looked to my bedside clock, and it was also off.

The power had gone out.

The icy hand I had kept quiet and contained for the past three months sprung to life, clawing me as if my insides were the wall of a well and it was desperately trying not to drown.

It's just a power cut, just a tripped switch, I told myself, hearing the tremor in my inner voice. *Get up, Claire, sort it out.*

Obeying my own instruction, I swung my legs out of my bed and when I tried to stand they felt numb. I took three measured breaths, calming myself, reminding myself Paul was in jail, and power cuts happened all the time. Finding my phone, I lit the torch and made my way to the stairs, holding onto the bannister as tight as I could to stop me from falling as I descended.

I checked my front door, and it was still locked, still untouched. I breathed a sigh of relief, and as I turned the torch beam towards the kitchen, something caught my eye on the ground, a foot away from the entrance. An envelope. Stooping down I picked it up and looked at it. There was no address on the front, no stamp. Just my name, and I knew the handwriting. It wasn't Mum's or Geoff's, so it must be Penny's – perhaps she'd dropped me a note, something sweet, something kind. Once I had the power back on it would be something I could read to help with my anxiety.

Holding it in my hand I made my way to the cupboard under the stairs and examined the fuse box. I tried to flick the power on, to see if there were any tripped switches, but it wasn't working. There was nothing coming into my house. Feeling panic rise, I hobbled through to my lounge and looked outside. The houses around were also dark, the streetlights off.

It's just a power cut, Claire. Take a deep breath...

I sat on the sofa and forced myself to calm down, before I hyperventilated and passed out. If I could just focus on my breathing, the power would eventually come back, and I would be another step closer to living as a fully independent adult: if I could do this now, I could do it for the rest of my life. I told myself I wasn't in any danger. Power cuts were just a thing.

With my breathing under control I felt better and to further help myself I looked at the envelope in my hand. Opening it, I'd expected to pull out a handwritten note from my best friend. She would make me smile, make me feel OK. There were several pages. As I turned them over, I saw it wasn't from Penny at all, but someone else. The back page fell from the stack and I picked it up, reading it.

Hello, Claire,

I have waited for this moment for a very long time. I have wanted you to know, to see, to understand.

I suspect right now you are confused, wondering why the lights are out. You're probably trying to convince yourself it's just a regular power cut – it has to be? Because the Black-Out Killer is in prison. Well... I've got a surprise for you.

My heart skipped a beat and I ran to my front door and looked through the peep hole to see if anyone was outside. But in the darkness, I could barely see the footpath. Whoever posted this was playing a cruel joke. I knew I should put the letter down, and yet, I couldn't.

Why did I come back? Why, after ten long years, have I made a reappearance? The answer is simple: it's you. You're the reason. A long time ago, I had to punish bad men, men like my own father. He didn't start out as a bad man. I remember moments when I was young where he cared. He listened. He looked after my mother and me. But then things changed, and I learnt I could challenge men like him – men who need to learn to undo their wrongs. That's what I tried to do at first. But then, I realised – it wasn't only their fault.

Your husband wasn't good to you. He hit you. And I know your secret, Claire. I know you wanted to leave, to start again without him. I waited for you to leave, but you didn't, you couldn't. Because you were weak...

He knew my secret. The secret I couldn't even share with my own family. He was someone close.

I planned to kill you for that weakness, to spare you a life of always being a victim. That night in the bathroom in Ireland, I saw that you weren't weak after all. I saw you fight, I watched you burn yourself to survive. And it filled me with hope. You had become someone who could show others a strength they didn't have, and so I let you live.

Then you met Paul, a man with a past. Claire, did you never wonder why he didn't drink? Did you never ask what happened to end his marriage before you? He was a man who hit his wife. The world knows that now. He is a man just like the man you married when you were young. When I discovered his secret, which was easy – so easy you could have too, if you'd tried – I understood that you had become weak again. So, I returned. Targeting the others who were just like you. I gave you a chance to see, but you have let yourself be blinded once more.

Framing Paul was easy. His work dictated where he would be and I could plan my kills to place him near the scene around the time. And plant the compelling evidence found in the boot of his car. The day I came into your house, I found his spare key. It was one of those small things I knew you would never notice was gone.

I expect you are confused right now. Wondering how this letter came to you. Wondering who I am if I am not Paul.

You will find out very soon, because I'm closer than you think.

I dropped the letter, along with the others, all in the same hand, all starting with my name. As they scattered on the floor, I saw a Polaroid photo slide out from the middle of the stack, face down. I slowly turned it over.

In the light from my phone torch, I saw the picture was of me. Dazed, semi-conscious. I was staring up at the camera, my eyes glazed and unfocused. Beside me was the bath, Owen's arm hanging out. Only now, looking at the picture, I could see it wasn't Owen's arm at all, it was just the sleeve of a top – one of Owen's tops. But he wasn't in the bath at all. Beside me on the bathroom floor, tucked under the sink was a small pool of blood, and in it small white objects that looked like teeth, alongside a pair of bloodied pliers. I recalled how they identified Owen by his dental records, by the teeth on the floor beside me. But my husband had never been in the bathroom with me. And if my husband hadn't been in the bathtub, then where was he? The image of the dark, cavernous mouth that haunted my dreams came fresh to me, telling me the worst.

Dropping the picture along with my phone, I let out a sob before running to my front door. As I got there, the keys were missing. Had I taken them out when I got home? Were they there only a moment ago when I checked to see if the door was locked? I couldn't remember. Panicking, I made my way towards the kitchen but before I opened the door, I heard a noise from the other side. A muffled crack, like glass being broken under material. Someone was in my house.

With nowhere else to go I ran upstairs, into my bedroom, slamming the door behind me. Then using all my might, I dragged my bed to block it, before cursing myself for dropping my phone in my haste. Holding my breath, I waited to hear something – footsteps, Mum's voice calling to me, Geoff telling me I was safe. But I heard something else. Something which confirmed my fears. I heard the sound of rain, and a piano chord played. A few seconds later a rumbling of drums, like thunder. It was that song. *Owen's song.*

The music grew louder, the sound coming up the stairs. Looking around, I tried to find something I could use as a weapon, and remembering the small nail scissors in my bedside drawer I moved quickly and found them. They were hardly dangerous, but they would have to do. I was the third version of myself now and would kill the man on the other side of the door. Holding them above my head like a dagger, I waited. The music grew louder still, and footsteps made their way across the landing to my door. And I waited. My heart pounded, the icy hand playing along with the song I'd once danced to in my living room, the night I drank too much and woke in a blackout.

The Black-Out Killer was never Killian, it was never Paul. But the first man in my life.

Then, over the song I heard a voice. One that was light. A voice I hadn't heard for so long. He was singing along to the lyrics. A voice that was supposed to be dead.

I held my scissors high. My heart was pounding, and I knew I would die tonight, unless I killed first. I had beaten him once, and although he would be ready this time, I could beat him again. I had to. The door handle turned and slowly the bed began to move as he pushed it. I dropped to the floor and using my feet I pushed. I didn't have enough strength to close it, but I could just about hold him back. Then he stopped pushing and the door closed again. Keeping my feet wedged against the bed base I waited to hear something. All was quiet.

Gripping the scissors so tightly my knuckles whitened, I slowly got to my feet. For a moment, I thought he was gone. I thought something had startled him and he had fled. But, then, the door handle moved.

'Have you worked it out yet, Claire? Are you now enlightened?' he said, his voice taking me back to the times I tried not to think about. I attempted to piece together my broken memory of that night ten years ago. I couldn't understand why I, why everyone, had thought he was dead. Then, I remembered the picture he had taken. The blood on the floor, the teeth, and the dark, cavernous mouth that haunted my dreams. That night, he had pulled out his teeth to fake his own death.

'Claire? do you want me to say it out loud, will that help?'

He waited for me to respond, but I wouldn't give him the gratification, and I didn't what to hear.'

'I was never in that bathtub Claire. The unidentifiable remains they found were of someone else. A homeless man from Cork I placed at the end of our garden a week before. One of those no-one cared about and wouldn't miss. I placed my teeth where I knew they would be able to get my DNA. It's funny what people will assume, with a little guidance.'

Suddenly, there was a surge against the door and the bed jolted a few inches. After a second, another surge. I hoped he had left, I hoped someone would come to save me. But the fact was, he would get into the room and he would try to kill me. I took a step away and held the scissors in front of me. I told myself tonight I wouldn't die. Tonight, I would instead end the life of a man who died a long time before.

After a few more surges the door was open enough for him to slip though. He stepped over the bed and stood in front of me. For a moment neither of us moved. My husband died ten years ago, and yet, despite the superficial changes, the new teeth I could clearly see in the dark as he smiled at me, I could tell that it was him. It was my husband. He was the Black-Out Killer. And if I let him, if I didn't fight back, he was going to kill me.

'Hello, Claire,' he said quietly, barely whispering my name.

'Hello, Owen.'

Acknowledgements

I used to think once that writing a book was a lonely task. But, as I've compiled this list of people I wish to thank, I can see that although it may feel isolating at times I haven't been alone on this wonderful journey. Firstly, I would like to thank my agent, Hayley Steed at Madeleine Milburn Literary, TV and Film Agency. We met at the start of this book, and I want you to know your kindness, support and faith has changed who I am as a writer. I also want to say a huge thank you to Madeleine, Giles, Alice and Georgia, for making me feel so welcome in the Agency family.

I would like to thank my editor, Dominic Wakeford – your faith and understanding has inspired me to work with more self-belief. You've always been on the end of a phone to answer the questions raised when writing *Closer Thank You Think*. I hope you know how much I value your ideas and suggestions. And thank you to Victoria Moynes, Anna Sikorsa, Jon Appleton and Dushi Horti. Your tireless efforts in making *Closer Than You Think* as good as it can be will never be forgotten. I'm truly honoured to have such support. Lisa Milton and Nia Beynon, I'm blessed to be a part of the HQ family, and I'm truly grateful to you.

To Ross Futter, thank you for your guidance in helping me understand a little about the building trade, and to Richard and Graham Harris, thank you for your guidance in helping me understand how electricity works – without your help The Black-Out Killer wouldn't have had the ability to do what he does so well. Another thank you is needed to my lovely writer buddies who keep me going through the tough times. So, Louise Jensen, John Marrs, Phoebe Morgan, Lisa Hall, thanks guys. You're all blooming legends in my eyes.

To my lovely family in Ireland, Bill, Helen, Laura and Christine Murphy. Thank you for housing me on my research visit. I had such a lovely time and cannot wait to see you all again soon.

Thank you to Kath Brinck for allowing me to use your name in my book, and to Shelley Pope for helping me name The Black-Out Killer. I'm truly, very grateful. And thank you to Tracy Fenton and The Book Club (TBC) – without such a wonderful, supportive place for readers and writers alike, I would never have met Kath and Shelley.

Thank you to the guys at my local Costa Coffee for allowing me to buy one cup and drink it over a course of six hours. and thank you to Chris Kay, the manager at that Costa, for lending me your surname to create the infamous Tommy Kay.

To Wendy Clarke and The Fiction Café Book Club, thank you for your support and generosity. You have been such a champion of the work I do since I first popped up with *Our Little Secret*, I will always be grateful to the club.

To you readers. The support you have shown and kind words you have shared have been overwhelming and wonderful. Without the retweets, posts in book clubs and word of mouth discussions, I wouldn't be in the place where I am now. And this place is the dream!

Finally, to Ben. I've said this once, but I need to say it again. You deserve all of the praise. Without you, there would be no motivation, no determination and no inspiration. And I will forever try to repay you for this.

Dear Reader,

When I set out on this amazing journey of creating books, I couldn't see how I could write even one. And yet, here we are, three books in.

Three. A hat-trick of novels. It still blows my mind.

And it's all because of you!

The support shown for my journey has been overwhelming. Because my first two stories have been shared, talked about and reviewed, I've been able write this third from a place of real joy. I'm motivated to keep going, to keep telling stories, and to try to make the stories I tell more entertaining, more engaging.

As I've mentioned, *Closer Than You Think* has been the most fun I've had in writing. I set out to achieve a story about a woman who is a hero in her own life. A hero because of the courage she shows in going out of her front door. In doing so, I have fallen in love with the person Claire Moore is. I hope you have too.

If you liked *Closer Than You Think*, please feel free to leave a review or get in touch. I'd love to hear from you, and reviews really help us writers find new readers.

When I'm not sitting in front of my laptop, which isn't often, you can find me on social channels: @darrensully. My wonderful publishers, HQ Digital and HQ Stories, are on Facebook and Twitter too. Follow them, they are doing incredible things in publishing.

Finally, I want to say that I am living my version of a dream come true, and there will never be enough words to show how grateful I am.

So, here's to you, your passion and kindness. And here's to many more adventures in writing.

You're all bloody amazing.

Darren x

Thank you so much for taking the time to read this book – we hope you enjoyed it! If you did, we'd be so appreciative if you left a review.

Here at HQ Digital we are dedicated to publishing fiction that will keep you turning the pages into the early hours. We publish a variety of genres, from heartwarming romance, to thrilling crime and sweeping historical fiction.

To find out more about our books, enter competitions and discover exclusive content, please join our community of readers by following us at:

🐦 *@HQDigitalUK*

📘 *facebook.com/HQDigitalUK*

Are you a budding writer? We're also looking for authors to join the HQ Digital family! Please submit your manuscript to:

HQDigital@harpercollins.co.uk.

Hope to hear from you soon!

Turn the page for an extract from
the thrilling *Close Your Eyes*...

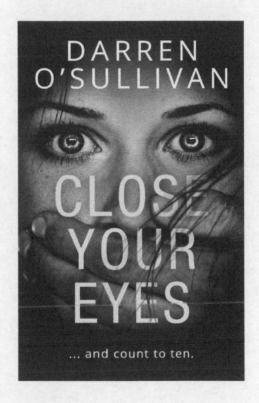

Prologue

Daniel
Sheringham
5th January 2018

Breathe.

Just breathe.

That was all I had to do. And yet it was impossible. Lying on the ground, the cold seeping through to my back and chest, I stared up at the sky. Unblinking. A sheet of nothingness stretching in all directions. Flat and smooth and devoid of anything I could identify with, devoid of anything I could latch hope onto. Just grey. I looked anyway, for something, anything that meant there was more. My eyes stung, I needed to blink. But I didn't dare. I knew if I did, my eyes might not open again. And grey was better than the black of what was surely to come.

Ironically, grey was the colour that made up my past, made up who I was, made up my memories. I had fought against it, now, it was all I had left. The only thing to hold on to. Grey was a friend all along.

Breathe.

303

Just breathe.

The pain was too much, the knowledge of what was coming next too constricting. I knew I would pass out soon. I could feel it creeping up my arms and legs. A stillness as my extremities conceded defeat. The blood flowing from my body was unstoppable, it came from too many places. My life was leaking out, a millilitre at a time, forming a pool in which I lay. It warmed the concrete around me, inviting me to relax, to accept. And it didn't hurt, it didn't matter.

I wasn't scared of what was next, part of me knew it was inevitable. It didn't even matter where I went once I died, all that mattered was that life would continue. The storm would end, spring would come. Summer would burn and then winter would return. It would do so for many, many years. There would be laughter and love. There would be success and change. There would be children growing to become adults who would have their own children one day. Then there would be peace as it came to an end, only to be replaced with another winter, another summer for ever and ever.

I was just a very small part of a much bigger picture.

I was just a single paint brush stroke on a canvas that was the entire world. A single small stroke of paint. One that was never very vibrant or colourful. More shading than subject.

Just before I closed my eyes for the final time there was a small gap in the grey, just enough for me to see beyond it. A small space of the brightest blue I had ever seen. Pure. Untouched by the past five days.

And that bit of blue, it told me everything would be OK, for the one person that it was all for.

And that was what mattered.

One week earlier

Chapter 1

Daniel
Stamford
29th December 2017, 7.48 a.m.

A long time ago I was told that the moments that were truly important in life were the moments we carry forward and recall on our deathbeds. Things like the perfect sunset. The moment we fall in love. A passing of someone dear.

As I lay in my bed, I was doing exactly that, as coming from the room next door was the sound of Thomas and Katie, talking and playing together. Their voices were my two most favourite sounds. Katie said something I couldn't quite make out, but whatever it was it made Thomas laugh and I couldn't stop myself from smiling. I wanted to join them. But not yet, first I would use my senses as I had been taught.

It was a doctor who told me to let my subconscious take over when it mattered. A doctor who was one of the many I had fifteen years ago in the days, weeks and months after I woke up in a hospital bed. But he was the only one I would never forget. He was the one who first told me what had happened and helped me understand my life had begun again. He helped me make sense of the facts. I was a broken body that didn't know where it was. A broken body that didn't know its name. A broken body whose even more broken mind couldn't comprehend that it once had a past that it may never see again. Its memories, my memories, like all memories, tiny bubbles that contained joy and happiness, sadness, fear. Only mine had all been popped.

Our conversation, the one that helped to save me from the pit of despair I was in, came on a grey February morning. I was sitting staring out of the window nearest my bed, trying to find a reason to carry on and he, doing his morning rounds, approached. Noticing I was lost in thought he asked me what I saw. I told him I saw drizzle, darkness before looking away from the window, back to nothing in particular.

'What about the trees?'

'What about them?'

'What do you see when you look at them?'

Sighing, I looked outside again, to humour the doctor. Thinking if I did he would go away and leave me alone.

'They look dead,' I said, holding his eye. I almost followed it up with a comment about how they were lucky, but stopped myself. The doctor sat on the end of my bed and looked outside. I watched him, wondering what he was doing. Doctors usually rushed in and out. I didn't blame them retrospectively, I was intolerable to be around. I waited for him to say something, but for a long time he just sat, looking out of the window, a small smile on his face. The silence was too much.

'What do you see?' I questioned.

'The same as you at first glance.'

'So then why ask?'

'Because I wanted to see how hard you looked.'

'Doc, you aren't making sense. If you don't mind, I want to be left alone.'

He looked at me, the smile unmoving and nodded.

'Before I do, Daniel, humour me once more and look again at the trees, but this time, look closer. Focus on the tree tops. Look at the way they are moving in the wind. Look at the very tips of those branches. What can you see?'

Reluctantly I did what he said and looked again, having to hide my astonishment when I focused on where he told me to. The trees may have looked dead at first glance, but as I focused I saw their tips starting to show the signs of sprouting buds that would become leaves eventually, they would attract birds who would nest and raise families. As he spoke I could almost smell the sweet scent a sapling gives off in spring. But I didn't remember any springs, or summers, or autumns. Only winter, the one I watched from my window. I learnt that the small act of stopping to let my senses work properly helped me see something wonderful that was always there, and the morning wasn't quite so dreary anymore. As he left my hospital room he told me if we embrace the stillness from time to time, we capture the moment entirely. His final words to me were that letting myself see the small things that really mattered wouldn't help me remember my past, but it might just help me have a future. That day, I knew I could learn to hold on to the precious moments that were to come in my life. Things I would experience going forwards, and they could be wonderful if I let them, despite not knowing anything about the past. Shortly after that moment with the smiling doctor I was told I would be going home soon. I never saw that doctor again.

I have had several moments in the fifteen short years that I can remember where I have done exactly that. I stopped, I became still, and in doing so I made sure those moments were branded permanently in my mind so that no matter what may happen I would never forget them. Moments like the two occasions I have fallen in love. The first time to Rachael, traditional, sweet, and almost as far back as I can remember. Two people who were nervous and excited. Full of possibilities. That first kiss suspending me above myself. I didn't know then, but that first kiss would eventually lead to another wonderful moment when Rachael told me I was going to be a dad. A box presented to me, inside being a positive pregnancy test, a card and baby grow. Tears that fell and warmed my cheeks. Her smile, unfiltered.

The biggest moment of all is reserved for the day my son was born, six years ago. Although it feels like six minutes. His tiny body helpless and defenceless. His beautiful little head that fitted perfectly in my palm as I carried him towards his mummy who lay on the operating table post-caesarean. His cry, his voice. As I carefully moved towards her, his eye found mine and changed everything I assumed I knew about myself.

But there is also the second time I fell in love, more recently, to my Katie. Our meeting and dating coming from a place that was wiser, but no less powerful.

I may have had more of these moments in the years before 2003. But I would never know. Mum prefers never to speak of the time before the accident; it's not important, she tells me. I know that they're memories that she doesn't want to relive and I'm not interested in finding out about them, not when I have no way of remembering. She's more focused on the man I am now – on rebuilding my life after what happened. She has spoken of my kindness though, my ability to love others and to jump into situations too quickly. Sometimes I will catch her staring into space and I just know she's recalling another time, another me.

In some ways, me losing my past is harder for her, she has to mourn for the man I once was without mourning at all, and I knew, despite how much I wanted to know about the me before, that if I asked her outright, she might break her silence, spilling the bottled-up emotions she held on to for my benefit. Something I couldn't do to her; she has been through enough. So I left it alone and focused on the now and the future. Which was Thomas and Katie.

From his bedroom I heard Thomas tell Katie what Santa had

left him at Mummy's house before, asking her to build a tower from the Lego my mum had bought him. His voice was followed by the crashing sound of hundreds of plastic blocks being poured onto his bedroom floor. It wasn't the words spoken or the sounds of Katie and Thomas building that would form into a lasting memory, but the context.

The woman I loved and the boy who means more than anything else in the world to me had formed a relationship that didn't need me to mediate. I wasn't required for them to be able to play and talk. I wasn't needed for them to be able to know and care for one another. And, with what I had planned for after New Year, Katie and Thomas caring for one another in such a way was essential.

Katie still thought I was asleep. I knew because she was speaking in her quiet whispery tones despite Thomas not lowering his voice at all. Truth was, I'd not really been asleep since just after 4 a.m. A dream, my dream, waking me early. The same one I had been having for over a year. The one of the accident that took away my memories and the life before.

Slipping out of bed I tiptoed towards Thomas's room. As I stepped in, I allowed myself a moment to enjoy the sight of them sat next to each other, him leaning into her as they built some sort of tower that stood about eighteen inches tall. Katie saw me first as Thomas was concentrating on his building task, and she smiled, looking from me to Thomas before resting her chin on his head. Her eyes told me everything. She was happy that he let her be close, she was content. After just over a year, he was treating her like part of his family. She mouthed a good morning to me, and I mouthed it back before turning my attention to my fixated boy.

'Morning, Thomas.'

He looked up at me, a smile spreading across his face.

'Daddy, look at the robot Katie and me made.'

'Wow, did you two really make this?'

'Yep.'

'All by yourselves?'

'Yep.'

'That's amazing. You are both very clever.'

'Well, Thomas did most of the building, I just helped where I could,' Katie said, focusing on Thomas as she spoke.

'Well then, I'm even more impressed. Bit of a clever one, aren't you?'

'Am I?'

'Yes, look at your robot. I doubt there is anything you can't do. Are you two hungry? Shall I make some breakfast?'

'Not yet, Daddy.'

'OK, no rush.'

'What time are you meeting Will today?' Katie asked, her smile shrinking, morphing into a tight one that she always held firmly in place when she was trying not to be worried about how I would feel after seeing my therapist.

'Not till 2.30, so we can take our time this morning.'

'Do you want me to come?'

'No it's OK. I'll drop Thomas back at his mum's earlier than usual this week.'

'Daddy, can I stay up here and play a little longer? I want to build a racing car.'

'Of course you can. Do you want me to help?'

'No. I want Katie to.'

'You want Katie to?' I said looking once again to my girlfriend, not even trying to suppress my smile.

'Right, I'll leave you two to it. I'll be downstairs, come down whenever you're ready.'

Once downstairs I flicked on the kettle before sitting at my kitchen table. I quietly drank my coffee and looked into my garden as the lazy sun forced its way over the horizon and listened to them talk above my head. Thomas laughed, his infectious giggle making Katie laugh as well.

Not knowing my past is a huge part of my present, and the questions that remain unanswered about me will be ones I will carry for ever. But, listening to my son and my love playing in a bedroom above me, I let myself believe that the questions I had, scars I carried, wouldn't be the future of me.

The future was now. The future was upstairs and everything about it was definitely real.

If you enjoyed *Closer Than You Think*, then why not try another heart-racing read from HQ Digital?